BULLETS IN THE BRIAR

Kimber Silver

Silver Plains Publications

First Edition published 2024
Silver Plains Publications

Copyright © Kimber Silver 2024

The right of Kimber Silver to be identified as the author of this work has been asserted by him in accordance with the Copyright, Designs and Patents Act 1988

All rights reserved. This book is sold subject to the condition that no part of this book is to be reproduced, in any shape or form. Or by way of trade, stored in a retrieval system or transmitted in any form or by any means, electronic, mechanical, photocopying, recording, be lent, re-sold, hired out or otherwise circulated in any form of binding or cover other than that in which it is published and without a similar condition, including this condition being imposed on the subsequent purchaser, without prior permission of the copyright holder.

Author disclaimer:
This is a work of fiction and any resemblance to any person living or dead is purely coincidental. The place names mentioned are real but have no connection with the events in this book.

Printed in U.S. by IngramSparks

Typeset and cover design by www.bookstyle.co.uk

A CIP catalogue record for this book is available from the Library of Congress in the U.S.

ISBN 979-8-9860836-0-5
Also available as an eBook
ISBN 979-8-9860836-1-2

*For my husband, Gabriel,
who gave me space to dream.*

Even in ruin, there is beauty.

CHAPTER ONE

Bushwhacked

Harlow, Kansas, 2015

Gabby Chambers looked out the front windows of the sheriff's office at a row of burning trees half a block away as a firetruck wailed in the distance. "I suppose I'll be off work today unless they can get the power back on. That lightning strike probably fried the electrical box on the other side of that tree inferno. I better call Rural Electric," she said, returning to her friends.

"Isn't that Layton's job?" asked Kinsley, referring to Josh Layton, the interim commissioner.

With a heavy exhale, Gabby reached for her phone. "He makes me do all the crap work. As if he would lift a finger to do anything other than preen like the peacock he is."

Kinsley picked up a profile sketch from Charlene's desk. "Who's this?"

"The murder victim in this new case. Lincoln was going to show it to the press to see if anyone could help identify the man. That bunch down on the state line won't give an inch," the head dispatcher huffed.

Gabby, on hold with the utility company, listened to their conversation. Curious to see the drawing, she peeked over Kinsley's shoulder and suddenly let out a muffled shriek.

Kinsley turned on her heels and was staggered by Gabby's now-ashen appearance. "What is it? Do you know this guy?"

CHAPTER TWO

End Of An Era

One week earlier...

Lincoln crushed an election debate speech he'd been working on into a ball and flung it across his office. He watched it bounce off the back of the door, roll a few feet, and come to rest against one leg of a small conference table laden with campaign signs that should have been put out weeks ago.

He'd been elected sheriff when no one else wanted the job, and now that it had become so intensely important to him, some vainglorious out-of-towner was trying to take it away. His leather chair let out a withering sigh as he relaxed back to consider what his life as an ex-sheriff might look like.

A sharp rap at the door abruptly ended his deliberation. "Yep!" he called out.

Charlene swept into the room carrying a steaming mug of coffee. Giving a loud tut, she stooped to pick up the discarded paper ball with her free hand. "How goes it, Linc?"

He rested his boots on the desk and rubbed his eyes. "As good as can be expected, I suppose."

"I can practice debating with you, if ya want,"

Charlene shot back, while planting the coffee on his desk. She uncrumpled the wad of paper and smoothed it out on the blotter in front of him.

Lincoln thanked her for the coffee and gave a halfhearted grin. "You afraid you're gonna have ta work for Fancy Pants?"

"I'm afraid I'm gonna need a new job. Because if you lose, I'm blowin' this pop stand."

Lincoln was well aware of Charlene's abiding loyalty, and felt that his losing this bid for sheriff shouldn't put her in a financial bind. "You know, I don't expect ya to quit if he wins—"

"I know you don't, but I wouldn't want to work for that poser." She cleared her throat nervously. "In any case, why are we even talking about it? You're not going to lose."

"I hope you're right, my friend," he said, surveying the election paperwork scattered across his desk.

"Just be your normal charming self. You've got this," Charlene advised before rushing off to answer a ringing phone, leaving Lincoln to contemplate his opponent, Trenton Crawley.

Crawley had moved into town when the boom from the Skelly trials was at its height, and he'd established fast friendships with the most influential residents of Stevens County. His connections had come together so quickly that it felt to Lincoln like a deliberate plan to oust him. If that were the case, the sheriff had to give credit to whoever recruited Crawley because they couldn't have picked a more ambitious specimen.

Something of a dandy, Crawley had become the talk

of the county with his silver-tipped cowboy boots and flashy Audi convertible. Fiona Belton, a checker at the grocery store, reported that his sports car was custom-made just for him. Local farmers couldn't see the point of such a vehicle since several of them had towed Crawley out of their sandy driveways as he'd made his way around the county to—in his words— "win the hearts of the yokels."

Lincoln smiled as he recalled a conversation he'd overheard in the donut shop. "Why in Sam Hill does the boy have silver stuck to his boots?" Bobby Ulrich had wondered out loud to a group of farmers gathered for coffee.

"Them ain't boots. Them's genie slippers," Jack Levine threw in. His remark had everyone within earshot rolling with laughter.

Lincoln had often wished that Mr. Crawley would hop on his magic carpet and fly away. It was clear that he saw the sheriff's job in an up-and-coming county as an avenue to make a big name for himself. Unfortunately, he also fit the bill for those Harlownians who wanted law enforcement in their own pockets.

Lincoln would be damned if he'd roll over and let Crawley win. He slid his feet off his desk and picked up the paperwork for the impending debate. Scanning a list of possible questions, he read the first one aloud. "Why do you want to be sheriff? Well, it sure ain't because I'm gettin' rich doin' it," he muttered.

"Linc, we have a call," Charlene relayed over the intercom. "Trouble at Weatherby's place. Scott said he'd meet you at the road."

Lincoln pressed the talk button to reply. "Be right out."

He tossed the bundle of papers onto the overloaded pile that served as his in-tray and gladly left them behind. Years of service to this community would have to be his ace in the hole because if debates and grandstanding were the roads to being the sheriff of Stevens County, then the position was very likely out of his reach.

CHAPTER THREE

Remains Of The Day

The buzz of an early lunch crowd at Mario's could be heard beyond the semi-private room Kinsley had reserved for her and Gabby's lunch meeting. The women were scrutinizing a half-dozen professional photographs of Gabby that they had spread across the table.

"I like this one." Gabby dragged one of the proofs they intended to use in her campaign to be county commissioner closer. "I don't look so terrified."

Kinsley picked up the photo. "I like it too. And you don't look terrified in any of them. Commissioner Gabby Chambers—that has a nice ring to it." She smiled at her pal as she set the photo aside and swept the rest out of the way to make room for their incoming pizza. She thanked the server, then grabbed a spatula to serve them both a slice of the 'Thomas Special' that had become her future stepson's claim to fame.

Gabby took a bite and chewed as she silently read through the tasks listed in the notebook next to her plate. Swallowing, she said, "I'll send that photo to the print shop, and they can make up my campaign signs. Good thing they have a quick turnaround. What should we work on next?"

Kinsley leaned over and read through the list. "Looks like we're back on track. What else can I help with?"

"As if you don't have a million things to do already!"

"How about that radio interview?" Kinsley pointed to an entry near the top. "We can practice if you want."

"Um—Thomas already volunteered," Gabby admitted hesitantly.

Kinsley's eyes widened. "Did he now? He's been awful helpful lately."

A blush rose over Gabby's cheeks. "Yeah, since he heard my relationship with Dusty was on the rocks."

"Fascinating," Kinsley grinned.

"Stop teasing me!" Her friend gave an uncomfortable laugh. "He's a good kid, and he's your family. I swear nothing is going on with us other than friendship."

"Uh-huh. Whatever you say," Kinsley joked. "Looks like you have yourself the start of a fan club, Miss Chambers." Secretly she was highly curious about what Thomas was up to with her best friend, but he was twenty-one and capable of handling his own affairs.

"How's the wedding planning coming?" Gabby asked, keen to change the subject. "Is there anything you need?"

"There isn't really much to plan. A dozen people out at the farm, short and sweet. I'm tickled that your dad has agreed to officiate." Kinsley took her last bite of pizza and set her plate aside.

"He's tickled you asked him. I can't get him to shut up about it. Now he thinks I'm going to take the leap, which is not going to happen." Gabby pulled a face. "The after-party that Frank is planning should be a hoot. Last I heard, the whole town is invited."

Kinsley smiled as she thought about the planned

wedding reception for Lincoln and her. It promised to be a celebration Harlow wouldn't soon forget.

***

Lincoln's black Chevy rumbled to a stop while a following dust cloud coated everything in a fine powder. He climbed out of the truck and warily studied a dark wall of thunderheads that was building to the south before turning his attention to Scott Weatherby, who was sitting atop a red roan mare on the other side of the barbed-wire fencing that lined a ditch.

As the sheriff approached, the rancher removed his baseball cap to reveal a white forehead that contrasted starkly with the brown leathery skin on the rest of his face. Using the sleeve of his plaid shirt, he wiped the sweat from his brow, leaving behind a muddy smear.

"Hey, Sheriff. Thanks fer comin'."

Lincoln adjusted his black Stetson to block the glare of the afternoon sun as he cast an eye over a vast expanse of prairie grass. "Sure thing. What do we have goin' on out here?"

"It's best if I show ya." The farmer's eyes wandered to his cattle as they edged closer in single file. "They reckon I'm here to feed 'em. We should get goin'."

Lincoln found Scott's reluctance to get to the point worrying. "Lead the way," he said and returned to his truck.

"Better lock it in or ya won't make it," Scott shouted as he turned his horse. "Pretty rough out yonder!"

Lincoln crawled into the pickup's cab and tugged the four-wheel-drive gearshift into high before heading for an opening in the fence a quarter of a mile away. Rattling across a cattle guard, he followed Scott off a two-lane path onto an open range littered with sagebrush and briar. The inhospitable vegetation tore along the sides of his pickup with a dull screech, and he winced as he imagined the damage to his paint job.

After a two-mile crawl across rugged terrain, Weatherby reined in his horse and signaled for the sheriff to stop.

Lincoln parked, grabbed his gloves from the console, and joined the rancher at the edge of a short drop-off. A few hundred yards away sat a small clapboard structure sporting a rusted metal roof. The bones of an old windmill stood beside it. Window openings that had long ago lost their glass, forlornly kept watch from either side of an open door.

"That's where we're goin'." Scott pointed toward the house. "Keep your eyes peeled. Been a bumper crop of rattlers this year." With a click of his tongue, he urged his horse forward.

Boots planted at a forty-five-degree angle, Lincoln made his way down an embankment as loose-packed earth threatened to send him headlong into thick patches of cacti. When he reached the bottom of the depression, he surveyed the property looking for anything out of the ordinary.

Scott dismounted and joined him, and the men fell into step. Finally, the rancher revealed the reason for his call. "This mornin', I was out checkin' cattle, and I noticed the front door was open when it's always closed." He stopped and regarded their destination uneasily.

"It was the smell that made me look inside—but I never expected to find a dead man."

Lincoln narrowed his eyes as he looked at his companion. "Did you say a *dead* man?"

Scott swatted at a blowfly that was taking an interest in his left ear. "Yep. See fer yourself."

The sheriff's long stride had him on the porch in moments. A rotten stench coming from inside the dwelling stole his breath instantly. He tucked his gloves under his armpit, pulled a red bandana from a back pocket, and tied it bandit fashion over his nose and mouth. With gloves back in place, he stepped toward the door. The time-worn floorboards protested under his weight, threatening to send him plunging below deck.

Squinting as he entered the gloomy space, Lincoln noted several sets of footprints on either side of drag marks in the thick dirt that covered the plank flooring. Scott hollered directions from outside to guide him toward what had once been a kitchen at the back of the dwelling.

Lincoln reached a doorway through a commotion of blowflies and peered into the next room. Shafts of sunlight streamed brightly through the missing cladding, and the source of the disgusting odor was starkly revealed. A white male, arms hanging limply at his sides, was kneeling in the middle of the space; a rope wrapped around his neck and tied to a rafter of the low-ceilinged room was keeping him upright.

As Lincoln inspected the victim, his focus kept returning to a single bullet wound to the forehead that lent a third-eye feel to the corpse.

The sheriff pulled off his gloves and stuffed them into his back pocket as he entered. He retrieved his phone and a couple of quarters, then placed the coins by boot prints that surrounded the body as a point of reference before he snapped pictures. The powdery dirt didn't allow for crisp impressions, but it was clear that one set was much smaller than the others. He moved around the dead man, noting a large exit wound at the back of his skull and a lack of blood spatter in the area.

In need of fresh air, Lincoln retraced his steps to the entrance. Once outside, he pulled down the bandana and breathed deeply before scrolling through the photos he'd just taken. With a weary sigh he placed a call.

"Hey, Linc," his dispatcher chirped.

"Hey. I'm gonna need backup at Weatherby's old homestead—and the coroner, if you could please, Charlene. We have a homicide."

Without hesitation the seasoned employee smoothed out a plan. "I'll dispatch Butch and Doc Geller right away. Anyone else I should call?"

"Could you please tell Kins I'm gonna be late?"

"Of course," she replied. "Who is it?"

"Don't know him. I can send ya a picture."

"Send it over. I'll see what I can find out."

Lincoln heard her start typing; if anyone could uncover the man's identity, Charlene could. "Thanks," he said before disconnecting the call.

He nodded curtly at Scott, who had taken up a spot in the shadow of his horse some distance away. Surveying the immediate area, Lincoln noticed off-road tire tracks that came right up to the porch. After snapping a few pictures of them, he returned to the victim.

There was something in the breast pocket of the man's faded cotton shirt. Lincoln gently slipped in two fingers and retrieved a ticket stub, similar to those he'd seen used in local raffles. A swift inspection of the deceased's jeans' pockets for a wallet or identification proved to be in vain.

Small puddles of blood directly beneath the dead man's hands caught his attention. Lincoln squatted and turned on his phone flashlight to get a better look. Several of the man's fingernails had been forcibly removed, adding another layer of evil to an already gruesome scene.

He stood and rechecked the area. Then, with nothing more to do until help arrived, he went to talk to Scott.

Weatherby rose from a squatting position and dusted the dirt from his jeans as the sheriff approached.

"You said you went into the house this mornin'?" Lincoln asked.

Scott nodded. "I did, but only fer a second. Didn't make it past the doorway to the kitchen before I ran back out and lost my breakfast. I've hauled off dead cattle, but I've never smelled anythin' like that." He tugged the brim of his cap lower, shielding his eyes.

"The smell of a dead body can make even the strongest men sick," Lincoln said, hoping to alleviate the farmer's discomfort. "Do you come by here every day?"

"I check my cattle several times a day, but it's been a solid week since I was out this way. I didn't get a good look at him, but no one should be here."

Lincoln watched him intently for any tells. "Have you had any issues with people bein' here who shouldn't be?"

Scott squinted as he looked out across his land. "To be honest, Sheriff, since the Skellys went away, we've had nothin' but trouble 'round here."

Lincoln removed his Stetson to slap off some dust. "Trouble? What kinda trouble?"

"Skelly kept things in line. I know he was a criminal, but he never let anythin' get out of hand. Now…" The farmer hesitated and a troubled look crossed his face.

"Go on," Lincoln urged.

"Well, now it seems them crooks are fightin' over who's gonna be in charge. It's been a hell of a mess."

That declaration caused Lincoln a hefty dose of guilt; he should have known about this sooner. "Scott, why didn't you call us? We wouldn't have let this go on."

Weatherby couldn't meet his gaze. "Because people get killed fer stickin' their noses where they don't belong. I have a family to protect, Linc."

The sheriff could see that Scott was holding back. Suspecting it was out of fear, Lincoln felt a slow-burning rage start to build in his chest. The repercussions of the Skelly family's actions continued to haunt his district, but he refused to let the county residents suffer because of them.

"I assure you, anything that has been goin' on will cease. We will protect you *and* your family."

Scott nodded. "I appreciate that. Look, I gotta get home. Ya need me fer anythin'?"

"Not at the moment. I'm sorry for the trouble you've been havin'," said Lincoln before shaking the man's hand.

Weatherby gave a short, sharp whistle, and his horse plodded over to nuzzle her master.

"Pretty neat trick," the sheriff grinned.

Scott winked before grabbing the reins and swinging smoothly into his saddle. As he urged his mount into a trot, Lincoln watched him ride away.

The tire tracks outside the house caught his eye again, and he followed them away from the crime scene. Memories about all that had happened since the Skelly trials almost a year ago dogged his every step. It had taken months after the final verdict for the fuss to die down and a semblance of normality to return to their small town. However, national exposure had brought in new people, and the population of Harlow had exploded. With those new residents came startup businesses and better job opportunities—but also more crime.

The tire marks led into a field overgrown with sweetbriar. Lincoln surveyed their zigzagging path: it looked as if someone had been riding an all-terrain vehicle for fun. It seemed unlikely the imprints had anything to do with the murder, but he'd keep them on the list.

The sheriff stepped into the field and inhaled deeply. He hoped the apple-scented briar would overpower the stench of death that was still clinging to him, but it was a wasted effort.

A roiling dust cloud to the east signaled the arrival of his backup. As he returned to the crime scene, Lincoln waved to his undersheriff, Butch Pate, who was unloading gear at the top of the rise.

Though murder was always a heinous crime, this killing suggested something more sinister. Lincoln couldn't help but wonder if a storm was blowing in that he might not be able to stop.

CHAPTER FOUR

Home Front

Kinsley's eyes wandered to her computer clock, but only five minutes had passed since the last time she'd checked. It felt to her like time had slowed to a crawl.

A new addition to her bi-monthly abuse survivors' group was haunting her. Casey, who had declined an invitation to share more than a first name, wore her desolation like a shroud, and that had Kinsley concocting several awful scenarios that might explain the stranger's sad state. She hoped Casey would return for their next meeting because the woman looked like she could use a friend.

The thrumming bass from a car passing the front of the house floated in through an open window, triggering memories of warm summer nights spent cruising Main Street with Gabby and Dusty. The couple's split had put a strain on the three of them doing anything together, but perhaps with time their friendship could be restored to some version of what they had once shared.

Shifting to a new sitting position, Kinsley refocused on the laptop screen and watched the cursor blink a few times before her mind wandered to a recent decision to create a new piece of software to license and distribute widely. It was a significant challenge, but, if she did it right, this venture could become a jewel in her company's crown. Tackling complex scenarios was where she usually thrived, and fear of failure had never stopped her—though it certainly was slowing her down this time.

Kinsley clicked on a file she'd saved to her desktop and opened a set of blueprints for her new office complex that a high-school pal, Darren Barnes, had sent. A brilliant architect, Darren had recently returned to Harlow to care for his ailing mother, and he and his husband Frank had become a welcome addition to their circle of friends.

Kinsley's decision to open a brick-and-mortar office in Harlow would create a more productive work environment than her dining-room table. Her budding intern partnership with a community college in the neighboring city of Liberal also meant that she needed additional space. Giving up the convenience of working from home would be her only regret.

She looked over a rendering of what would become the home of KDR Enterprises, and a smile played across her lips. The warm, Spanish-style office building, with its terracotta-tiled roof and creamy stucco exterior, would be a beautiful addition to Harlow's business landscape. However, Kinsley knew that once her new headquarters were completed, hiding how well she'd done for herself would prove impossible.

Kinsley closed the drawing, and that cursor was back, taunting her from the end of a blank line that should have been written already. Groaning, she pushed back from the table and went to the kitchen for a glass of water. A glance at the microwave's digital display showed half past eleven. Lincoln was rarely out this late…

That thought had just evaporated when the familiar rumble of his pickup prompted her to cross the room, take leftovers from the refrigerator, and place them on the counter.

"Kins!" Lincoln called out as he came into the house.

"Kitchen!" she hollered back as she placed her favorite cast-iron skillet on a burner and turned it on. She retrieved a pot from a lower cabinet and set it next to the pan.

Kinsley smiled as he came into the room. "Hungry?"

"Always. Thank you for savin' me somethin'." Lincoln rounded the island and gathered her close.

"Of course." Kinsley rose to her tiptoes and gave him a quick peck. "Tell me what you've been up to until all hours."

He released her and took his place at the breakfast bar while she forked a Salisbury steak into the heated pan. "Well? Are you going to share?" Kinsley probed as she spooned potatoes into the pot.

Lincoln placed his hat on the stool next to him and ran his fingers through his hair. "There's been a murder."

His shocking response made her lose track of what she was doing and a pat of butter meant for the mashed potatoes slipped off the end of her knife and hit the vegetables with a plop. She laid the knife aside. "Someone we know?" Her heart squeezed painfully with the still tender loss of her dear grandpa Henry to the same fate last year.

"No one I know, and Charlene didn't know him either." Lincoln scratched his neck. "I'm pretty sure he's from that religious settlement out near the state line."

"What makes you think that?" Kinsley asked as she

returned to her task. "And I think they call themselves 'The Order', last I heard." She turned the steak, poured mushroom gravy over the top, and placed a cover on the pan.

"Yep, that's the one. His clothes are homemade like the ones they wear." Lincoln yawned and put his forearms on the bar as he inhaled. "Dang, that smells good."

"Jalinda gave me her recipe after they invited us to dinner and you about ate her out of house and home," Kinsley teased.

"If the food is good, I'm gonna eat it." Lincoln grinned. "How was your day?"

"I met with Darren and finalized plans for my office and training center. He is amazing. It's going to be nice to have a proper workspace."

"I like that you're keepin' everything local and hirin' Francisco's construction company. He'll do a good job. How's Darren? And Frank?"

"They're great. We should have them over soon. By the way, I talked to Frank about heading your nonexistent election campaign, and of course he said yes. Expect a call from him."

Lincoln shook his head as he watched her stir the vegetables. "I hate that I need a campaign."

Kinsley plated his meal and placed it in front of him. "I know you do, but that snake Crawley is out shaking hands every day while you're busy keeping us safe." She moved to the sink to wash the dishes. "Frank will make sure they know how valuable you are."

Lincoln speared a mushroom and popped it into his mouth. As he ate, he thought about the race for sheriff and how the town would react to the news of another killing. He had to solve the case before the election, and that was all there was to it.

CHAPTER FIVE

The Early Worm

Lincoln's blacked-out Chevy pickup, tucked in amongst a few stunted cherry trees, would be difficult to spot from the road that led to Weatherby's farm. He sipped coffee from Henry's old thermos and the nutty aroma awakened his senses as he examined the predawn horizon for the third day in a row. There wasn't much going on at a quarter to four in the morning. Still, the landowner's report of nefarious activity could not be ignored—especially with the high priority of their new murder case.

He and Butch, together with the coroner, had searched every inch of the ramshackle dwelling on the day the body was discovered. The bullet that had caused a gaping hole in the victim's skull was nowhere to be found. With no indication of a struggle and hardly any blood surrounding the body, they'd agreed that the shooting hadn't happened in that house.

They had dusted the door frames for fingerprints, but only came up with partials. The walls in the house were coated in dirt and they had recovered an almost perfect palm print next to the corpse, but it hadn't led to a break. At least not yet.

The young male's homemade jeans and simple cotton shirt immediately pointed them to a religious group that had set up shop decades earlier near the state line between Kansas and Oklahoma. The Order seemed to have adopted the practices of several religions, including the Amish. They were a close-knit clan that kept their interactions with the outside world to a minimum, and there had never been an ounce of trouble from them in all the years Lincoln had been sheriff. Most of the men worked in and around Harlow, and, as a whole, they had an upstanding reputation.

Lincoln had taken a picture of the deceased to the settlement, but the members had formed a united front against him and revealed nothing, which left him wondering why they wouldn't come forward to claim one of their own. Finding the next of kin seemed less likely with each passing day, and keeping the news of a murder suppressed in Harlow for long would be next to impossible.

Light from an almost full moon bathed the flat expanse of land in a milky glow. A scraggly coyote trotted into sight, and when it stopped a few yards in front of his pickup, Lincoln wrapped his arms around the steering wheel to study the animal.

Seconds after hearing the report, bullets pinged off his pickup. Lincoln dove across the bench seat and reached for his sidearm that lay holstered in the passenger floorboard. "Son of a bitch!" he hissed.

Breathing in deeply through his nose, he exhaled and slipped his Sig Sauer from its holster while listening for whatever was coming next. When no more bullets hit his truck, he reached for the key in the ignition, cranked the engine, and peeked over the dashboard.

Several more rounds were fired, but this time they were moving away from his position. Lincoln watched a flatbed Chevy with a dog box attached rocketing across the rough terrain ahead of him: coyote hunters.

Dropping his pickup into gear, the sheriff took out after them, laying his palm on the horn. *These idiots could kill somebody by hunting in the dark,* he thought.

The jalopy he was chasing slowed and finally rolled to a stop. Lincoln slammed his vehicle into park, radioed in the tag number, his location, and a request for backup. Steam had started to rise from under the hood of his truck, confirming that the bullets had hit something vital. He reluctantly added the need for a tow truck.

Lincoln's headlights illuminated the scene. He aimed his pistol through the rolled-down window space as he slid out of the driver's seat, using his pickup door as a shield. "Exit your vehicle with your arms raised!" he shouted.

The dogs, caged in boxes on the back of the truck, bayed loudly, increasing the tension in an already charged situation.

"Shit, Sheriff, don't shoot! It's me! Johnny Ray!" The man swung his pencil-thin legs out the open door of his pickup and moonlight glanced off a rifle that lay across his knees.

"Put that gun down, Johnny. You shot at me, and I'm in no mood to mess with ya," Lincoln warned.

"Oh, hell! I was shootin' at the coyote. Sorry." Johnny climbed out and laid the Remington on the truck bed. "I wouldn't shoot ya on purpose."

Lowering his gun, Lincoln moved around the door of his vehicle. "Who's with ya?"

"My brother." Johnny Ray turned his head and hollered over his shoulder, "Jed, get out here!"

Jed Ray rolled out of the truck and rested his forearms on the bed. He peered at Lincoln from beneath a dark curtain of unkempt hair. His face was as round as a dinner plate with little slits for eyes placed closely together. A wide grin revealed an incomplete keyboard of teeth. "S'up, Linc?" His gaze wandered to Lincoln's pickup, and the tower of steam rising into the night dimmed his sunny smile.

"You boys are huntin' illegally. I know Scott Weatherby doesn't allow hunters on his land. You shot at me. I'm gonna have ta take ya in." Lincoln studied the pair. The Ray brothers had never been a violent lot; they were more often found sitting on their porch getting drunk than doing anything harmful.

Johnny begged for a reprieve, "Aw, come on, Linc. We're sorry. We didn't see ya. I didn't mean ta shoot yer truck."

The sound of a far-off siren rose and fell. "I ain't goin' ta jail!" Jed yelled. "Ma'll skin us!" He lurched across the uneven ground like a parade balloon ripped free from its tether.

"Dammit, runnin'll make it worse. Get yur giant butt back here!" his brother screeched.

The escapee only made it a few yards before he bent forward, placed his hands on his knees and started wheezing.

"You're an idjit, Jed," Johnny announced as he approached the sheriff with his arms held high in surrender. Lincoln signaled for him to put his arms down. "Ain't ya gonna cuff me?"

Lincoln arched one brow. "Do you need to be cuffed?"

A crooked grin appeared on Johnny's face. "I ain't never been arrested afore, and this don't seem like how it oughta go."

With a tight-lipped grin, Lincoln stuck his gun in the waistband of his jeans and reached back to pull the cuffs from their holder. "Put your arms out."

He read Johnny his rights as he adjusted the metal restraints; even on their smallest setting they were loose around the prisoner's slender wrists. Presumably, the man wouldn't try to escape since he'd asked to be restrained. That was the first time in Lincoln's career as a law enforcement officer that anyone had ever asked to be cuffed.

Undersheriff Pate brought his SUV to an abrupt stop next to Lincoln's vehicle, hopped out and surveyed the scene. "What the hell happened to your pickup, Linc?"

"We shot it," Johnny Ray piped up, then ducked his head sheepishly. "But it were an accident."

Butch suppressed a laugh before he set out across the field to bring back the out-of-breath runner. He and Lincoln stepped aside to talk once the brothers were secured in the back of Butch's vehicle.

"Dusty sent for one tow truck. I'll call for another to take this back to the Rays'." Butch tipped his head toward the coyote wagon.

Lincoln considered the agitated hounds locked in their crates. "No, I'll drive Johnny's vehicle out to their place and unload those dogs. We can't leave 'em cooped up like that."

Butch grinned and slapped him on the back. "Good luck with Ma Ray—you still have a good chance of gettin' shot today. I'll send help if we don't see ya pretty soon."

Lincoln chuckled. "Thanks for comin'. I'll wait for the tow."

The undersheriff returned to his vehicle and waved goodbye out the open window as he bumped across the uneven ground, dodging yucca plants along the way.

Lincoln put a hip against the flatbed of Johnny Ray's truck and spoke softly to the howling dogs. Pulling a packet of beef jerky from his vest pocket, he dropped a few pieces through the tiny cage windows. He had seen too much death over the years, and the idea of hunting for sport held no appeal for him.

His gaze wandered to a rise where the coyote that had caused this morning's ruckus was sitting, still as a statue, watching him. The fading moonlight illuminated the animal's silvery coat as it ruffled in the south breeze. The coyote bowed his head before he rose and trotted into a cornfield beyond.

After a considerable wait, Curly Jenks, the only game in town when it came to wrecker service, finally arrived. As he drove unhurriedly across the rough ground, the sun broke the horizon with jeweled tones of rust and gold. Chains attached to his rig plinked out a tinny melody to accompany his arrival.

He unloaded and took a lingering look at the steaming Chevy. "Sher'f, yur ride give out on ya?"

Lincoln tapped the broken grill. "Bullet took out the radiator, along with other things, I'd imagine. Could you please tow it over to Junior's garage for me?"

"Sure 'nuff." Curly bent to look at the holes in the vehicle before he scuttled off to bring his wrecker around.

Once his truck was on the way to the repair shop, Lincoln's thoughts turned toward the Ray brothers. He was sure this wasn't their first late-night hunting excursion, so it was possible that they had witnessed something pertaining to the murder and didn't know it. A thorough questioning would be in order when he returned to the office.

Lincoln knew they had meant him no harm, but they needed to curtail their unlawful activities; intended or not, they could have shot him instead of his pickup, or they could have hit one of Scott Weatherby's cows. The whole situation was a recipe for disaster.

When Lincoln tugged open Ray's vehicle door, the smell of stale chewing tobacco slapped him across the face. He took a deep breath of fresh air before pushing the seat back and crawling into the cab.

***

As Kinsley approached her house at the end of her morning run, a passing wrecker loaded with Lincoln's truck sent panic coursing through her. She ripped her phone from her pocket to speed dial his number. "Please let him be okay," she begged as the phone rang.

"Hi, sweetie." Lincoln's warm tone provided instant relief.

"Oh, Lincoln, thank God! I saw your pickup on the tow truck. What happened?"

He quickly relayed the morning's events as he approached his target location. "I gotta go. I'm out at the Rays' farm. We can talk more at lunch."

"Of course. Be careful out there. Those people are

outlaws." Kinsley could envisage June Ray standing on her porch in a flowered nightdress with a shotgun tucked under her arm.

Lincoln chuckled. "I'll watch myself. See ya in a few hours," he said as he navigated a bend that led to the Rays' homestead.

Kinsley exhaled, disconnected the call, and stepped onto her porch.

"Out for a run?" a male voice asked from the direction of the rocking chairs at the far end of her veranda.

Startled, she took a faltering step before regaining her footing as the unexpected guest rose to greet her. Josh Layton, former deputy mayor, was sizing her up as he approached. She noted his crisp white shirt and the navy slacks that fitted him to a T. Somewhere in his late forties, his golden hair and cornflower-blue eyes painted a misleading picture of a boy next door, but when he flashed his politician's smile, a mouthful of sparkling white teeth revealed his truer nature: a great white shark on the hunt.

"What can I do for you, Josh?" Kinsley responded coolly as she maintained her distance.

"All business, I see. I'll get right to the point. I need some webwork, and it's been said that you're the best in the area. I'm here to hire you." He rested his shoulder against the door jamb, positioning himself between her and the front door.

"I'm not taking on any new work," Kinsley replied. She had no intention of ever working for this impudent upstart.

"You mean you won't take on *my* work? There's no

need to cut your nose off to spite your face. I'm willing to pay what I'm sure will be your exorbitant price," he crooned as he moved into her personal space. "Miss Chambers has no chance against me in the race for commissioner. You must see that."

"No, I don't see that at all." Kinsley sidestepped him to unlock the door. "You're right—I won't take you on as a client, but not for that reason. Thank you for considering me." Her intention to leave him on the porch was crushed as he followed her into the open doorway.

She stopped short to keep him from coming inside, which left him close enough for his minty breath to tickle the hairs on the back of her neck.

"This is a small town, and I have powerful friends," he murmured.

His velvet-over-steel tone pushed her into fight mode. She turned around and backed him across the door's threshold. "You start stirrin' shit, and you're bound to get some on ya. You don't need that with an election coming up. Do you?"

"Miss Rhodes, you've misunderstood." Josh's fake, public-servant persona clicked into place. "I only meant that working for me could gain you some much-needed respect." He narrowed his eyes. "It could help your little business."

Kinsley had to fight back laughter. "My *little* business is doing just fine without you and your friends. Have a good day." She stepped into the house, shut the door with a solid crack and flipped the deadbolt into place.

Toppling the Skelly regime had promised a brighter future for Harlow, but the corruption ran deeper than

Kinsley had imagined. A line had formed to be the next evil bastard in charge, and Layton had excellent qualifications.

She entered the bathroom, stripped off her clothes while the water for her shower warmed, then stepped under the spray to wash away the creepy start to her morning. The future of Harlow would be decided on election day. If they were to have any chance at cleaning up their town, Gabby and Lincoln had to win their bids.

CHAPTER SIX

In The Boondocks

Lincoln drove cautiously onto the Rays' property; the family took their right to privacy seriously, and an unexpected visit would not be welcomed. Parking at the front of the house, he exited the noxious vehicle and took a cleansing breath as he scrutinized his surroundings.

The unkempt clapboard residence sported a copious amount of bare wood. Years of rain mixed with rust from metal window screens had stained the cladding at the corner of each opening, creating an illusion that the house was weeping bloody tears. Dead cottonwood trees looked on like silent mourners.

A yellow cat with a crooked tail wandered out of a barn and eyed Lincoln with mild disinterest. When the caged dogs yapped, the tabby skittered under a heap of metal that had once been a vehicle.

Lincoln spotted several kennels next to a shed on the far side of a neglected lawn. He reached into the truck to get the leashes, skirted the vehicle, then took a giant step onto a hitch and another onto the flatbed. Squatting, he quickly slid open one of the access doors in the center of the cage, and snapped a leash onto the first dog's harness ring before the hound knew what had hit him. He repeated the process, then slipped each animal a piece of jerky to remind them he was a friend.

"Back away from them mutts!" A sandpaper voice boomed from the direction of the dwelling. "Raise yer hands where I can see 'em."

Lincoln dropped the leashes and stood slowly. "Mrs. Ray, it's Sheriff James."

"Yeah, I knowed. Johnny called me from the station. I should shoot ya fer jailin' my boys." She had one eye on him through the sight of a double-barrel shotgun. A lit cigarette was precariously perched at the corner of her mouth, and the smoke was tangling in her messy curls. Stains and patches dotted her work-worn overalls.

June Ray was a force to be reckoned with, and Lincoln wasn't looking for a fight. "Mrs. Ray, I'm just bringin' your dogs home. Johnny and Jed shot at me. I couldn't allow that. You understand, right?"

He watched her warily as she contemplated what he'd said before lowering her shotgun. "Them boys are plain no good. Take after their pa. May he rest in peace." She leaned the weapon against the house and came down off the porch. "Let's get them dogs put up."

They each took an animal and crossed the lawn to the kennels. Lincoln stepped around circular patches of goat-head stickers that were the only signs of life in the carpet of brown. After they had secured the dogs, they began their trek back across the lawn.

"Wanna beer, Sheriff?" June asked.

Lincoln had to suppress a smile at the question. Firstly, it had just passed six-thirty in the morning, and secondly, he was an officer of the law on the clock. He did admire June's gumption, though. "I'm on duty, Mrs. Ray, but I do thank you for the offer. I'm gonna take Johnny's pickup in so they can get home when we release 'em."

June nodded. "I'm gonna skin both of 'em alive. I taught them idjits not ta shoot at the law." She grasped Lincoln's hand roughly and pumped it like she was drawing water from a nearly dry well. "Do what ya need ta do. They deserve what they get."

He extracted his hand from her steel grip. "They'll be home by supper time. Thank you, Mrs. Ray." He considered Rays' farm and its proximity to Weatherby's homestead; it was within a few miles of the crime scene. "Have you had any problems out here lately, Ma'am?"

Her bushy brows knitted together. "Whatcha gettin' at?"

Lincoln continued cautiously. "I mean in general. Everything goin' well out here? No issues with anyone?"

June's brown eyes twinkled as she took a long drag from her cigarette, tossed it down, and ground out the stub under her booted toe. "We're the trouble, Sheriff," she said, before bursting into raucous laughter.

Lincoln couldn't help but laugh. This morning, he would have to agree with that statement.

"Hang on a minute. I got somethin' fer ya," June said before she shambled off with surprising speed and disappeared around one corner of the house.

Lincoln leaned against the truck bed and looked at cattle pens that were in dire need of repair. The Rays' barn was missing so much wood that there was little more than the framing remaining. If he thought she'd accept help he'd send out Thomas and his friends, but he knew better. June Ray was a proud woman.

A prickly pear cactus had grown around the base of a rusted water pump next to a dry stock tank. Brilliant yellow flowers smiled at him from atop each teardrop-shaped pad.

"Even in ruin, there is beauty," Lincoln observed aloud.

"Here ya go." June hurried toward him holding out a bluetick coonhound pup. "Fer 'em boys of mine doin' ya wrong. She's the best in the litter. A good 'un."

"Oh, Mrs. Ray, I couldn't take your dog."

She pressed the whimpering pup against Lincoln's chest. "Take her. She'll be a good hunter."

"I…" Lincoln stumbled over his response as he took hold of the animal. "I don't know what to say. Can I buy her from ya?"

"Nope. That gal o' yourn like dogs?"

"Kinsley'll be very happy. But I'd like to pay ya somethin'."

June gave him a snaggle-toothed grin as she patted the pup's head before stepping back. "You keep on bein' sheriff. How 'bout that?"

He tipped his hat. "I'll do my best. Thank ya most kindly, Mrs. Ray."

Lincoln rubbed the dog's ear as he climbed in the coyote wagon and placed the puppy on the seat next to him. The Ray's washboard driveway nearly loosened his teeth before he got back on the blacktop. The bluetick bundle curled against his leg when the road smoothed out.

As the sheriff did his best to ignore the vehicle's odor, which he was sure would stick with him for the rest of the day, he stroked the pup and thought about the morning's events. Rays' farm was only a few miles from the settlement where Lincoln was sure the murder victim had family, so there was a good chance that June Ray knew more than she was saying. If she wouldn't spill, maybe her sons would, though he wouldn't put any money on what those boys knew.

Butch had heard some gossip at the hardware store recently about illegal immigrants staying with The Order. It was little more than hearsay, but if they were harboring illegals it would be one more reason for them not to come forward with information. Ultimately, the group mistrusted outsiders; what Lincoln needed was an insider.

CHAPTER SEVEN

Breaking News

Lincoln flipped back the covers and swung his legs out of bed. Sitting on the edge, he rubbed his face with both hands. The long days were starting to take their toll; nearly a week in, and they weren't any closer to solving this new murder than they had been on day one.

He and Butch had decided to release the news about the dead man to the public. They needed to identify their victim, and someone had to know who he was. It had been a minor miracle to have kept a murder secret in a town the size of Harlow for as long as they had.

Unsurprisingly, the Ray brothers didn't know a thing. Lincoln had let them go after confiscating their weapons and charging them with the unlawful discharge of a firearm. Their mother had no doubt passed judgment and doled out punishment more severe than any court could when they returned home. Jail might have been kinder.

Lincoln went into the bathroom, turned on the shower faucet, and continued ruminating as the water warmed. Unfortunately, what they knew about the victim was much less than what they didn't know. The coroner had put the man's age in his late thirties. He was fit, and his calloused hands gave the indication of manual labor. Strangely, the victim's sharply pointed, Mexican-style boots were out of sync with the rest of his homespun clothing: one would not expect highly polished footwear that barely had a scuff on the sole with near-threadbare jeans.

Dreading the day that lay ahead, the sheriff stepped under the warm spray and closed his eyes.

***

Kinsley listened to Lincoln whistling as he finished his morning shower routine. She absently flipped sausages in a pan as she considered how much this new case would impact both him and the town. Having a full staff to back him would help with investigating, but it wouldn't stop the discord that was sure to come his way after they released the information about this latest murder.

Lincoln wandered in and poured them both a cup of coffee. "Where's the pup?"

Kinsley smiled. "Out back—and her name is Maizey."

"I guess that means we're keepin' her?" Lincoln teased, knowing she had immediately fallen head over heels for the furry bundle.

"As if you have to ask. Thomas and I are smitten." Kinsley plated the sausages and cracked eggs into the hot pan. "Any luck with those people out at the settlement?"

"Nope, they're shut up tight as a drum." He kissed her cheek before taking a seat at the bar. "What I can't figure out is why. I know he's one of theirs."

"What did they say exactly?"

"A whole lot of nothin'. The guy at the gate glanced at the photo, said he didn't know the victim, and that was that. I was summarily dismissed."

"That is weird. You don't suppose this has anything to do with my grandpa and the Skellys, do you?"

"I don't, but the murder has certain hallmarks that worry me." Lincoln gazed out the kitchen window while he sipped his coffee. "When you lived here before, was there ever talk about cartel activity?"

Kinsley plated the remainder of their breakfast while she contemplated what evil might have invaded Harlow. Taking a seat, she said, "When I was in high school, there was a murder out in the country just across the Oklahoma state line. I remember the news report saying it had certain hallmarks, too." She tried to shake off a creeping sense of dread. "The rumor was that a Mexican cartel was responsible. Then it faded away as if it had never happened. I don't remember the crime ever being solved, but I wouldn't swear to that."

She hadn't thought about that killing in years. Grandpa had told her the death was drug-related and used it as a vehicle to teach her about the dangers of 'mixing up with the wrong sorts.'

"I don't remember the news mentioning those people being members of any religious sect." Kinsley watched Lincoln as he processed this new information.

He took her hand and kissed her fingers. "Kins, don't worry. We'll stop whoever did this."

She couldn't ignore the deep lines near his mouth that spoke the real truth of the weight he was carrying. Adding to his load would do no good. "I'm not worried. You're the best sheriff there is." She squeezed his hand and changed the subject. "I go for my final dress fitting this week. You haven't changed your mind about making us official, have you?" she teased.

"Nope. You're stuck with me. Do ya need me to do anything?" He took the last bite of sausage on his plate.

"Just show up on time. I have everything arranged."

"I look forward to us being husband and wife—officially." A sly grin spread across Lincoln's face.

"If you don't want to be late for work, you'd best put away that naughty smile, Sheriff," Kinsley warned him lightheartedly.

"I'd love to be late, but I do have a news conference scheduled. Maybe I shouldn't show up with scratch marks and hickeys."

She snickered as she cleared the plates and put them in the sink. "As if I've ever marked you."

Lincoln came up behind her and wrapped her in his arms as she continued. "Well, except for the time we broke the dining-room table. But that was hardly my fault."

They reminisced about that particular hot summer encounter. He had sported a shiner for days, picked up from the arm of a chair he'd hit as they'd tumbled to the floor. "It was worth the black eye," he said, nipping her earlobe. "I'll see you at the courthouse at eight."

"I'll be there."

Lincoln turned her around and kissed her lips softly. "You'll stay in and run on the treadmill, right?"

She met his gaze. "I promise."

"I'm the luckiest guy," he said before reluctantly letting her go and heading out.

Kinsley let Maizey in and watched the dog sniff around Lincoln's barstool before returning to sit in front of her. "It's just you and me, girl. Wanna watch me run in place?"

The puppy's tail thumped excitedly against the linoleum.

"I wish I was as revved about it as you are. You need to get big quick so we can run together." She scratched behind the pup's ear. "Come on, Maiz. Let's do this."

After several starts and stops, Kinsley convinced the dog to lie down with a chew toy and watch instead of attempting to get on the treadmill with her. Gradually increasing the speed, she broke into a run.

Certain hallmarks? What could that mean? Whatever they were, they worried Lincoln enough to ask her to change her routine. With an upcoming election, this was the last thing he needed, and she wished there was something she could do to help. Watching out for herself and Thomas would have to do for now.

CHAPTER EIGHT

In A Flash

Lincoln made his early morning rounds in the country as he had every day since the discovery of their latest murder victim, but, yet again, he returned to town empty handed. The criminal activity Scott had mentioned had ceased—at least for now.

Charlene had ordered dozens of donuts for their press conference, which was set for eight a.m., and his next task was to pick them up before going into headquarters. He still had his reservations about asking the public for help, but there didn't seem to be another way to move the investigation forward since the stonewalling he'd received from The Order.

The deceased's identifying markers had been entered into every system available to them—both state and federal—but it was as if the man didn't exist. Lincoln would have preferred to have told the victim's parents before releasing any information, but it was likely they already knew.

He trekked down the long, narrow hall from the back door of the Donut Shop and emerged into a packed house: the six o'clock crowd had this place humming. Most of the long communal tables were filled with local farmers chewing the fat and solving the problems of a small town, or so they thought. All eyes turned to Lincoln as he approached the register.

"Hey, Sheriff. Grab a cup and join us," Jack Levine called out.

Donna Davies, the bright-eyed shop owner, pushed through double swing doors behind the counter as she came out of the kitchen and presented Lincoln with a steaming mug of coffee.

"Thanks, Donna," he said.

She patted his arm. "Don't let 'em fill ya full of bull, Linc."

Lincoln gave her a wink then moved toward Levine's group. "Hey, everybody," he said as he took a seat. "What's the word?"

"We should be askin' you that, Sheriff." Jack reared back in his chair and studied Lincoln over the rim of his coffee cup as he noisily took a sip.

"You'll know soon enough. I'm sorry I can't share anything yet. Y'all understand, right?" Lincoln did his best to smooth the waters; he didn't need a pack of angry farmers to add flavor to his chaos stew.

"Yeah, we do," Jack said. "It gives us ol' coots somethin' to wonder about fer a change." His deep laughter spread among the others. "We hear ya tried to get into the compound out south the other day. How'd that work out for ya?" The amusement on his face was positively wicked.

"Not that well," Lincoln acknowledged. He took another sip of coffee and listened as the conversation at the table turned to talk about the settlement.

"My wife was one of 'em. Private bunch," Stanley

Cooper threw in. "She still has a sister in there. They like to keep to themselves."

Lincoln made a mental note of the association. "It's their right," he offered.

A large industrial-type clock fixed to the wall near the front door told him he'd best be on his way. "Men, I thank ya for the chat. I hafta get donuts back to the office."

"Better get with it, or Charlene'll have yer hide," Jack teased, which pulled another round of chuckles from the onlookers.

"You ain't kiddin'," Lincoln said, joining in the friendly ribbing before scooting away from the table. "I'll see y'all in a bit."

As he drove through the waking town, Lincoln wondered how congenial those men would be once he revealed another murder.

Approaching the office, Lincoln groaned upon seeing several news vans already parked along the curb. Pulling into his reserved spot, he braced himself, stepped out of the truck, and headed inside where he was greeted with microphones and deafening chatter.

He had lived through much of the same during the Skelly trials, and his finesse had greatly improved. "I'm sorry, folks. No comment at this time. Please join us at the courthouse at eight, and I'll answer all I can." Lincoln wore a practiced smile as he moved beyond the secure door, forcing the reporters to pack up their disappointment along with their equipment and leave.

"You got the donuts, right?" Charlene asked from across the room where she was deftly filing paperwork.

"I did. I know better than to mess with your plans."

The dispatcher snorted and turned around to face him. Lincoln noticed her less dramatic makeup and new hairstyle. "You look real pretty today. Somethin' special happening I should know about?"

"With all this media, we're on TV constantly. I saw myself on the news, and I can't go on lookin' like that." Charlene cringed. "Kins gave me the name of her hairdresser gal in Liberal. I just wish this publicity merry-go-round would stop. I want off."

Lincoln agreed wholeheartedly. He had more attention than he wanted, including everything that came with being voted sexiest sheriff in a local publication. A grin peeked at the corner of his mouth as he thought of how Kinsley had almost fallen over with laughter when *that* announcement came out.

"Well, don't you just look like the cat that ate the canary?" Charlene observed.

His smile spread as he switched the focus to his dispatcher's new relationship. "How's Dixon?"

His question brought about a crimson flush to the roots of her red locks.

"Oh, that good, huh?" Lincoln chuckled and headed down the hall to his office. He was glad Charlene had found someone to date.

Dixon Carlisle, his new deputy, was a quiet sort. A thin scar sliced through his eyebrow, giving him a fearsome look; when coupled with his bodybuilder physique, it discouraged most people from trying anything foolish. On more than one occasion Lincoln had heard Charlene and the ladies tittering about Dixon's big biceps.

He rounded his desk and sank into his chair. The new deputy fit in well with their crew. He hoped everything would work out with him and Charlene because if those two parted on bad terms, things could get mighty uncomfortable around the office.

A sketched likeness of the victim lay on his desk, next to a photo Lincoln had taken. He and Butch had agreed it would be better to show a drawing rather than an image of a dead man with a bullet hole in his forehead, and he had to hand it to the artist: the rendering was excellent.

He put the pictures aside and moved to a file that contained an autopsy report on the decedent. The official cause of death was a blow to the head resulting in a traumatic brain injury, but the man also had massive internal bleeding. Lincoln rubbed his forehead while he read the laundry list of injuries: broken bones, extensive bruising, scrapes, and cuts. Removing the deceased's fingernails and the gunshot to the forehead postmortem were out of place.

Why desecrate a corpse? he wondered. *Was it a calling card?* He scribbled a note to look for other murders with these unusual markers, including the one Kinsley had mentioned.

His cellphone rang and interrupted his rumination. "James," he answered.

"Hey, Linc. Crawley is giving his own press conference in front of the courthouse. Really layin' it on thick about what a terrible sheriff you are," Butch said grimly. "And it looks like we got one hell of a storm blowing in from the south."

"Thanks for the double warnin'," Lincoln replied. "Crawley can spout off all he wants, but the proof is in the puddin', right?"

"It sure is. He's a pompous ass. If it wouldn't get me arrested, I'd take him down a notch or two."

"Guys like Crawley usually get what's comin' to 'em… eventually. I'll be there in fifteen." The sheriff ended the call and sat back in his chair to gather his thoughts before heading to the courthouse and the spectacle that would inevitably follow their announcement.

He longed for the peace and small-town friendliness that used to define Harlow.

CHAPTER NINE

The Devil You Know

Kinsley made her way past the gathering crowd at the courthouse and sprinted up two flights of stairs before turning down a wide hallway. The familiar scents of old paper and floor wax that permeated the courthouse ticked some box that lightened her heart. She had loved going to the municipal building with her grandpa; from its highly polished floors to the expanse of glass in the lobby, she'd dreamily considered it a flatlander's castle.

As she neared Gabby's office, Kinsley suddenly remembered that her friend used to live out at the settlement.

The memory of the first time they'd met played out in cinematic quality. As per the daily summer ritual, thirteen-year-old Kinsley and her grandpa had stopped by the diner to eat breakfast with his friends before going to the farm. Surprised to see someone her own age, Kinsley had watched the disheveled girl slip into a corner booth. Finger-shaped bruises on the girl's bicep would have been impossible to miss, and she had poked her grandpa to get him to quit entertaining the troops long enough to look.

Henry's eyes swung from the new arrival, who was counting the change she'd dumped on the table, to his granddaughter. Without speaking, he pressed a few dollars into Kinsley's hand and nodded for her to go. If memory served, she had faked a trip to the restroom so she could strike up a conversation on her way back. What she'd said, she couldn't quite remember.

Though rightly standoffish, by some miracle Gabby had decided to let Kinsley sit with her, and they'd ordered food. By the time Grandpa joined them, Gabby had revealed she was without means and out of options.

Kinsley hadn't known it at the time, but she had met the best friend she would ever have.

Rejoining the present, Kinsley glided into Gabby's workspace and addressed her friend. "Hey, gorgeous, ready for this?"

"Just a sec. I need to file this paperwork." Gabby hurried through to an adjoining room.

Hateful-looking storm clouds were framed by windows that lined the far wall. Kinsley hoped they wouldn't bring hail this close to harvest. Turning to the county maps tacked up on corkboards along the edge of the room; she searched the numbered plats for her farmland. A large chunk of the county now belonged to her. Grandpa would have teased her about being a land baroness, but secretly, he would have been proud.

"Let's get this show on the road." Gabby returned, linked arms with her pal and the pair went down the service stairs at the back of the building to the ground floor.

The banquet hall was buzzing like a beehive as they entered and found a place to stand at the back of the massive space. Kinsley watched the people mingling before her gaze drifted to Lincoln, who was standing on a stage at the far end of the room. Engaged in a conversation with Butch, he seemed relaxed despite the upcoming announcement. It amazed her how he could look so at ease when such a large group would be hanging on his every word.

The sheriff rolled down his shirt sleeves and buttoned the cuffs. The sky-blue cotton tugged against his chest, which took her thoughts in a whole new direction. He searched the crowd until their eyes met, giving her a smoky smile.

Gabby leaned in and whispered, "Jeez, Kins, control yourself. You two are setting the place on fire with those looks."

Kinsley couldn't hide a knowing grin as she shrugged. "Hey, on my way to your office this morning, I remembered that you used to live out south of town. I never think of you as that person anymore."

Gabby spoke softly. "Because I'm not her. What made you think of that?"

Kinsley turned to her friend. "This press conference—" Suddenly, a high-pitched screech filled the room and everyone grabbed their ears.

The young tech assistant flushed with embarrassment. "I'm sorry. Sorry…" he muttered as he scrambled to fix the system.

Kinsley reached for Gabby's hand and squeezed it. "We'll talk later."

Lincoln twisted the coupling on the mic stand and raised it as the obnoxious sound came to an end. "Good mornin', everyone. Thank you for comin'. We called this meet —"

A blinding bolt of lightning illuminated the room

through the windows behind him, followed immediately by a clap of thunder that vibrated through the building and its inhabitants. The power went out, leaving everyone in the dark. Outside the windows, a row of cedar trees that lined the lot between the courthouse and the sheriff's office began to burn. The blaze quickly moved from one tree to the next until the entire row resembled medieval torches.

Panic started to set in once the initial shock subsided. From his place on the stage, Lincoln yelled at the murmuring crowd, "Looks like I have a fire to put out, folks! Let's move in an orderly manner toward the front doors of the building!"

Dropping from the riser, he moved through the horde. A spiderweb of cracks that were now decorating the laminated glass indicated an escalating crisis.

He gathered Kinsley and Gabby on his way out the door. "I'll meet you at home later."

"We'll go to the office and check on Charlene," Kinsley countered.

Lincoln nodded and began steering people away from gawking at the blaze.

Kinsley and Gabby took a wide path around the fire and entered headquarters. Charlene released the secure door to let them in. "Holy moly!" She wiggled her finger in her ear as if clearing an obstruction. "That lightnin' strike was too close for comfort."

Gabby looked out the front windows of the sheriff's office at the row of burning trees half a block away as a firetruck wailed in the distance. "I suppose I'll be off work today unless they can get the power back on. That lightning strike probably fried the electrical box on the other side of that inferno. I better call Rural Electric," she said, returning to her friends.

"Isn't that Layton's job?" asked Kinsley, referring to Josh Layton, the interim commissioner.

With a heavy exhale, Gabby reached for her phone. "As if he would lift a finger to do anything other than preen like the peacock he is. He makes me do all the crap work. He's Skelly all over again."

Kinsley picked up a profile sketch from Charlene's desk. "Who's this?"

"The murder victim in this new case. Lincoln was going to show it to the press to see if anyone could help identify the man. That bunch down on the state line won't give an inch," the head dispatcher huffed.

Gabby, on hold with the utility company, listened to their conversation. Curious to see the drawing, she peeked over Kinsley's shoulder and suddenly let out a muffled shriek.

Kinsley turned on her heels and was staggered by Gabby's now-ashen appearance. "What is it? Do you know this guy?"

***

Gabby ended the call, placed her phone on the desk, and reached for the sketch. She gripped the edges of the print and stared at the likeness as her past blasted into the present. "It's the man they were going to give me to," she croaked. Raising her gaze to her friends' worried stares, she shook the paper. "This guy is dead?"

Charlene nodded in response.

"Jacob Miller," Gabby whispered. The name was like acid on her tongue.

Kinsley placed a hand gingerly on her friend's forearm. "What do you mean they were going to give you to him?"

"Arranged marriage. It's not uncommon within the group." The pointed shards of those painful memories sliced through the box Gabby had kept them in, and everything began to spill out.

Considered a great catch, Jacob had been a strapping man with dark hair and chocolate-colored eyes. He cut a fine figure, but Gabby had only been able to see his coal-black soul. She'd wanted nothing to do with his extravagant house or wicked ways.

"Gabs, are you feeling all right?" Kinsley moved closer and tugged at the crumpled sketch. "Here, have a seat. Do you need some water? You're as white as a sheet."

Gabby began to sit when a clap of thunder shook the building. She jumped in fear and squatted down in front of Charlene's desk like a cornered animal.

"Gabby, please say something. You're scaring us," Kinsley pleaded. She crouched in front of her friend and then helped her up and into a chair.

Traumatized by the events of the past hour, Gabby continued to stare at the floor.

"What can I do for you?" Kinsley asked.

"Nothing can be done. This is bad," Gabby said. A tear slipped from her lashes and splashed onto her bare arm, which lay limply against her legs. She wondered what kind of monster it would take to kill Satan himself. "I need to tell Lincoln what I know."

CHAPTER TEN

Broken Halo

After the chaotic press conference followed by the unsettling reveal of the murder victim's identity, Kinsley and Gabby had reached their threshold for drama. They escaped to the solitude of Kinsley's house, where a suede leather couch and a promised glass of bourbon welcomed them in.

As the patter of rain on the roof became a steady thrum, Kinsley considered her puppy in the backyard. "Do you mind if I let Maizey in?"

Gabby drained the glass she held and looked up, as a sparkle crept into her eyes. "I'd like that."

Hurrying through the house, Kinsley corralled the dog in the mud room with a towel and vigorously rubbed her to dry her off. But full of youthful energy, Maizey slipped her mistress and darted away. She was wiggling around Gabby's feet by the time Kinsley caught up to her. Gabby stroked the pup's forehead, murmuring to her until she calmed.

Kinsley took the bottle of bourbon and refilled their glasses, smiling down at the now well-behaved animal. "You're a regular dog whisperer."

"This is a good one, aren't you, Princess?" Gabby received a tail thump in response.

"How are you doing, Gabs? I can't imagine what a shock it must have been to find out the murder victim was your ex-fiancé."

"I never considered him my fiancé. He was an obligation I was expected to fulfill. That's why you were thinking about my past, isn't it?" Gabby asked.

"Yes." Kinsley paused, then said, "I often forget that you had a completely different life before I met you."

"I never talked about it much, even with you—I wanted to leave it behind. Jacob and I grew up together. He was ten years older than me, and his father owned the house next to ours. He would come over and help my father when I was a little girl." Gabby lifted her glass and swirled the amber liquid. "I don't remember a time when he wasn't in our lives."

Kinsley pushed a chew toy toward the dog with her toes. Maizey took the hint and lay down, contentedly gnawing on the fuzzy orange bone.

Gabby continued, "Within our community, jobs were doled out evenly and pay was split among everyone through the church. It was meant to be a fair system to ensure that the elderly and infirm were cared for, but some received a bigger cut. Jacob Miller got the lion's share, and he became well off. There was a quiet rumbling about the methods he and his goonish pals used to keep the peace, but no one dared step out of line for fear of a visit from him and his crew."

Gabby paused as she considered the promise of marriage her father, Aaron, had made that she had been tasked to keep. "Jacob's father, Abraham Miller, was an elder of the church, and he granted his son whatever his heart desired. I was at the top of Jacob's list. I had no choice in the matter—I was still a little girl when my parents told me. He was a handsome boy, so I thought it would be fine. But things changed the spring I turned eight."

She closed her eyes as the memories took hold. "One of my chores was milking the cow, and I remember being excited because the cat had just had kittens. I couldn't wait to see if their eyes were open yet. I'd sneaked into the barn and was surprised to find Jacob in the horse stall bent over the box where the kittens were. He must have been about eighteen years old then."

She swallowed hard. "The kittens were mewing loudly and I shouted at him to leave them alone. He leaped up, pinned me to the stall boards with this forearm across my throat, and told me he would do what he wanted and if I didn't keep my mouth shut he'd shut it permanently."

A single tear escaped and landed on Gabby's leg. "I never told anyone. That was the first horror in a long line of cruelty I was privy to over the next five years. Jacob knew I was trapped, and that gave him license to open the door to his demented world."

Kinsley took her hand. "I'm so sorry."

Gabby squeezed her friend's fingers. "Jacob was the source of work outside the community, and he was the law inside it. Though I use the word 'law' loosely."

She drained her glass and set it on the coffee table. "His parents are Abraham and Rachel Miller. I'll tell Lincoln anything I can, but I haven't had any interaction with Jacob since the day I left, so my information will be old news. The people who live out there aren't bad, and most of them abide by their faith, but just like anywhere else there is bad among them. It's a hard life. I was never going to fit in, so I left. It was the only way to protect my family and myself."

She met Kinsley's steady gaze. "I don't know if I can get anyone out there to talk to me, but I'll try. Maybe we could find out what Jacob was doing lately."

"I understand how difficult this must be." Kinsley said and gave her friend a warm smile before she pulled her in for a hug.

From the outside, Gabby looked as fragile as a China doll, but she bent like a willow in the wind when trouble came calling.

CHAPTER ELEVEN

Revelations

Gabby lay in bed for hours, but sleep had been hard to come by since the day of the fire at the courthouse. Memories of her previous life haunted her until she could no longer stand the unanswered questions. Her brother, Amos, was still with The Order and she had communicated with him for years via notes passed on by the local lumber-store manager. A few days ago, she'd sent a message asking if Amos could get away to meet her. He'd sent word that he would meet her before dawn today at the cottonwood that grew at the edge of Kinsley's land.

Gabby turned on her side and watched the clock tick off another minute before she closed her eyes and relived one of the last times that she'd heard her biological mother's voice.

"Sweet girl, you must accept the ways. It's a good life. Please, Patience. They will shun us. What will we do for work? Where will we live? Think of your family, of your little brothers. Do you not care what happens to us?"

Gabby hadn't thought about her Christian name in a very long time. When she'd started a new life in Harlow and the Chambers had stepped forward to adopt her, she had changed her name legally from Patience Lapp to Gabriella Chambers. To her blood relatives, Patience had died the day she'd chosen the outside world, so it was appropriate to lay her old identity to rest and allow Gabriella to rise from the ashes.

Sighing, she threw back the covers. She might as well get ready since lying in bed was doing no good.

***

Gabby's Toyota Corolla's engine purred as she searched the dark fields in the pre-dawn hours. Without warning, a figure appeared at the roadside, and she brought her car to a sudden halt.

She hit the button on the armrest to unlock the door. "Hurry," she hissed, urging her brother to get in the car. Before he was fully ensconced in the passenger seat, she took off.

"Gee, Patience. Slow down. You're likely ta kill us," Amos groused.

A few miles down the road, she veered onto Henry's land and pulled her car between a barn and a row of trees. Gabby killed the engine and turned toward the large blond man next to her. A light mounted on a post at the corner of the barn illuminated the interior of her car, and her eyes roamed over his changed features. She hardly recognized her little brother; he had filled out since she'd last seen him, and now he looked more like a misplaced Viking than the kid she remembered. His cornflower-blue eyes were glassy with emotion.

"Give us a hug 'den, Sis." He held his arms wide.

Gabby flung herself against him and held on tightly. Her brother was the one thing she missed from her old life. They were five years apart in age, but they had been inseparable from the time he was born until the day she'd chosen the outside world to that of The Order. Memories of that little towheaded boy tearing at their father's overalls as he tried to save her from being punished made her chest hitch, and she fought back tears.

"Don' cry, Patience." The deep timbre of his changed voice comforted her as they sat back in their seats.

"I'm so happy to see you, Amos. It's been too long." Gabby managed a trembling smile.

He smoothed the hair back from her face. "You're different."

"Yeah, my friend Kinsley gave me a new look. She said she let my butterfly out." They both chuckled.

"You 'ave a suitor 'den?"

"I did," Gabby replied as the break with Dusty flitted through her thoughts.

"Gud." His warm smile made her heart overflow.

"Leave the settlement. Please, Amos. I can help you," Gabby pleaded. But it was the same argument she gave every time they met; she knew he wouldn't listen now any more than he had before.

"Dat and Mawem need me."

Gabby hugged him again. She had missed his lovely mixture of English and Dutch. As she let go, she asked the burning question: "I know you don't have much time. What can you tell me about Jacob Miller?"

"I know 'e's dead." Amos's statement hung in the air between them. "The sheriff was out wit' a picture of 'im."

"Why didn't his parents tell Lincoln who he was?" She watched her brother's face for any unspoken clues. "Amos, what's going on?"

He took a deep breath through his nose and exhaled slowly. "'E turned dark, Patience. So much more dark dan when you were 'ere."

Amos launched into the story of Jacob Miller's descent. His need for power, cruelty, and money had corrupted their community. "'Is father was powerless ta do anyting. The last few years 'e was usin' our compound ta hide shipments as a favor fer someone in Mexico." He stopped and looked at his sister. "'E fell in wit' bad fellas an' 'e brought da dirt home wit' him. No one was safe, not even 'im."

"You're saying a Mexican gang killed Jacob?" Gabby's chest felt like it had caved in.

"Maybe." He fiddled with a pen in a cup holder on the console. "Dey are in control out at da place, Patience. We can't stop 'em. Anyone dat tries disappears."

Suddenly her car felt uncomfortably confining. "I'll tell the sheriff. He'll get rid of them." Gabby grasped Amos's hand. "Maybe you should get out for a while."

"If ya care about dis sheriff, ya better tell 'im ta stay away, or 'e'll be dead too." Amos listed the horrors the gang had perpetrated on their community since Jacob's death, and it was dizzying; it seemed that corruption had a stranglehold on the settlement.

"Amos, I promise I'll find a way to help."

He nodded, but Gabby could see he had little faith she could solve the issues he'd revealed.

Driving him as close to his home as she dared, he climbed out of the car and slunk away. Gabby watched his broad back vanish into the darkness before she swung around and took the blacktop toward town.

The news Amos had shared was much worse than she had expected. Now, afraid to tell Lincoln what she had learned because it might endanger his life, Gabby was stuck with what to do.

As she reached the city limits, morning light skimmed the horizon. A church spire rose above a sleeping Harlow and whispered to her troubled soul. Suddenly Gabby knew where she had to go.

CHAPTER TWELVE

Expect The Unexpected

Headlights pierced the darkness ahead. Lincoln retrieved his night vision binoculars from the passenger seat to get a better look at a vehicle that had stopped less than a quarter of a mile away at the end of a cornfield.

The sheriff watched as a man exited the car, slipped into the six-foot-high rows of corn, and disappeared. The Corolla then sped away toward Harlow. As he put the binoculars on the seat, Lincoln wondered who Gabby Chambers was meeting at this early hour.

He started his pickup and followed, but dropped back when the sun broke. The morning light would reveal his presence, and he wasn't quite finished with this particular surveillance.

Hours after the failed news conference and ensuing calamity, Lincoln had dragged himself home only to learn that Gabby had been previously betrothed to the victim in his case. He finally had a name: Jacob Miller. Gabby's revelations about being a member of The Order, and that her family was still with them, had nearly knocked him off his feet. It didn't escape his notice that Kinsley had failed to mention her best friend's affiliation to the group, but he wasn't about to stir that hornet's nest. He knew now, and that would have to do.

It was apparent that Gabby's cooperation thus far was borne out of her love for Kinsley. Lincoln hadn't pressed too hard that first night; he knew that Gabby would come around. In his experience, digging up the bones of one's past was never pleasant. Still, she had agreed to help, and Lincoln wasn't going to turn her down. If he were to guess, he'd say she'd found someone to question under cover of darkness.

When Gabby turned off City Limits Road onto Washington Street, Lincoln was sure he knew her destination. He took the long way around to Reverend Chambers' house; from several blocks away, he could see Gabby's car parked in her parents' driveway.

Fearing he'd be discovered if he got any closer, Lincoln detoured toward Pearl's to pick up breakfast for Charlene. Gabby Chambers was up to something, but he'd let it lie for now. He'd eventually discover what she'd uncovered if she didn't volunteer the information first. Like cream, the truth had a funny way of floating to the top.

CHAPTER THIRTEEN

Hidden Pasts

Gabby sat in her car and watched the warm morning sunlight inch down the front of her adoptive parents' blond-brick home. The neighbor's sprinkler ticked an almost hypnotic rhythm as she thought about how they would likely react to what she had to say.

Reverend Harold Chambers was a play-by-the-book kind of fellow, not prone to shades of gray, but he was always fair and forgiving. Her mother, Marilyn, was an angel in disguise; no matter what Gabby said or did, her love would not be diminished.

Divulging what she knew to anyone was dangerous, but Gabby needed advice. Going to Kinsley was out of the question this time because she would undoubtedly tell Lincoln. No: Harold and Marilyn Chambers were her best choice.

She shoved her shoulder against the car door. As it opened, a screech of metal against metal echoed off the surrounding houses and shattered the peaceful morning. Retrieving a newspaper from the lawn, she peeked inside through a glass storm door — her mother was bustling around their kitchen. Gabby tapped lightly on the door frame to get her attention.

Marilyn looked up, smiled brightly, and waved her inside. "You're an early bird, dear. I've just taken a pan of cinnamon rolls out of the oven. Please have a seat. Your father will be here any minute." She patted her daughter's back as she drew near.

A round oak table nestled cozily into a bay window. Gabby pulled out a ladder-back chair and the rush seat issued a pleasant creak as she settled in. The toasty smell of cinnamon and pastry gave a welcoming warmth to the kitchen.

"What brings you by?" Marilyn asked.

Gabby fiddled with the silverware that lay neatly upon woven-rattan placemats. Finally, she replied, "I was out."

She looked up and saw her mother's trusting smile, which again had her debating what to do. Everything that was going on at the settlement would come to a head eventually, even without her intervention, but she worried that her brother would be killed before that happened. And the Chambers couldn't protect themselves if they didn't know about the evil that was stirring nearby. Their blood would be on her hands if she stayed silent and something violent turned up on their doorstep.

"Gabriella," Marilyn said as she closed the space between them. "You can tell us anything, sweetheart."

Gabby couldn't meet her mother's eyes and lie. "I just missed you guys," she replied, dodging the invitation to divulge her secret.

"I've been talking to you for five minutes. You were off in your own little world." Marilyn perched on the chair next to her and grasped her daughter's hand. "What's happened?"

Harold Chambers lumbered into the kitchen and stopped short when he saw his daughter. "Gabs, how wonderful. I was just thinkin' about you. I must have pulled you in with my powerful *ESPN*." Harold fancied himself quite the comedian; his bad-dad jokes rarely landed, but there was something to be said for his persistence. His snow-white beard and round belly were reminiscent of old Saint Nick, and his laugh matched his jolly appearance.

"Hi, Dad." Gabby rose and hugged him tightly as Marilyn went back to the kitchen.

By the time the pair took their places at the table, Marilyn had returned with plated cinnamon rolls. Gabby took a bite and closed her eyes as she savored the buttery-rich pastry melting on her tongue.

"Gabriella was about to tell us something important," Marilyn stated.

Gabby's eyes flew open like window shades someone had released too quickly. Her parents looked at her in anticipation as she struggled to swallow. These wonderful people had taken her in when she was at her lowest; she would have to trust them with this.

She shared a condensed version of all that had gone on, beginning with her past ties to Jacob Miller, and ending with her meeting Amos in the predawn hours. Gabby was breathless when she finished, and her parents were looking on in stunned silence. She'd never told them much about her life before she came to live with them, and they'd never asked. Gabby wondered if this information overload might make them regret their decision to make her part of their family.

"I came straight here after talking to Amos," she said. "No one knows he talks to me. Lincoln would no doubt go after these men if I told him, and I'm afraid they'll kill him—but I'm afraid they'll kill my brother if I *don't* tell him. What do I do?"

A fat tear rolled down Marilyn's cheek as she rose and pulled Gabby against her chest. She seemed to be reading her daughter's mind. "My sweet, sweet girl, I'm so glad you came to live with us." She released Gabby and turned to her husband. "Well, Harold, what do you say?"

Harold balanced his chair on its two back legs and stroked his beard thoughtfully. "We have ourselves quite a dilemma here." He grunted, much like he did when he wrote his sermons. "Yes, quite a predicament. These folks operate outside the norms of society, and to stop them, we need people who also don't necessarily abide by the law."

"Sounds like this might be my territory." A gruff voice from the direction of the hallway drew all eyes to a new arrival.

Harold chuckled as he set his chair down and pushed the last empty seat back with his foot. "You are just the man for the job. Looks like your visit might have been divine intervention."

Gabby's eyes were focused so intently on the unknown male that they nearly watered. He was absolutely the tallest human she had ever seen.

"Harold, you've been keeping secrets," the mountain of a man said. He stopped next to Gabby's chair and asked, "Who is this goddess?"

"Dean, don't go spillin' that charm of yours all over the place. This is my daughter Gabby."

"Daddy…" she chided, then stood and held out her hand. "I'm Gabriella, but please call me Gabby."

The stranger took her outstretched hand, turned it over, and kissed the back as his olive gaze held hers. "Gabriella, you are a gem. I can see why your father has kept you hidden."

Gabby blushed and lowered her eyes to check out the patches on his vest.

"Honey, this is Dean McCormick. He's the president of a club I belonged to years ago in California. He stopped by for a visit on his way east," Harold explained.

The clean, crisp scent of Irish Spring soap mixed perfectly with the earthy tones of the stranger's leather riding gear. What her father had said finally sank in, and Gabby turned her attention toward him. "Did you just say you belonged to a *biker* gang?"

Dean and Harold chuckled as Marilyn jumped up and said, "I have an old photo album somewhere." She darted to the living room and dug around in a cabinet under the television.

"Here it is," she announced as she rejoined the group and lay the book on the table. "Close your mouth, sweetheart, or you'll catch flies," she teased Gabby, then headed toward the kitchen to get their newest guest a mug and plate.

Dean winked at Gabby before pulling out a chair. She wondered briefly if the antique seating would hold him.

Harold addressed his guest. "Gabby has a boyfriend, so don't go gettin' any ideas."

"Dad! Really?" Gabby wanted to crawl under the table.

"McCormick's uncle and I were best friends back in the day," Harold continued.

Marilyn set a cup of coffee and a roll in front of Dean before opening the photo album. "Your father wasn't always a preacher. He has a past, just like we all do." She flipped through a few pages. There, in his black-leather glory, was Harold Chambers, proud member of a motorcycle club.

Marilyn ran her finger over the photo. "He was a handsome devil." Her wistful look said more than words. "My father forbade me to see him, but nothing could have stopped me. He left the club, and we were married. But Harold's kept in touch with them. They were his family before I was." She smiled at Dean as she reached out and rubbed his shoulder.

"I was a hunk, wasn't I?" Harold grinned as his focus moved from the photo to Gabby.

"You were." Gabby giggled and rolled her eyes before addressing Dean. "And you run this club now?"

"I do. It wasn't the plan, but my uncle passed away unexpectedly and left us in the lurch. I stepped in to keep things afloat. I intended to move on, but that was a decade ago, and I'm still in it." He shrugged.

Harold leaned in as they looked at more pictures. "It isn't easy to leave the life."

Gabby listened to his tales of bike rallies and all manner of wild-boy antics she'd never imagined her dad, the reverend, would have been involved in. When the conversation waned, Dean cut to the chase. "So, tell me, Gabriella. What shady dealings have you uncovered?"

She looked at her father. "Tell him, sweetheart," Harold urged. "If anyone can help, Dean can."

CHAPTER FOURTEEN

Would You Like Fries With That?

Kinsley pulled into her driveway and took a few moments to enjoy the resplendent sunset as she thought about what had been accomplished today. A wooden barn that had stood on their land for several generations had been losing its battle with the elements for quite a while, so she'd recruited Thomas and some of his friends to help her get it back into shape. They'd completed the necessary repairs, but applying apple-red paint and trimming the building in a brilliant white would take several weekends. Thankfully, her stepson and his pals worked for the price of cheeseburgers and gas for their vehicles.

They also planned to put up some fencing to stop people from parking between the building and a row of trees. From the fresh tire tracks Kinsley had found, she assumed teenagers were using it for a make-out spot.

She took a deep breath and shifted her thoughts to the night's festivities. The get-together Frank had arranged would be the first big push in Lincoln's bid for sheriff and Gabby's for county commissioner. It had been a miracle that Kinsley had talked Lincoln into doing anything in the way of campaigning; he'd been dead set against it.

Exiting her vehicle, Kinsley made her way down the side of the house to the back garden, where she was sure she'd find Frank in the throes of party preparation. As she stepped through an open gate, the transformed space looked nothing like it had before. Twinkly lights lay along the top of the fencing, and citronella torches had been placed strategically to ward off mosquitoes. Small strings of LED lights lined the middle of each red-and-white checkered, cloth-covered picnic table. The glow highlighted the centerpieces of wildflowers arranged in Mason jars. She had to hand it to Frank: it was undoubtedly country chic.

The man in question sidled up next to her to admire his work, and she caught a whiff of birchwood and plum with a hint of leather. Frank's perfectly fitted slacks and designer shirt put him in the magazine-cover category rather than someone attending a backyard barbeque.

"Do you like it?" he asked, putting an arm around her shoulders and hugging her to his side. "Good gawd, I hope you're going to shower before this shindig!"

Kinsley burst into laughter. "Are you saying I stink?"

"Well, you're no spring bouquet." Deep dimples punctuated his teasing smile. "I don't mind, but our guests might take offense."

She slipped her arm around Frank's waist as they looked at the magical space he'd created. "You're amazing. Thank you for doing this."

"It was a great idea, Kinsley — a perfect way to showcase our dream team. Once people hang out with Lincoln and Gabby, they'll fall in love. And this party will help prepare Gabs for those baby-kissing events I have planned."

Kinsley gave him a little squeeze as a flurry of giggles came from the direction of the gate. "The girls from the college dance team have arrived."

Frank glanced down at her. "Go get spiffy for this hoedown." He started to walk away then stopped and looked back over his shoulder. "Speaking of hoeing down, I brought Darren's portable turntable. Bring out some of those old country records when you come back, okey doke?"

Frank wasn't a country music fan, but the way he made fun of the genre kept them in stitches. "You're the best, Frank."

"It's a burden I'll have to bear." He feigned weakness as he joined the twittering young women gathered by the grill.

Kinsley hurried over to Lincoln's house to check on Maizey. The fur ball came barreling toward her as soon as the gate opened. She fended off being tackled and patted the dog, then threw a tennis ball a few times before slipping away across the lawn and straight to the shower.

Mentally checking off a list of safe conversation topics to bring up at the party, she rolled through the guests they had invited and hoped she hadn't left anyone out. It wouldn't do to make voters mad at this late stage.

Hazel Bishop had agreed to attend and bring her cronies. Lincoln needed the 'silver set' on his side, and it wouldn't hurt for them to get to know Gabby in the process. Thomas had invited kids in his age group who were of voting age. Winning that demographic would be significant.

The sound of metal hitting the tile floor just outside the shower caught her ear, and she smirked as her fiancé opened the frosted-glass door and joined her. "Why, Sheriff! What are you doing in my shower?" She slipped her arms around his neck.

"I couldn't resist, knowin' you were in here naked." He bent and gave her a toe-curling kiss.

"I'm glad you didn't listen to your better judgment, cowboy," Kinsley said as she pressed herself against him. "You're rarin' to go."

Lincoln grinned and turned her away from him. "How could I not be? Just look at you." He kissed a small scar on her shoulder as his hands slid over her wet skin.

***

Kinsley put the finishing touches on her makeup then turned to watch Lincoln shave. "That was some spectacular showering, Sheriff."

With a gleam in his eye, Lincoln leaned in for a kiss. "Mmm. It certainly was."

"Meet you in the kitchen." Kinsley winked at him and turned to go.

Opening the refrigerator, she removed a tray of meat and placed it on the counter. Lincoln approached, wrapped her in his arms, and kissed the nape of her neck. "You're awful lovey," she teased.

He chuckled as he released her and retrieved the tray filled with burgers, bratwurst, and hotdogs. "I'll take this for you."

"Thank you. How do you feel about tonight?"

"I appreciate you puttin' this together for me and Gabby. These relaxed social gatherings are much easier to navigate than public speakin'."

"Frank did all the work. He's a godsend." Kinsley took the vegetable trays from the refrigerator and closed the door with her hip. "People enjoy being around you. You're kinda charming — but don't get a big head over it."

Lincoln wore a playful grin as he held open the back door with his shoulder and swatted her rear as she passed. Kinsley laughed as she headed toward the condiments table while Lincoln was on a mission to deliver his bounty to the grill master.

Frank bustled around giving the dance-team ladies instructions on refilling drinks and general service tips. They scattered as the sheriff approached. "Here comes the man of the hour with a ton of meat," Frank joked.

Lincoln hooted in response. "How have ya been?"

"Our social calendars are simply overflowing." Frank smiled and pointed to the table next to the grill. "Put that meat down and tell me what I can do to help get you re-elected."

Lincoln unloaded the tray and rested his shoulder against a brick archway connected to the outdoor kitchen. He picked absently at the vines that grew wild over the structure, which stirred the heady smell of honeysuckle.

"I really couldn't say, though I appreciate your willingness. Havin' to fight for this position is new territory for me." He met Frank's gaze. "I guess they'll re-elect me or they won't, and I'll have to live with whatever happens."

Frank flashed a sly smile. "Oh no, we aren't leaving this to chance. We're going to make these townsfolk want you so badly, they'll rush the polling stations to put their votes in."

The corner of Lincoln's mouth pulled up. "Oh, yeah. How are we gonna do that?"

"Well, if it weren't for little Miss Hot Pants over there," Frank tipped his head toward Kinsley, "I'd book you in for a kissing booth. That would send you zooming past your competition. But since she would have kittens, we'll have to come up with something else."

Lincoln grinned and shook his head.

"You're a charismatic man. For tonight, be yourself," Frank suggested. "That should lay a good foundation for me to build on." He raised the top of the grill and placed burgers in neat rows on the hot surface.

Lincoln contemplated Frank's words as he looked across the patio at the throng of people who had just arrived, led by his son.

Thomas left the group in his wake and made straight for his father with Maizey in tow. "I brought some friends. Kins said I should." He looked over his shoulder at his pals as they mixed with the young ladies from the dance team. "They're eligible to vote, and they're all yours, Dad."

Lincoln pushed off from the wall and grasped Thomas's shoulder; he and his son were nearly eye to eye now. "Thank you. I'll do my best to win 'em over." He glanced at Frank and gave him a cockeyed smile. "Orders from my campaign manager."

"Mmm-hm." Frank winked, then turned back to the barbeque with a spatula in one hand and a glass of wine in the other.

Thomas grinned. "These guys are well in hand, thanks to Kins."

As the starry eyed lads swarmed around the dancers, Frank joined the James' men and whistled low. "Dang, your woman is brilliant."

Lincoln nodded. "She sure is."

A hubbub at the gate pulled his gaze toward a gaggle of the September set led by Loretta Jenkins and Hazel Bishop. In their attempt to be at the front of the pack, the ladies had stuck themselves solidly in the opening, and neither would back down to clear the tangle. Lincoln could see Darren's head peeking out behind the two older women as he tried to help them through.

"Ladies!" Darren shouted. "There is room for everyone. Please, let's take turns."

Frank lost his composure and snorted as his husband tugged on Loretta's arm to try to dislodge her. Maizey bayed over the commotion, and Lincoln bent to rub the pup's neck.

"Kindly ask Mrs. Bishop to remove herself," Mrs. Jenkins replied haughtily. "I've received a personal invitation from Miss Rhodes. She came to my house for tea."

Hazel heehawed, then pushed harder on her rival. "Tea? Goodness, Loretta, what kind of airs are you trying to put on?"

Darren gave them both a solid nudge and the grandmothers, followed by their granddaughters, stumbled into the yard. Hazel and Loretta stopped to straighten their suits and hats while burning each other down with their looks.

Frank leaned toward Lincoln. "There is your audience, Sheriff James. Generations of women to woo to your side. Go get 'em."

That comment was more than Lincoln could take, especially after witnessing the elderly women's version of the 'Charge of the Light Brigade,' and he burst out laughing. Afraid he'd offend the ladies with his levity, he turned away from the crowd and feigned interest in something at the back of the yard. Suddenly, a memory of a fight between the same pair of ladies years before sprang to mind, and he fought to suppress more laughter.

Hazel and Loretta had been at an auction, both bidding on a simple, oak, dining table. The back and forth went on for a long time, with each woman only raising by five-dollar increments. Gradually the price of the table crept past the two hundred dollars it was worth; by the time the bidding reached two thousand dollars, both women were in a tizzy trying to outdo one another.

When Loretta jumped her offer by five hundred dollars, that was the tipping point. Hazel grabbed a little ceramic figurine from a nearby display and beaned her challenger with it, which started a wrestling match that Lincoln had to break up. In the end, neither woman was arrested because no one had pressed charges, but it was a catfight that would live forever in the memory of this small town.

Lincoln gathered his composure as he faced the partygoers again. The gate debacle had the women shooting daggers at one another from across the yard as a charming Darren flitted between their tables, plying them with drinks and hors d'oeuvre. Lincoln couldn't suppress a grin: Mr. Barnes would need every smooth move he possessed to calm those ladies down.

When Gabby arrived with her parents, Lincoln

watched the trio closely. Reverend Chambers left his wife and daughter with Kinsley and joined the sheriff and Frank at the grill. "Hey, Rev, whatcha know?" Lincoln asked.

"Not a thing, not a thing…" Harold watched Frank flip burgers. "What is there to know in Harlow?"

The three of them chuckled at his apt observation, but Lincoln noticed that the reverend was refusing to make eye contact with him. That was new; he and Gabby's father had always been very friendly. He had his suspicions about the reason for the change, but it pained him to think Harold and his daughter were being intentionally deceptive.

Maizey whimpered as she looked up at her master. Lincoln squatted and ran his knuckles over her back. "What do ya think, Maizey girl?" he asked quietly. "Anyone here spark your interest?" The pup thumped his boot with her tail. "You let me know if ya smell anything rotten."

As he stood, he tried to decide which group to approach first. If nothing else, the eclectic mix of attendees would make for an interesting dynamic as the night wore on.

CHAPTER FIFTEEN

Point Counterpoint

An uncomfortable, hard-plastic chair coupled with his impending primary debate, was making Lincoln squirm. Why the powers-that-be felt the need to hold events in this cavernous banquet hall at the courthouse was beyond him. They had yet to fix the sound system that had blown out the day of the lightning strike, which meant he would have to shout so everyone could hear him.

As the room began to fill, the crowd split into his side and his opponent's side. For the first time, Lincoln had visual confirmation of Trenton Crawley's supporters—and it was more than a little concerning. Granted, he had not done much campaigning except for the party they'd hosted recently, but Lincoln had given one hundred percent to the job each day; surely that had to count for something.

Recalling the 'you can do it' speech Kinsley had given him over breakfast, he bent forward, placed his elbows on his thighs, and laced his fingers together. When he looked up, she was watching him. He gave her a wink as his opponent strutted into the auditorium like a big rooster in a yard.

Trenton worked the crowd, glad-handing people on Lincoln's side of the aisle. There was something to be said for his oily kind of schmoozing, but it wouldn't work on everyone. The sheriff glanced over Crawley's supporters and spotted Sheila from the diner. That was no surprise: she wasn't a fan of his after he'd let her know that they would never be more than friends.

The person who did give him a bit of a shock was Hazel Bishop. He and Mrs. Bishop had always had a friendly affiliation — at least, he'd thought they had. She had attended their barbeque and acted as pleased as punch at being there. If he lost her vote, she would take a big chunk of the bridge-playing set with her.

When he saw Loretta Jenkins sitting across the aisle from her, he realized that this was a personal struggle between the two women that most likely had nothing to do with him. Still, it was not ideal for anyone to be feuding when he needed solidarity.

Lincoln raked his fingers through his hair and stood as Crawley approached the stage. "Linc," his opponent said with a nod.

It irked Lincoln to no end that Trenton took such a familiar approach. They hadn't said much to each other since the man had landed in town, and they would never be friends when this race was over, no matter the outcome. "Crawley," he returned as they took their places behind their respective podiums.

The mediator was Selena Trujillo, a local radio-station host chosen for her unbiased position. The original plan had been to have one of the commissioners mediate, but all of them had strong Crawley leanings, and Lincoln had quickly shot that down. He couldn't cave if he were to have any chance in this debate.

The mediator shuffled her paperwork and Lincoln's stomach churned. He had no doubt about his ability to be sheriff, but public speaking was not his cup of tea.

"Gentleman, I believe we are ready to get started," Mrs. Trujillo stated loudly, which brought the chatter in the room to an end.

Lincoln gripped the edges of the podium as if they were a lifeline. Out of the corner of his eye, he could see his opponent looking as cool as a cucumber.

"First question: Why do you want to be sheriff?" Selena began. "Sheriff James, start us off if you would, please."

Lincoln rubbed his thumb over the smooth wood of the stand while he thought about what to say. "I've made Harlow my home for the past decade. Recently, my son moved here, and he has been welcomed with open arms by the people who make this town great. It's my number one priority to protect everyone who lives in this county."

"But you haven't protected the people who live here, have you?" Trenton interrupted.

"I've done my best, Mr. Crawley. Most would agree Harlow has been a safe place to live—"

"I disagree. Two murders in as many years hardly constitutes a safe place to live. That is a failing on you and your team, Mr. James."

Lincoln couldn't hold back an incredulous look. "Murder happens even in the safest communities. Over the past ten years—"

Trenton stepped from behind his podium and poked his finger at Lincoln. "Over the past ten years, you have run the city and county into the ground. It is time for that to stop."

Half-turning, Lincoln faced his accuser. "That's not the whole truth. The budget was held hostage by the former commissioner who painted my team and me into a tight corner."

Trenton smirked as he faced the crowd. "Now you're going to blame the inefficiencies of your office on someone who isn't here to defend himself?" he scoffed. "If you knew your business, Mr. James, you would have known that it was illegal for the law enforcement budget to be cut so severely, wouldn't you?"

Charlene shot out of her chair. "Hey, now! You weren't here, and you don't know what you're talkin' about, Crawley!"

The crowd erupted. Selena called over the rising commotion, "Everyone! Everyone! Let's calm down. Sheriff James, please continue. Mr. Crawley, hold your comments until it's your turn."

Charlene continued her rant as she turned to the audience. "Trenton Crawley isn't from here. He doesn't give a rip about any of you. Lincoln kept y'all safe, even when he wasn't gettin' a dime of pay. Do you think Crawley would do that? Linc is the best man for the job, and you know it!"

Selena waved to the undersheriff, signaling him to take charge of the fuming dispatcher. Butch crossed the room and urged his workmate out of the row of chairs. They edged toward the door at the back of the hall, but Butch couldn't hide his smug smile as he took his time walking her to the exit and Charlene continued her tirade.

"You all need to think long and hard about who you

have watchin' out for you. When times get rough, Linc won't give up on any of you!" she shouted as she was ushered outside.

Once the crowd had calmed, the mediator addressed Lincoln again. "Please finish what you were saying, Sheriff James."

Lincoln looked at Kinsley. Although she was smiling, it did little to mask her worry.

"This is more than a job to me. Many of you are my friends, and we've been through a lot together. I'll continue to perform the duties of sheriff to the best of my ability if I'm given the chance." He left it at that and stepped back, watching the crowd, and drawing strength from those who smiled or gave him a thumbs-up.

Crawley took his turn and rambled on about the department's incompetence and poor management. The man had the audacity to make a dig about how Lincoln worked alongside his employees instead of being an overseer. "Case in point," Trenton sneered. "That dispatcher is out of control. You wouldn't have that with me as sheriff. I run a tight ship."

The fact that this stranger to Harlow couldn't even call Charlene by her name as he insulted her threw gasoline on the fire burning in Lincoln's chest. "Mr. Crawley, I suggest you lay off my employees. You don't know 'em," he warned.

Trenton ignored him and continued. "That woman will be the first one gone when I'm elected. I haven't met anyone currently employed by the sheriff's office or the city who is worth keeping. The citizens of Stevens County will get their money's worth with me." His open palm connecting with the podium put an exclamation point on his declaration.

That pushed Lincoln over the edge; he threw up his hands in frustration, grabbed his Stetson from under the podium, and stepped off the stage to address the crowd.

"For near on a decade, I've built fences and rounded up cattle. I've babysat your kids and showed up at a moment's notice day or night when I've been called. I love this county and everyone in it. Either vote for me because you believe in me or don't, but I won't stand for a stranger runnin' down good people who have given everything ta make this a town worth livin' in. Those people he's puttin' down are your friends 'n' family. If he'll do it to them, ya can bet he'll do it to you next."

He crammed his hat on his head and headed for the door, his heavy footfalls echoing sharply in a room that had gone ominously quiet.

When Lincoln reached his pickup, he laid his arms across the truck bed's railing and exhaled as the scene he'd just created spun around in his head. "Good Lord, what chance could I have now?" he murmured to himself.

Kinsley's soft touch brought him out of his contemplation. "Are you doing okay?"

Lincoln turned his head and peered at her from under the brim of his hat. "Got any room on that computer team of yours for an ex-sheriff?"

She slid her arm around his waist and hugged him as he stole a quick kiss.

Thomas jogged up and joined them. "You did great, Dad. People won't forget what a terrific sheriff you are."

"Thank you, son. I hope you're right. That wasn't how I saw today goin', but I guess it's done now. I'd best get back to the office and see how things are there." He straightened and tucked Kinsley under one arm while he put his other around Thomas's shoulders.

As Gabby rushed up to them and rattled on about how exciting the debate had been, Lincoln scanned the parking lot. His eyes landed on a blood-red Chevy Nova with a person sitting inside. He dropped his arms from around his family. "Charlene," he muttered.

Charging across the lot toward her car, he bent to look in through the driver's side window. Lincoln's heart seized when he saw his dispatcher slumped over the wheel, and he whipped open the door.

Charlene shot up as if she'd received an electric shock. "What in the—?" she exclaimed while looking at the people gathered around her car. "Shit," she spat and wiped her face with a tissue, smearing black streaks of mascara across her cheeks.

"Get out here, ya fireball." Lincoln stepped back so that she could climb out, then immediately pulled her into a hug. "Thank you for today, Charlene. You're the best friend a guy could have."

"I've messed up the whole thing with my big mouth," she despaired.

Kinsley rubbed her back. "You were perfect, and what you said *needed* to be said. You and Lincoln both gave that snake what for."

Charlene stepped back and her eyes skipped between Kinsley and Lincoln. "I don't understand."

Thomas jumped in. "It's true. Dad gave the whole

town a talkin' to after you left. That should give 'em somethin' to mull over."

"You didn't…" The dispatcher breathed the words as she looked at Lincoln.

"I did, and I'm not a bit sorry." Lincoln gave her a wide smile. "Let's go get somethin' to eat, and I'll tell you all about it."

CHAPTER SIXTEEN

Wild-Eyed Boys

Lincoln was sitting in his pickup in the parking lot of the local discount store, trying to decide if he needed a candy bar, when a horde of passing motorcycles made the ice in his tea-glass rattle. As he watched them, the patches on their leather cuts made it clear that these weren't weekend ride-for-fun guys—they were a club.

He had some experience with their type in town. They generally kept it to a low roar and were gone in a day or two. He'd had less trouble with the motorcycle clubs than with the harvest crews that rolled through town every summer; those country boys were always out for a good time.

Lincoln hoped this group would be on their way soon. The last thing he needed was more trouble after yesterday's debacle of a debate. Ditching the idea of an afternoon snack, he followed the motorcycles out of town and was relieved when they crossed into the next county.

He took a left at the last paved road in his county and drove south toward Weatherby's farm. Guiding his pickup onto a two-lane dirt path, he stopped at the edge of the drop-off that overlooked their crime scene. Other than the depression where the structure sat, the land was flat and without an obstacle to block a person's view.

The sheriff rubbed his knuckles over his jaw as he thought about the case. Coming up with no new revelation, he hopped out of the truck and walked along the rise until he was even with the dwelling.

A glint in the powdery dirt at his feet caught his eye, and he squatted to inspect it before pulling out his pocketknife. He carefully dug around the spent shell, stuck the knife in the open end, and held it up. A twenty-two casing or a spent rifle cartridge wouldn't be unusual — but this was a nine-millimeter, and it hadn't been there long. As he stood, he eyed the distance to the house, guessing that it couldn't be more than two hundred yards away.

Lincoln shaded his eyes and looked beyond the house for anything that might reveal a clue as to why someone had picked this specific spot for a body dump, but other than its remote location, he had yet to find any connection between Miller and the farmstead.

A lone figure walked out of a cornfield on the other side of the depression. When Lincoln waved, the young woman paused, turned around, and disappeared back the way she'd come. He looked at the space briefly before taking the casing back to his pickup and dropping it in an empty cup holder. The victim had been shot with a nine-millimeter gun; it couldn't be a coincidence that he'd found a spent shell of the same size so close to the scene.

From the moment he'd seen the body, he'd been positive the murder hadn't happened in that house. The autopsy had given solid proof: Miller had been arranged in the position they'd found him in. It was like some elaborate production, but the reason why someone had gone to such trouble continued to elude him.

Lincoln had thoroughly researched the Weatherby family and found nothing to indicate a criminal background; they were just your everyday farming family who kept it between the lines.

The sound of a four-wheeler brought him back to the present as an ATV zoomed up and stopped next to him. "Hey, Sheriff. Can I help you?" the young driver asked.

"I was just out here makin' another sweep of the scene. Scott Weatherby gave me permission to be here."

"Yeah, he's my dad." The boy held out his hand to shake. "I'm Greg."

"Nice to meet ya, Greg. I was just about to leave. Sorry to alarm ya." Lincoln stepped toward his pickup then turned back toward Weatherby's son. "Has your dad ever hired help that you can remember?"

The kid eyed him before he answered. "Sometimes my buddies help during harvest, but they aren't really hired. That's it."

Lincoln nodded. "I didn't know you had a sister."

"I don't."

"I just saw a girl in your cornfield."

Greg glanced toward the field in question. "It's probably one of those folks from the settlement. Dad lets them pick sweetcorn. See ya, Sheriff." He kicked up a rooster tail of dirt as he made for home.

Lincoln watched the young man for a moment before returning to his vehicle and heading into town.

***

Once he reached Harlow, Lincoln's first stop was the morgue housed in the basement of the hospital.

He took the stairs two at a time and ducked to avoid a low door frame at the bottom. The harsh fluorescent lights flickered overhead as he strode the lengthy cinderblock hallway toward the last door on the left. As he grasped the cold, metal door handle and entered the somber world of the Stevens County coroner, Dr. Delbert Geller, an acrid smell of bleach and death that permeated the space pressed him to finish his business and be on his way.

Dr. Geller had held his position for years. As Lincoln entered, the rail-thin man unfurled himself from his seat and held out his hand in greeting. "What a surprise, Sheriff James. I don't get many visitors."

Lincoln shook his hand, noting the coroner's monotone voice was as dull as his surroundings. "Hey, Delbert. I came by to ask you some questions about the autopsy on Jacob Miller that I'm not quite clear about."

"I doubt there is anything that I've missed," Dr. Geller replied sharply.

"No, no, Delbert. You've done a fine job. I'm just the curious type, ya know." Lincoln attempted to disarm him. "Your report stated that the gunshot to Miller's forehead was not the cause of death."

"No, the shooting clearly happened sometime after the person died."

"Along with some of the other damage to the body, like the fingernail removal? That happened after the victim was dead, too, didn't it?"

Dr. Geller fixed Lincoln with an icy stare. "Hum,

that's an interesting question, Sheriff. What exactly are you driving at?"

"Nothin' really. I just was thinkin' that a pretty severe beatin' occurred, and the official cause of death was a blow to the head. I'm wonderin' why someone would damage the body in such a way after death."

Delbert sat and motioned for Lincoln to take the chair in front of his desk. He pulled open a drawer and laid a file gingerly on his pristine desktop, ritualistically folding back the cover as if he were handling the Declaration of Independence. He flipped through several pages while Lincoln waited. Finally, the doctor cleared his throat. "I did note here that his fingers were broken."

Lincoln sat forward and listened while the coroner read from the report word for word. "The hands were clenched, the fingers laid against the palms." Delbert paused and danced his fingers across the papers in front of him. "Yes—"

The sheriff was on pins and needles to hear what Dr. Geller would reveal.

"I attributed all of the injuries to a severe beating, one of the worst I've ever seen. If I didn't know better, I would say the man had been in a car accident and was thrown from the vehicle. His skull was cracked and nearly every rib was broken, along with his arms and legs in several places." Delbert looked up from the file. "But only the first joint on each finger was damaged."

"Like someone unfurled a clenched fist that had rigor mortis?" Lincoln suggested.

Delbert nodded. "Exactly. Sometimes, rigor mortis can set in instantaneously, especially in the hands. Having so many broken bones but only the first joint of each finger injured is unusual. I noted that here in the margin."

Lincoln contemplated this new piece of information. "So, besides the gunshot wound, it's probable some of the damage to the body happened after he died."

"It is certain," Delbert confirmed. "Also, there were marks all over his body from blows made by something cylindrical, like a pipe. Those wounds also indicated that they were inflicted after he died."

Lincoln stood. "You've given me what I came for, and I thank ya."

"You're welcome," Delbert replied. "If you don't mind me saying so, you have my vote, Sheriff James."

"I appreciate that more than you know, Delbert." Lincoln smiled at the stoical individual and thought he caught a flicker of a grin pass across the man's otherwise unchanged face.

As he returned to his pickup, the sheriff's thoughts centered on the injuries inflicted after Jacob's death. Beating someone once they were deceased suggested a passionate kind of rage, as if someone had tried to take back something personal that Jacob had stolen from them. Something that even his death could not repay.

CHAPTER SEVENTEEN

Best-Laid Plans

As Gabby passed out of the shadow of the courthouse into the blazing sunshine, she fished around in her purse for car keys. She stopped, looked into the pit, and pushed aside her billfold and several stray receipts to no avail.

A rumbling motorcycle caught her ear; although she cautioned herself not to look, her curiosity paid no mind. She watched as Dean McCormick brought the kickstand down with the heel of his boot, leaned his Harley into position, and removed his helmet. While he ran his fingers through his blond mane, Gabby examined his face. When their eyes met, one corner of his mouth pulled up. *It's a sin for any man to smile like that*, she mused.

The biker dismounted and approached with colossal strides. "Gabriella," he purred.

Gabby tried to avert her gaze but found it impossible to look away. Swallowing hard, she spluttered, "M–Mr. McCormick. What brings you to our courthouse?"

"Oh, my, so formal. Have I done something to offend you?" Dean asked as he moved closer.

"Na—No, nothing." She glanced away from his sultry stare. "I—uh." Gabby silently chastised herself for her inability to keep it together around a good-looking man. "I need to go," she added breathlessly, and turned to leave.

"I'm here to see you," he said.

She stopped so suddenly that the sole of her shoe squeaked against the concrete. Unsure if she had heard him correctly, or if it was just wishful thinking, she didn't dare turn around.

"I thought we might go to lunch," Dean proposed.

Gabby picked up on the smile in his voice, and her heart took on the patter of a hummingbird's wing. There was a time when she would have given anything for a man like this to show her attention, but she was fresh off a breakup with Dusty, and her dad had made it clear that Dean McCormick was forbidden fruit.

She dropped her head back and looked at the clear blue sky, then turned to face him. "Look, you are—" She hesitated, searching for an acceptable excuse. Anything other than the truth. "You are—"

Dean stepped even closer until they were almost touching. "Please, have lunch with me." His whiskey voice left a tingle in its wake.

Gabby opened her mouth and let everything she felt fly. "You are hands down the most gorgeous man on the planet, and I — God help me — want to strip you down and ride you like a wild bronco. But I promised my dad I wouldn't get involved with you."

A hearty laugh rumbled deep from within his chest. "Gabriella Chambers, you are the most unusual woman I've ever met." He backed off giving her space. "If you come to lunch with me, I promise I'll not let you do anything that would cause you distress concerning your oath to your dad."

Gabby narrowed her eyes at him. "You won't tempt me?"

"I will be a perfect gentleman."

"From what I've heard, I doubt that's true," she muttered.

Dean chuckled. "I'm far from an angel, but I am a man of my word."

She watched him skeptically.

"Additionally, if you rode me like a wild bronco, as you suggest, the Rev would hunt me down and remove the offending part. I'm partial to my part," he teased.

Gabby burst into laughter. "Yes, he just might do that. Okay, but this outing has to be public…and friendly, nothing more."

"Follow me to the park. I have food and drink. We can talk about how I can help with your issue." He waited, but she didn't answer. "Is the park public enough?"

She nodded and hurried to her car to follow him.

***

Gabby watched Dean scoot in on the other side of a picnic table and open a paper sack. He placed a packet in front of her. "Pearl said this is your favorite."

She thanked him. "You aren't what I expected," Gabby said as she unwrapped her sandwich.

"No?" He smirked. "My uncle, the previous club president, sent me away to school in Massachusetts. He wanted a different life for me, but I was the club members' choice to take over when he died."

Surprised by this new information, Gabby looked up at him. "What school did you attend?"

"Harvard." He took a big bite of his club sandwich.

She wrinkled her nose. "You expect me to believe you went to Harvard?"

Dean shrugged as he finished chewing and swallowed. "Believe it or not, it's the truth. I was a good student. My parents were killed in an automobile accident when I was eight, and they left me a large trust. My uncle kept me on the straight and narrow."

"I'm really sorry about your parents." Gabby's heart hurt for the loss he had suffered, and he accepted her condolences with a nod. "What did you study?" she asked curiously.

"Law," Dean replied. "Though I wish I'd gone into criminal justice."

"If you're a lawyer, why would you choose to be the president of a motorcycle club?"

He laughed. "Methinks you might be a bit judgmental, Miss Chambers. All clubs aren't what people assume they are. Ours has evolved over the years, and we keep our activities on the legal side of the line. We do a lot of good. When the Rev was with my uncle back in the day, things were, shall we say, less wholesome. My law degree has not gone unused."

Gabby looked away. "But what we're asking of you—it's not exactly above board."

"I hope we have to do nothing more than scare whoever it is away, but we are prepared should removing the problem require more persuasion. We can be very daunting as a group."

She took a bite of her bacon, lettuce, and tomato sandwich as she considered what he'd just said.

"Why don't we go over exactly what you know?" Dean prompted. He listened intently as she shared the detailed information Amos had given her before he asked, "Who is your source?"

Gabby's gaze skittered away, and she focused intently on some children playing baseball nearby.

"Is this person reliable, or are they prone to exaggeration?" Dean persisted. "I want to be prepared for what we are walking into."

Gabby folded the paper wrapper around the remaining half of her sandwich. "You won't tell anyone?" She locked eyes with him.

He took her hand and held it. "I will tell no one. I promise."

"It's my brother, Amos. And yes, he is reliable. He wouldn't say something that isn't true. But if anyone finds out he talks to me, The Order will kick him out—although that might be a good thing."

"You were one of them? I thought the Rev was your dad."

"Harold and Marilyn adopted me. I was nearly fourteen when I left the community."

Dean squeezed her fingers lightly then let them go. "Thank you for telling me, Gabriella," he said as he cleared their trash and rose. "Your lunchtime is nearly over." As he came around the table and helped her over the bench, she looked at him longingly.

He didn't let go of her hands. "Gabriella Chambers, if you ever find you'd like to, I'd love to do something about that look you're giving me right now." He lifted her hand and placed her palm against his chest.

She stepped into his orbit and breathed in his earthy, leather essence. "Yeah," she sighed, regret coating every letter of the word. Then she regained her composure and slid her hand away from him. "Thank you for lunch. It's nice to know more about you."

He walked her back to her vehicle and opened the door. Once inside, she rolled down the window and he squatted beside her car. "Thank you for trusting me," he said. "I hope you'll go to lunch with me again before I leave."

"Sure. Give me a little notice next time, won't ya?" Gabby retrieved a business card from the console and handed it to him. "No excuse for you not to call."

A smoky grin whispered of promises unspoken as Dean tucked the card into his vest pocket and patted the spot where it lay near his heart. He gave her a parting wink before he mounted his bike, fired it up, and sped away.

Gabby gripped the steering wheel and laid her forehead against the backs of her hands. "What am I going to do about Dean McCormick?" she moaned.

As she returned to work, visions of a green-eyed, motorcycle-club president dominated her every thought.

CHAPTER EIGHTEEN

Tread Lightly

Kinsley peeked over her shoulder again at the open door near the rear of the church meeting hall. Her optimism had grown thin that Casey, the pregnant young lady with whom she'd become acquainted during the past two meetings, would appear. Gleaning any new information from the woman was like squeezing blood from a rock. Still, from the look of her, Kinsley couldn't help but feel that her new acquaintance must be in an abysmal predicament, so she couldn't stop hoping to make a connection.

Returning her attention to the speaker at the front of the room, she tried to concentrate on what was being said, but her mind continued to wander. She hoped that Casey was all right wherever she was tonight.

Fifteen minutes before the meeting was due to end, the chair beside her squeaked. A quick scan of the new arrival revealed dark circles under Casey's eyes. "It's good to see you. How have you been?" Kinsley whispered, trying not to disturb anyone around them.

"I—" Casey hesitated as she picked at what was left of her bitten nails. "I'm fine." When her gaze met Kinsley's, nothing even close to fine was reflected in those dismal depths.

"You don't know me well, but I want to help if possible." Kinsley turned to face Casey more fully. "If you're in trouble or just want to talk, I'm here."

The dam that was holding back the woman's tears started to crack. "There's nothin' no one can do."

Kinsley took her hand. "I felt the same way, and as long as I kept everyone on the outside it proved to be true. I had to let someone in."

Casey's eyes darted to the other people in the room and back.

"We can go somewhere else if you want," Kinsley offered.

"I cain't."

A cold chill ran through Kinsley. "Is the baby's father watching you?"

Casey shook her head as another fat tear rolled down her cheek.

"I'm sorry. I won't pry. But if you need out of whatever you are in with whoever you're afraid of, say the word and I'll get you out."

The scruffy girl shook her head. "I made my choices."

"No one deserves to be mistreated."

Casey searched Kinsley's face but said nothing. They turned their attention to Dr. Linda Towner, who was giving the closing remarks from the front of the room.

Kinsley's concern drowned out what was being said as she mentally ran possible scenarios about the girl's circumstances. She knew full well that little could be done until Casey decided to get out. Pulling a card from her wallet, she pressed it into the girl's hand. "My cell phone number is on there. If you change your mind call me anytime—day or night."

"Thanks," Casey whispered. She hugged Kinsley's neck tightly before she rose and melted into the pack of people who were leaving.

Kinsley ran up the back stairs and looked out of a window to see who had come to collect her, but the girl had vanished. When she returned to the lower level to help put the meeting space back in order, Dr. Towner pulled her aside to discuss a low-cost healthcare venture they were starting together. "I have some exciting news and a few hitches. Do you have time to talk?" she asked.

"I do. Let's set up shop over there." Kinsley indicated a small conference table at the edge of the room.

Linda laid her bag on the table and removed a stack of papers. "We have plenty of nurses and nurse practitioners ready to help. What we need is a doctor. Do you know anyone?"

Kinsley thumbed through the impressive stack of applications. "Not right off hand, but there must be someone. Do you have any friends like that, *Doctor*?"

Linda smiled at the nod to her profession. "I wish I did. What I do know is that this won't work without an MD on staff. Let me do some digging, and I'll see what I can come up with." The psychiatrist changed the subject. "Who is your friend?"

"My friend?" Kinsley lowered the applications she held and frowned. "What friend?"

"The young girl you've been sitting with at meetings."

"Ah. Casey No-Last-Name. I don't know her, but I wish I did. She may be stuck in something bad," Kinsley explained as she returned to the paperwork and separated the preferred applicants from the secondary choices.

"Be careful how involved you become. Domestic violence situations can be treacherous," Linda cautioned. "You're welcome to send her to me anytime. I'll see her free of charge."

Kinsley met the psychiatrist's worried look. "That's a generous offer, but I doubt she'd come even if she could get away to do so. I only see her here, but I'll extend your offer at our next meeting."

"You've come a long way from that broken woman I met nearly a year ago, Kinsley. This town is fortunate to have you."

Kinsley blushed. "I don't know about that. I'm trying to turn Harlow back into the safe place it was when I was a kid—only better."

"You're really not very good at taking a compliment."

Kinsley smiled knowingly before they turned back to business.

***

As Kinsley wearily climbed the stairs to her porch, her thoughts returned to Lincoln's bid for sheriff and a conversation she'd had with Charlene. The head dispatcher had rightly pointed out that the sheriff wasn't much for talking about his charitable acts, but if he was going to beat Trenton Crawley, he would have to change his mind about sharing them. The people of Stevens County needed to know what they would lose if Lincoln were no longer sheriff.

A perfect example was his involvement in the lives of the Lamar boys. Lincoln had joined an organization that helped foster children in order to watch over Lavonne and Garrett Lamar's children, who had been placed in the custody of a local family. The boys had adjusted well despite the dreadful circumstances surrounding their father's death and their mother's incarceration the previous year.

Only Kinsley knew about his support for those kids. Lincoln didn't do it for praise but because it was right. That type of commitment was the number one reason he should be sheriff, but convincing him to talk publicly about any of his behind-the-scenes good deeds would be nearly impossible.

CHAPTER NINETEEN

Fallen

Lincoln tapped a pen steadily on his desk as he made a mental list of the growing number of items that urgently required his attention. Unfortunately, the election kept floating to the top, despite his best efforts to ignore it. He picked up his coffee mug, took a sip, and thought about a conversation he'd had with Kinsley over dinner the previous night.

She'd suggested he hire a company to create a series of video advertisements to showcase the charitable works in which he was involved. Her recommendation surprised him because Kinsley was the last person to speak out about the incredible things she did for people. But the idea of using acts of kindness as a publicity stunt went against his grain; in his opinion, doing the right thing and then bragging about it took the good out of the deed. If that was the path to victory, it was time to turn in his badge.

The intercom squawked and Charlene came on. "Linc, Sam Lockwood called and asked specifically for you."

"Be right out." Lincoln closed the autopsy file on Jacob Miller. He'd intended to read through it again before he'd been distracted by thoughts of videos and campaigns. Coming into the front office, he stopped at Charlene's desk. She was taking another call. As he waited, he moved the pens in her holder that she'd separated by color into a random configuration.

Charlene pressed the disconnect button on her headset before smacking his hand away from the pen box. "You know I don't like it when you mess with my stuff."

Lincoln grinned mischievously. "Did Lockwood say what's goin' on?"

"He said you have to see whatever it is for yourself."

"That isn't suspicious at all," he muttered.

Charlene retrieved a pink message slip off her desktop, dramatically raised it to eye level, and cleared her throat. "*Send Linc out. There's somethin' he's gonna wanna see*," she recited. Dropping her hands, she lifted her eyebrows. "That is exactly what he said and nothing more."

"Okay, I believe ya." He shot her a cockeyed grin as he swiped his Stetson off the rack by the door, then headed for the rented pickup he'd traded for the ridiculous car they'd stuck him with initially. After one day of twisting himself like a yogi master to get in and out of that uncomfortable sports car, he'd had enough. When Lincoln had returned the vehicle and insisted that it wouldn't do, they'd fallen over themselves laughing. It seemed they had taken bets on how long he would keep the showy red ride before he stormed back in.

Opening the pickup door, Lincoln slid behind the wheel and cranked the engine. As he slipped the gearshift into drive, he chuckled. He had to admit it had been a good gag.

The two-lane county blacktop was deserted. As he drove past cornfields and pastureland, Lincoln wondered about the reason for Sam's summons. Lockwood had never before contacted the office for any reason that the sheriff could recall.

A stand of evergreen trees lined the mile-long dirt drive that led to Lockwood's farm, giving a pleasing visual break to the miles of flat terrain. Lincoln took a left off the blacktop and followed the tree line to the end of the lane, which ended in a circular drive at the front of a grand, white, two-story house. Double porches and oversized Roman columns dominated the structure in the style of an old Southern mansion. Like an iridescent pearl resting on a field of green chiffon, the house was in stark contrast to the acres of corn and soybeans that hugged its borders.

Lincoln stepped out of his pickup and walked toward the house, the clack of his leather-soled boots against a brick walkway was an affront to the silence of the morning. Before he had taken the first of the five steps that led up to a porch, a screen door slapped back against the cladding, and Sam Lockwood marched out to meet him.

The men clasped hands and exchanged a brief greeting. "What can I help ya with, Mr. Lockwood?" Lincoln asked.

"Come on out back, and yu'll see. We got ourselves an invasion, Sher'f," the silver-haired farmer said.

Lincoln followed as Lockwood rounded the side of the dwelling. "Now, I ain't scared or nothin', but the wife, she ain't none too fond of 'em bein' so close. I have to say, I ain't seen so many in one place. 'Specially out here."

They approached a towering oak tree toward the back of the property where the cultivated grass ended. Sam took a pair of binoculars from a picnic table and handed them over. "Take a look fer yourself." He pointed across an open field to a house that Lincoln could barely make out. "The old Gunderson place is full up."

Lincoln raised the field glasses and surveyed the land to the west. The motorcycle club he'd followed to the county line had found a place to roost, but the crew he'd followed through town was nowhere near as big as this gathering.

He lowered the glasses. "Gunderson passed away a few years ago. Do you know who owns the property now?"

"Harold Chambers," Sam replied as he sat on the tabletop.

Lincoln could not hide his astonishment as he turned to face the elderly man, who wore an impish grin. "The reverend?" he clarified.

"One and the same," Lockwood confirmed. "Now, ya tell me, why the hell would that many bikers be out in the country?"

The sheriff shook his head as he lifted the field glasses and took another look. "A religious revival?"

Sam heehawed. "That's some revival, Sher'f."

Lincoln handed back the binoculars. "Since Gunderson's house sits just across the county line, I'll call the Morton County sheriff and we'll check it out. Please assure your wife there isn't any need to worry."

"Aw, she's a worrier. Truth be told, they haven't done much of anything. Some whoopin' and hollerin' in the ev'nin's, but nothin' criminal." Sam stepped gingerly off the table and gave Lincoln a friendly slap on the back. "Young men like yurself get up to mischief. Ain't nothin' wrong with that."

"Still, it's odd they're there." Lincoln frowned as he cast an eye over the land that surrounded Lockwood's house.

"I wouldna called, but Genevieve wasn't gonna let it go," Sam said as the men started back. "I hear tell yur gonna find out about havin' a wife purty soon. Ya got yourself quite a woman."

"I did better than I should have," Lincoln replied with a wink.

The pair stopped at the steps of the front porch. "Fer what it's worth, you're one hell of a lawman," Sam said.

"Thanks, Mr. Lockwood. I appreciate that." They shook hands. "And thanks for callin' this in. We'll get some answers."

"Don't let 'em recruit ya," Sam teased, then turned, ascended the stairs, and disappeared into the house.

Lincoln returned to his pickup, took out his phone, and scrolled through his contacts until he found the person he was searching for: Nelson White, the sheriff of Morton County.

White had been a one-man show since his deputy had run off to follow a Lynyrd Skynyrd cover band that had been on tour a few months ago. A fellow veteran, he and Lincoln had a shared friendship with Henry Rhodes; they had spent many a summer night on Henry's front porch, trying to see which of the three could tell the biggest lie.

Lincoln grinned as he pressed the call button. Henry Rhodes had changed his life in ways he'd never imagined.

"Why, Sheriff Lincoln James, fancy hearin' from you. Lookin' for a job already?" White's rough laugh vibrated over the line.

Lincoln chuckled. "Not yet, but keep me on your list, just in case. I have another reason for callin'."

"Oh yeah? Do tell." A lighter clicked in the background as White lit a cigarette and took a deep drag.

"The old Gunderson place is burstin' at the seams with bikers. What do you know about what's goin' on out there?"

"Bikers? Well, I'll be damned. What in the hell would the Rev be doin' with them?"

"My question exactly. A welfare check might be in order. I'm willin' to back ya, and I'd like to see for myself, if you don't mind."

"Sure 'nuff. I'm clean across the county but I'll head that way. Meet ya in fifteen," Nelson confirmed. His vehicle engine roared to life before the line went dead.

A dirt road leading into the Gunderson homestead teed off the main blacktop. Lincoln pulled his pickup onto the shoulder and called in his location to dispatch while he waited until the whine of Sheriff White's diesel pickup announced his arrival. White threw Lincoln a shotgun wave as he turned onto the road, his dual-wheeled pickup kicking up a thick dust cloud that made it difficult to see the path ahead.

They passed through an open gate and navigated rows of bikes. Lincoln cast an eye over the tents and the men drinking coffee around early-morning fire pits.

The two sheriffs parked near the house and exited their vehicles. White hiked up his jeans with one hand. "Are ya checkin' out my fine figur'?" he joked as he patted his protruding belly that threatened to explode his wide gun belt like a blown tire. "No need to hide your jealousy,

Linc. That disgustin' flat stomach you got there can't compare."

They shared a laugh then turned to face the house. Sheriff White continued, "Don't look like the Chambers are around."

They approached the front door cautiously, keeping an eye on the men in the yard who were looking on with interest. Nelson unsnapped the thumb strap that held his sidearm in its holster and said quietly, "If they decide we ain't friendly, we're gonna be in deep shit."

"Let's hope that doesn't happen." Lincoln's gaze fell to Nelson's hand on the butt of his revolver. "Don't pull that smoke wagon unless everything goes sideways." Hyperaware of the situation they faced, he didn't need a nervous cop turning this into a shootout.

Lincoln knocked then stepped back as the door was flung open with such force that it stirred the dead leaves on the porch into a flurry. At six feet six, he was generally taller than anyone he met, but the man who filled the doorway was taller by a head. *That is one big son of a bitch,* he thought.

"This welcome to the neighborhood call took longer than I expected," the man stated.

"Good mornin'. I'm Sheriff James, and this is Sheriff White. We're lookin' for Harold Chambers." Lincoln stepped aside as the brute moved out of the house, coffee mug in hand, and closed the door behind him.

"Reverend Chambers isn't here. Is there something I can do for you, gentlemen?" The articulate individual watched the officers coolly, his mild demeanor only serving to abrade an already uncomfortable situation.

"I'm here to assist Sheriff White," Lincoln told him. "We're just curious why a club is stayin' at Reverend Chambers' house."

The biker took a sip of coffee from his mug but remained silent.

"You have his permission to be here, I assume?" Nelson asked.

The man issued a curt nod.

"Are you bein' intentionally evasive?" Lincoln challenged.

The man shook his head slightly as he met the sheriff's gaze. "No, Sheriff James, I am not. My name is Dean McCormick. Harold and Marilyn are friends of mine. We were nearby and I wanted to see how they were doing. It is as simple as that."

He pulled a phone from his back pocket and placed a call. "Harold, Sheriffs James, and White are here. From their body language, I'm certain they believe we've killed and buried you on the property. Will you please alleviate their fears?" He held out the phone. "You're on speaker."

"Hey, Linc." Harold's amusement filtered down the line. "The boys are okay. No need to worry."

They finished their conversation and Dean ended the call. "I didn't mean to be pushy, Mr. McCormick, but we've had calls about your presence," Lincoln explained.

"Yes, I'm sure," Dean replied. "If that's all, I have an appointment."

Now that the matter was in hand, Nelson puffed up a little. "We appreciate your cooperation, Mr. McCormick."

"We'll do our best to keep it down to a low roar until we leave town," Dean assured them.

Lincoln extended his hand. "Mr. McCormick, good to meet ya."

"A pleasure to meet both of you." Dean shook their hands in turn.

The officers returned to their trucks. Lincoln thanked Nelson for his assistance before he loaded up. As he took a back road and crossed into his own county, he speculated on how Harold Chambers and Dean McCormick might be acquainted. It seemed an unlikely friendship. That story Dean had tried to sell about him and his comrades stopping by for a visit was a load of crap. Something was going on with Gabby and her parents but putting pressure on Kinsley's best friend to find out the truth would be a delicate operation.

CHAPTER TWENTY

Hold The Line

Kinsley cradled her phone against her shoulder as she tugged open the front door. She smiled warmly at Phillip Faulkner, a friend of Thomas's, who was undecided about his college major—and he was thirty minutes early for his computer internship overview. Having met him only once, she hadn't got a computer programmer vibe from him, but one never knew what secret potential could be hidden beneath a baseball cap and a scruffy T-shirt.

She held up her hand and made the motion of a mouth talking nonstop. "Uh-huh," she said politely while listening to the person on the other end. Kinsley waved Phillip into the house and closed the door behind him.

Holding the phone away she whispered, "this call is almost through." Resuming the conversation, she proceeded toward the dining room.

Turning to signal which chair Phillip should take at the table, he was nowhere to be seen. Kinsley nearly burst into laughter when she realized he'd remained in the foyer. Quickly wrapping up her call, she returned to greet him properly.

"Hi, Phillip, please come in. Sorry about that. It's been a busy morning." The lanky young man tagged along behind her this time. "You can sit here," she indicated an empty chair. "Thomas will be right out."

Kinsley watched as he quietly inspected the dining room. Admittedly, his first impression of her could have been better. Having the intern program fizzle out before it even started wouldn't do. "I'm a bit of a whirlwind sometimes," she explained. "We're glad you came. Could I get you something to drink?"

Phillip held out a plastic wrap covered plate filled with cookies topped by a coral-colored gingham bow. "Ma said to give you this as thanks for helpin' me." When Kinsley didn't instantly take the gift, he fumbled it onto the table with a clatter.

"How nice. Please tell your mother thank you." The teen's tension was profuse, and the feeling transferred to Kinsley. "We'll try to make this fun. Please don't worry. There won't be a test afterward," she joked.

Phillip watched her with interest, and the corner of his mouth tugged up slightly.

"Why don't we start over?" Kinsley removed the plastic wrap and bow from the plate and laid them aside. "Thomas and I thought—"

Her stepson blasted in, interrupting her attempt to repair the rough beginning she'd had with his friend. "Damn, Phil! Tryin' to get in good with the boss by bribin' her?" He grinned, reached around Kinsley, snagged a cookie, and flopped down in his usual spot.

"Shit, no," the boy answered. "I—I mean shoot. I'm sorry I cursed, Miss Rhodes."

Thomas chuckled as he reached for a second treat. "Yeah, Kins is a delicate flower. She never cusses."

Kinsley laughed, more out of relief than anything else. Thomas's arrival seemed to have calmed his friend's jitters. "It's not a problem, Phillip. You can be yourself with us." She started toward the kitchen. "I'm going to get some coffee. Anyone want anything?"

"Uh—Yeah, a Coke, if ya have one," Phillip said as he slid into a chair beside Thomas.

"Me too, please," Thomas added.

Kinsley returned, placed sodas in front of the young men and dropped some napkins by the dish of cookies.

"You're sure it's fine I'm here, Miss Rhodes?" Phillip asked as he watched Thomas's screen intently.

"I can't think of any reason why not."

Phillip clarified his concern. "What about the sheriff?"

Thomas snorted. "Dad doesn't know anything about computers."

Kinsley suppressed a chuckle as a vision of Lincoln instructing someone on coding popped into her head.

Phillip tried again. "Na—no. What I mean is, will he be upset I'm here when he isn't?"

Kinsley's brows stitched together. "I don't understand."

Thomas filled in the blanks. "Phil wonders if Dad will be mad that you're in the house with a strange man."

"Oh…" Her eyes flicked from her stepson to Phillip. "Oh. No, Lincoln doesn't mind who I have over when he's not here." She wondered what the boy's home life must be like if he assumed it was inappropriate for a man to be in a woman's house without her husband being present. She wanted to believe it was a sweet throwback to a more innocent time, but it was a little weird.

"Thanks for the drink, Miss Rhodes."

"You're welcome. Please call me Kinsley. Thomas will walk you through the basics. Let us know if you have questions or want to see something else."

Phillip nodded and scooted his seat closer to his pal as Thomas explained the current project he was working on for school. However, Kinsley's curiosity would not let her remain quiet. "Who are your parents?" she asked.

"Jim and Patty Faulkner, Ma'am."

"I didn't realize you were Jim's boy. You live near Weatherby's farm, right?"

"Yes, we do, and that mess out there has caused trouble for us," he lamented.

Flummoxed by his sudden change in demeanor, Kinsley stumbled over her reply. "Ah—I—I'm sorry. I'm sure it has caused a ripple in the peace you usually enjoy."

"Yeah, we've had people looky-lookin' and tearin' up our land. It's pissin' us off," Phillip grumbled.

"I understand." Kinsley was shaken by the tension that had returned.

"Do ya think the sheriff will solve it soon? It would stop people comin' round if he did."

"I know he's working hard to solve it," Kinsley said.

As she opened her latest email, and processed what Phillip had shared, a remembered conversation with Lincoln about people who perpetrated a crime returning to the scene came to mind. *Maybe one of those trespassers is the killer*, she pondered.

***

All the evidence they had collected was spread out on the conference table in Lincoln's office, and he and Butch were silently contemplating the clues in front of them. One by one, the sheriff lined up the photographs he'd taken on the day of discovery and placed them in sequence. He continued the timeline with the coroner's autopsy pictures, studying each one, looking for anything they might have missed.

"I went to see the coroner, and he mentioned somethin' that stuck with me," Lincoln said thoughtfully. "He said the broken bones were unusual, like the man had been in a car accident." Lincoln picked up one of the autopsy photos. "What does that look like to you?" He pointed to a bruise on the deceased man's hip.

Butch pulled the photo closer to study it. "Looks an awful lot like diamond plate."

Lincoln slid a close-up of the man's face toward his undersheriff. "And that?"

Butch tilted his head, then rotated the picture. "Could be grill marks from a vehicle. I could gather pictures of different grills to see if we can match that mark. It might give us a vehicle make."

Lincoln stroked his chin. "Yep, that might give us a direction. It's possible the guy was hit and killed, and the driver panicked."

"They went to an awful lot of trouble to cover up an accident." Butch lay the picture back on the table.

"I agree. Maybe the person who did this was tryin' to intimidate Miller, and it got out of hand."

"Plenty of folks had good reason to want to scare the livin' shit out of him. I have yet to talk to anybody with a good thing to say about Miller. I can hardly believe that Gabby was going to marry the creep. Hey, speakin' of her, I saw somethin'."

"Oh, yeah?" Lincoln switched his focus from the pictures to his undersheriff.

"Now you know I'm not a gossiper, and I wouldn't say a thing, but..." Butch paused as the color rose in his cheeks.

Lincoln couldn't remember him turning red in all the years they'd worked together. "Damn! You're blushin' like a teenager. What did ya see?"

Butch grinned. "On my way here, I took City Limits Road into town. They built that new park, and it's a nice drive." He drummed his fingers on the table. "It's really none of my business, and I feel bad sayin' anything—but the guy was so big."

An image of a man who had filled the doorway at Harold Chambers' house flashed in Lincoln's mind.

"I saw Gabby Chambers and this huge stranger out there. He was holdin' her hand, and she wasn't resisting. I pulled around behind some trees and watched for a spell in case she was in trouble, not that I could have taken the beast. When they started gettin' more serious, I high-tailed it out of there. Gabby was obviously there by choice." Butch rested his hand on the table and looked at Lincoln. "I thought she was Dusty's girl."

"They've had a partin' of the ways, but you didn't hear it from me. Maybe what ya saw wasn't what it looked like."

Butch shrugged, but Lincoln could see he had made up his mind. "I won't tell anyone else. It just took me by surprise," the undersheriff said.

"The man you saw is Dean McCormick." Lincoln pushed his chair back from the table and stood.

Butch followed his lead. "You know him?"

"Nelson White and I went on a call at the old Gunderson place. Apparently, Harold and Marilyn Chambers own it and there's a bike rally goin' on there," said the sheriff as he crossed to the other side of the room.

"A *bike* rally?"

Lincoln nodded as he added new possible leads about a vehicle accident to the whiteboard. "It looks like a mini-Sturgis."

"And that's not troublin' you at all?" Butch stepped up next to his boss. "What's your plan?"

"I'm not gonna do anything. They aren't botherin' anyone. They have a right to be there, and that's that." Lincoln laid the dry marker in the tray, turned, and patted Butch on the back. "We better get to work solvin' this murder. It ain't gonna solve itself."

"Should we watch 'em?"

"I got my eye on 'em. Let's wait to worry. We have enough on our plates with a killer on the loose." Lincoln noted Butch's skeptical look. "They're in Morton County. If they cause trouble here, we'll pick 'em up. The fact that none of us knew they were at Gunderson's says quite a bit."

"True, true." Butch let out a breath. "I'm on edge with everything that's goin' on and this election in play. I'll feel a lot better once you've won and Crawley leaves town."

"I might not win," Lincoln suggested.

Butch shook his head. "It would take a bigger man than Crawley to beat you, Linc."

"Here's hopin' you're right," the sheriff replied.

CHAPTER TWENTY-ONE

Dirt-Road Detectives

Harold Chambers pulled onto the shoulder of a gravel road and slipped his vehicle's gearshift into park. Reaching across the console, he squeezed Gabby's hand briefly as the three motorcycles that had followed them came to a rumbling stop. The group converged at the front of the Chambers' SUV.

"There it is," Harold declared, indicating the settlement a few hundred feet from their location. A little over a half section was surrounded by twelve-foot chain-link fencing. "The front gate on the opposite side is the only way in or out."

Gabby inhaled deeply and the sweet scent of flowering alfalfa that was growing abundantly in the fields on either side of the road made her smile. "That's not entirely true. At the southwest corner the fencing is cut and held in place by one hook. We used to sneak out at night."

Dean reached into a knapsack that hung from his shoulder and pulled out a pair of field glasses. He reviewed the area she'd mentioned. "How do you know it's still that way? You've been gone a long time."

"I just know," she returned. "If you go to the front gate, they won't let you in. They already have one dead member, so they're probably a little out of sorts."

Dean lowered the binoculars and looked at her. "Who is dead?"

Gabby bit the inside of her cheek as she met his gaze. "Jacob Miller, the leader's son. He was murdered not long ago."

"And you're only telling me this now? We can't get mixed up in a murder investigation."

"The murder didn't happen in there," Gabby countered. "He was found a few miles away."

"Still…" Dean turned his attention back to the fenced area. "I assume it's an active investigation?"

"It is."

"If we get caught interfering, that's a serious crime."

Gabby pursed her lips as she considered the compound. "I understand if you can't help."

"I strongly suggest that you tell Sheriff James what you know."

Dean's attorney voice had taken over, but she couldn't do what he advised. "Kinsley is my best friend. If I get her fiancé killed, she'll never forgive me."

Harold pulled her to his side. "It'll be okay, sweetheart. I promise." He kissed the top of his daughter's head.

"Thanks, Daddy," Gabby said before she broke away from the others and walked down the road, scanning the fencing, hoping to glimpse Amos. If she could get him a message to get out for a while and take everyone with him, maybe they would be safe until she could find a way to stop what was happening to them.

"Hey," Dean said as he came up behind her.

"Hey," Gabby quietly responded without turning around.

"I didn't say I wouldn't help, but an open murder investigation does make things infinitely more complicated. You understand that, right?" When she didn't answer, he moved closer and touched her shoulder. "I'll do something. I just don't know what yet."

She nodded and bent to pluck a stem of wild wheat from the ditch, studying it intently as she spun it between her thumb and forefinger.

"I know you feel guilty about our little make-out session at the park," Dean went on. "We can stop seeing each other, if you want."

Gabby shook her head. "I don't want that. I kissed you first, remember?"

His boots crunched against the dry earth as he moved in front of her. "It is a moment I won't ever forget. Never has a picnic table been such an erotic setting—at least not for me."

A secret smile played across her lips as she recalled their afternoon delight, but when reality took hold, her joy faded. "I've never lied to my dad before. The guilt is eating me alive."

Dean reached out to comfort her, then stopped. He glanced toward Harold before pulling back his hand. "I understand. Secrets can be like poison, and you've got quite a few," he said. "I'd love to hug you, but I will refrain since we have an audience. Please think about telling your father what's going on with us. And while you're at it, you should tell Sheriff James the truth, too."

Gabby watched him steadily.

Dean tilted his head toward their companions. "I should get back before there are too many questions."

As he walked away, Gabby contemplated his advice. She had always prided herself on being honest, but since the day of the lightning strike, her life had turned into a web of secrets and half-truths. It wasn't a skin she wore comfortably.

CHAPTER TWENTY-TWO

I Spy

From an oil-well access road a quarter mile to the south of the settlement, Lincoln looked on with interest at the arrival of a familiar SUV and three motorcycles. He raised his binoculars and watched Reverend Chambers, his daughter, and three bikers survey the compound. Their presence stirred up many more questions about how involved Harold Chambers and Dean McCormick were in the death of Jacob Miller.

He looked away long enough to dial his dispatcher, then resumed watching the collective as they pointed toward the fencing at the back of the property.

"Hey, Linc," Charlene said when she picked up.

"Hey. Did you find anything new about Reverend Chambers and this McCormick fella?"

"The Chambers lived in San Diego before coming to Harlow, the same town as our mysterious biker. McCormick has no record to speak of, outside of a few speeding tickets. I did find something interesting, though, and I need to follow it up. There is a member of the California Bar Association with the same name."

Lincoln lowered the binoculars and pressed his phone tighter to his ear. "Come again?"

"A Dean McCormick is a member of the California State Bar. He's an attorney."

"Now that is somethin'." Lincoln closed his eyes and squeezed the bridge of his nose. "McCormick's stories are shot full of holes, and now they're out at the settlement."

"I can't believe Gabby would be involved in a murder, but it's getting harder and harder to deny," Charlene said. "What can I do to help?"

"Keep diggin'," Lincoln returned. "Find out if this guy *is* an attorney. That brings a whole new level of what-the-hell into this."

"Will do."

"Thanks, Charlene," he said, and ended the call.

What did Miss Chambers know, and how was he going to get it out of her without blowing up his whole world? That was the million-dollar question.

***

"Hey, missy. Those are my toes." Kinsley pulled her foot away from the nibbling puppy as she bent and looked at Maizey, who had made herself at home under the table. "Are you bored, Maiz?"

The dog whipped her tail around in response.

Kinsley sat up. "I need some fresh air, too. Running on the treadmill is a whole lotta no fun. It's a beautiful day. Surely that ol' sheriff wouldn't mind if we took a walk at high noon on a public street?"

Maizey crawled from under the table and waited anxiously for her mistress's next move.

"We'll leave him a note just in case he pops by. Otherwise, it'll be our secret." Kinsley penned a short message and left it on her closed laptop before she and her dog escaped the confines of their house.

They made quick work of their walk to Harlow's business district, where Kinsley slowed to a stroll as she window-shopped. Since the Skelly trials, new businesses had been blossoming downtown. A specialty tea and candle shop had just opened, and she hadn't had a chance to visit it yet. She examined the store's eclectic display through the window, then looked more closely at a menu listing various teas.

The pup suddenly stopped tugging at the end of her leash and bayed loudly. Kinsley whipped her head toward Maizey and found the source of the disturbance. A furry-faced, leather-clad fellow had knelt and was trying to pet the pup. Kinsley attempted to reel in the leash, but Maizey refused to budge, which forced her to move toward the dog.

A similarly dressed second stranger strolled out of the donut shop and approached the scene. The smell of freshly fried chicken coming from the bag in his hand made Kinsley's mouth water.

"Nice pup. Did you get him locally?" asked the man who was still kneeling in front of a growling Maizey.

"It's a girl. The Rays south of town have a bluetick hound that had a dalliance with a wandering stranger. She isn't fullblood."

The biker stood and nodded as he continued to look at the dog. Maizey was not warming to him in the least. "That's okay. It's great that she's already protective of you."

Kinsley reached down and scratched her dog's back. "We don't get out much."

"My name's Kenny Cooper," he offered. "Do the Rays have any more dogs for sale?"

As Kinsley gave him a once-over, his companion laughed. "Kenny, I assume she's wondering what you'll do with a dog. You need a shave. You're scaring the lady."

Kenny chuckled and pulled back his leather vest. He dug around in an interior pocket and produced a business card. "I'm an accountant, Ma'am. I'm not looking to hurt any dogs. I had a bluetick as a boy, and I'd like another."

Kinsley took the card and skimmed it. "You don't look like any accountant I've ever seen."

"You don't exactly fit either, unless everyone in Podunk Nowhere walks their dog in two-thousand-dollar Italian designer hiking boots," Kenny teased.

A blush peeked at the collar of her shirt as she grinned and held out one foot. "No one here would know what these are. Okay, Kenny Cooper, well played. I'll call the Rays and let you know if they have any puppies left. I'm Kinsley Rhodes, by the way." She tucked his card into her jeans' back pocket and held out her hand.

"Nice to meet you, Kinsley," Kenny returned as he shook her hand.

A horn tooted and they both looked at a dark-blue Dodge truck that was creeping down Main Street with a very interested occupant. Kinsley returned to her conversation. "I'll call you in a day or two. How long are you in town?"

Kenny looked at his pal, who shrugged. "We don't know. A week or so, could be longer. We have to…" He stopped abruptly. "We'll be here a while. Please call me."

"I will."

As the Dodge pulled in at the curb and Lincoln got out, the two men wasted no time on goodbyes. Kinsley and the sheriff watched them until they rounded one corner of the bank and disappeared down a side street. "What was that about?" Lincoln asked.

"It was weirdness." She pulled Kenny's card from her pocket and handed it to him. "That guy wanted to know if he could get a dog from the Rays."

"What else did they say?"

"Nothing, really. They're in town for a while, and he wants a dog. The Donut Shop must have fried chicken on special today because they had a sack of it, and it smelled pretty good."

"Did he tell you why they are in town?" Lincoln pushed.

"Dang, I didn't know I was a suspect. Are you gonna arrest me, Sheriff?"

Lincoln put his arm around Kinsley's shoulders and side-hugged her as he laughed. "I'm sorry. Let me take you and Maizey to lunch to make up for it. We can get some burgers and eat at the park. How about that?"

"We would love it." Kinsley slipped her arm around Lincoln's waist. "The guy did seem to stumble around how long they were going to be here, and he started to say they had to do something but stopped mid-sentence. Does that help?"

"It certainly does. Thanks." Lincoln walked her back to his truck and held the passenger door. The rumbling sound of revving motorcycles reached his ears.

Kinsley's revelation confirmed to Lincoln how imperative it was to obtain a warrant to get inside the settlement. While he'd tried several different tactics, Lincoln hadn't yet succeeded in coming up with something that would hold water with the judge, but giving up wasn't in his nature.

CHAPTER TWENTY-THREE

Musical Chairs

After he'd spotted Gabby and her entourage sniffing around, Lincoln spent much of his stakeout time for the next few days at the settlement. The Chambers had not made another appearance, and now that he thought of it, Gabby had stopped coming by the house when he was home.

The beat of a particularly bluesy country tune came on the radio, and Lincoln tapped his fingers on the steering wheel as a hot summer breeze ruffled the receipts that hung from a clip on the truck's visor. He took a left off the main blacktop onto a sandy, unpaved road and drove until he came to a stand of cottonwood trees, a quarter of a mile from The Order's compound. Pulling his pickup into the shade, he parked and killed the engine.

He was not alone on today's adventure. "Come on, Maizey girl. Let's take a little stroll."

When he opened the door, the pup leaped from the pickup and immediately put her nose to the ground. She moved around in circles until she caught a scent and followed it into a field of prairie grass across the road. Lincoln sauntered behind; he hadn't a clue what had grabbed her attention, but something had. Since she was a hunting dog through and through, and he didn't hunt, he would have to find something else for her to do to expend that energy.

He issued a brief, sharp whistle before turning back toward his vehicle. A few seconds later, Maizey came barreling up beside him. He reached down and brushed the dirt from her nose. "Let's see what those people at the settlement are up to, girl."

Back at his pickup, Lincoln opened the extended cab door, retrieved a metal bowl, and set it on the ground; he reached in again for a bottle of water, and gave the panting dog a drink. When she'd finished, Maizey jumped in the pickup and took her place in the passenger seat.

Lincoln emptied the bowl, tossed it in the truck, and closed the door. If the previous days' surveillance was any indication, they were in for a dull, hot day.

***

After a few hours of mind-numbing boredom, Lincoln was about ready to throw in the towel when a rental box truck trundled down the blacktop and turned onto the short entrance road that led to the compound. He raised his binoculars and watched. A horn sounded, and a large gate rolled back along a track to allow the truck inside. Laying the field glasses on the dash, he took down the out-of-state license-plate number and called it in to dispatch.

The transport was disappearing between buildings as Dusty returned his call. The truck had been rented in the border town city of El Paso, Texas. El Paso was around five hundred miles from Harlow, so something mighty important must be in there to take such a long trip. Maybe the rumor Butch had heard about The Order harboring illegals out of Mexico was true.

Lincoln raised his field glasses to take another look and swore under his breath as a sea-blue Audi crept into his field of vision. The car rolled to a stop beside his pickup, and the driver's window lowered. "Who are you stalking today, Linc?"

Maizey, who had been sleeping peacefully, sprang into Lincoln's lap and issued a warning bark. Scratching the pup behind her ear, Lincoln squinted at Crawley then focused on the settlement. "You'll get your snazzy car dirty out here."

"Just keeping an eye on the welfare of the residents. They'll soon be under my watch." Crawley's smug attitude was never in short supply.

The radio squawked with a request for Lincoln to return to the office, and he heard the call echo from Crawley's car as well. They'd had their suspicions, but this confirmed how Trenton was keeping up with every move the police made. Switching strictly to cell-phone use would nip his game in the bud.

"Good luck with that," Lincoln said, and tugged on the brim of his Stetson. He started his pickup, dropped it into drive, and kicked up a swirl of powder-fine dust and sand that he hoped would choke the irritant he'd left in his wake.

Lincoln fumed as he drove toward town and considered the number of police calls at which Trenton had miraculously appeared. It had started right after the debate: Crawley had become a consistent, unwelcome shadow, which frustrated Lincoln to no end. The situation had recently come to a head in the Donut Shop.

Crawley had swanned in while Lincoln was sharing a cup of coffee with some of the local farmers and had immediately begun the same bull about Charlene and the deputies being incompetent that he'd spouted at the debate. Lincoln should have kept his cool, but he'd had enough. He'd stood, towered over Crawley, and, with measured steps, backed him out of the establishment and onto the sidewalk, warning him to mind his manners.

Thunderous applause had welcomed Lincoln when he'd returned, but guilt pricked at him because it wasn't a proper way for a sheriff to behave. What's more, it wouldn't be beneath Trenton to file misconduct charges against him. Since then, he had walked a straight line where the wannabe usurper was concerned.

Lincoln pulled into his parking space at headquarters and shut off the engine, gripping the steering wheel tightly as he inhaled. Letting out the breath he was holding slowly, he was about to open the truck's door when his phone rang. He retrieved it from his shirt pocket and scowled when he saw his ex-wife's name on the caller ID. "Good God! Can this day get any worse?" he grumbled, hesitating briefly before ignoring the call.

The sheriff opened the door, whistled to Maizey, and exited the pickup. As they sailed through the outer office, he tossed a hello to Dusty. There was no time for pleasantries; he was on a mission to learn more about what was being transported into the compound and what a biker club, paired up with a local reverend and his political-leaning daughter, had to do with it.

Lincoln sat at his desk and turned on his laptop while Maizey found a comfortable spot near his feet. Preferring old-fashioned, boots-on-the-ground police work, this case had reached beyond the borders of his county, and he needed the internet's help.

As the computer came to life, he thought about Gabby and their friendship. Lincoln had difficulty believing she was up to no good, but the evidence against her was beginning to stack up.

CHAPTER TWENTY-FOUR

Passengers

Kinsley studied her fiancé as he moved his breakfast around his plate with a fork. She'd tried three topics and received nothing but grunts and one-word answers. It was out of character for him to play with his food, and he'd hardly eaten anything the previous night at dinner. She tried a new topic. "Gabby and Dusty are officially through. She thought they might get back together, but that's not going to happen."

"Yep," Lincoln responded.

"Yeah. Dusty said he was ending things with her because the moon is purple, and cats are living on it."

"Hmm."

Kinsley took her plate to the sink and leaned back against the counter. "What's a girl hafta do to get some attention around here?"

Lincoln looked up. "I'm sorry. What were ya sayin'?"

"Nothing important. What can I do to help?" Kinsley asked as she crossed the kitchen to stand beside him.

"Has Gabby said anything about what's goin' on with her lately?"

"No, other than the election and her breakup with Dusty."

Lincoln nodded and returned to pushing his breakfast around.

"Is there something else?" Kinsley asked. "There must be."

"She's been hangin' out with her dad and some of his friends. It's new, so I thought she mighta said somethin'."

"How much trouble could a girl get into with a reverend and a slew of parishioners?" Kinsley joked.

"Yeah, you're probably right." He stood and leaned in for a goodbye kiss. "Mmm. You taste like maple syrup." He kissed her again.

Kinsley lingered in his arms savoring the moment before she opened her eyes and smiled. "Go to work and try to stay out of trouble."

Lincoln chuckled as he let her go. "See ya tonight, gorgeous."

Maizey followed him to the door, and he reached down to pat her before he left. She was rambunctious, but they'd fallen hopelessly in love with the pup. It eased his mind that Kinsley had an added layer of protection when he wasn't there.

***

As the sheriff loaded up and headed out of town, his thoughts turned to Harlow's local lumber store. It had been a frequent haunt for Mr. Miller and his pals. When the sheriff had interviewed the employees, it was obvious that many were afraid to say much, except for Emily Patton, who had dated Miller for a short while. She obviously still carried a torch for Jacob, and her lovestruck view of the man had loosened her tongue. As she was extolling the virtues of the deceased, she'd named a few of his associates, which had given Lincoln a good place to start.

Pulling into the driveway of a farmstead that belonged to Jeb Paulson, the first name on his short list of Miller's cronies, Lincoln scanned the area before getting out. Alert to his surroundings, he approached the rickety dwelling; if Miller's dangerous reputation were true, his known associates would likely be more of the same.

Lincoln stood to the side of a case opening and gave a quick rap on a storm door that sat a bit cockeyed in its frame. It rattled as he knocked. "Sheriff's office!" He announced loudly.

A work-worn hand pressed against a rusty metal screen and pushed open the door. Bloodshot hazel eyes darted from the officer to the dirt road in front of the house. "I ain't done nuttin'," the man squawked.

"Mr. Paulson?" Lincoln asked.

"Yep," the individual confirmed. "But I ain't done nuttin'," he repeated edgily.

A toddler peeked around the doorframe; when Lincoln winked at the youngster, he was rewarded with a giggle.

"Get ye back in da house," the man scolded, sending the child scampering away.

"Mr. Paulson, I'm here to ask about your association with Jacob Miller. I was told you worked together."

Paulson looked out at the horizon before his focus skittered back to Lincoln. "Ye got yer facts wrong. I don' work for him no more. Let us be. We don't need no trouble."

Before Lincoln could respond, Paulson was pushed aside violently by a woman who charged out of the house and onto the porch, backing Lincoln to the steps. "Come to take the spawn of Satan with ya, lawman?" She had a hold of the small boy's arm and was dragging him behind her. "Take 'im! We don't need visits from his father or that lot."

She pushed the toddler toward the sheriff then wiped her hands on her flowered apron. "This is what we know of Jacob Miller. He whelped a bastard on our daughter and turned her into a whore. Take this…this…" The woman shooed the boy away. "Let us be. We want no part of it. And tell Miller to stay away from us!"

"Mrs. Paulson, if you're havin' trouble, I can help. Surely, ya don't mean to send your grandson away." Lincoln was struggling to get a handle on the unexpected development.

The woman's eyes landed on the child, who was now clinging to the sheriff's leg. "My husband invited evil in, and we'll have no more of it." She rushed back into the house, yanked her husband along with her, and slammed the interior door shut.

Lincoln looked down at the boy who was wrapped around his thigh. He ruffled the child's hair before he prized him from his leg and picked him up. "I got ya, young'un," he soothed.

A door slammed from somewhere at the back of the house and Lincoln took the three porch steps quickly to the ground. As he rounded the building, the sheriff saw Mr. Paulson on his way toward his barn. "Sir, wait right there!" He ordered.

The man stopped and turned slowly. "Take 'im, please. This is no place for da child," Paulson pleaded.

"Tell me what you know about Jacob," Lincoln countered.

"We were put out of da community because of what he did to our daughter. She's passed now, but da child remains. My wife has no love for da boy. You'll take 'im?"

"Where were you and your wife on the night of June tenth?" Lincoln asked.

"In Oklahoma wit' da wife's family." Paulson dug around in his front pocket and produced a wallet from which he pulled a piece of paper. "That 'dere is names and such. Call 'em. We were 'dere. I didna kill Jacob." He reached out and patted the boy's back. "'Is name is Levi. He's three." Jeb dashed away a tear trailing over his weather-beaten cheek as he turned and left the sheriff to ponder an extraordinarily odd start to his day.

Lincoln gazed at the boy in his arms. It was hard to believe this malnourished, unkempt child was three years old. "Well, Levi, it's you and me, buddy. This diaper isn't an appropriate uniform for a deputy. What say we find ya some clothes and somethin' ta eat?"

The youngster laid his face against the sheriff's shirt front as they returned to his pickup. Lincoln would never understand people as long as he lived. He strapped the boy in the back seat as best he could and drove carefully toward town, connecting with dispatch as he drew near.

"Hey, Linc!" Charlene answered with her usual zest.

"Hey. I need you to call Jenny Armbruster and have her meet me at the office in about an hour, please."

"The social worker? What's up?"

Lincoln looked at the child in his rearview mirror. "My interview at the Paulsons left me with an unexpected passenger. He's three, and cute as a button."

"That must have been some visit. Bring the baby on in. I'll have Dixon stop and get breakfast for us," Charlene replied. "Can't say bein' around you is ever dull."

Lincoln chuckled. "I can't have you gettin' bored. I hafta do a little shoppin' first, then I'll be in. Thanks, Charlene." He ended the call.

Parking his pickup next to a curb outside the only local general store, he shut off the engine. As he peered unseeing inside the building, the sheriff thought about Charlene and the rest of his team. If Crawley won the election and made good on his threat to fire everyone, Lincoln would need a Plan B for all of them, including himself. After meeting the private investigator Kinsley had hired last year, getting a PI license had crossed his mind. With thoughts of a new career starting to form, Lincoln climbed out of his vehicle and opened the back door of his pickup.

"Hey, little fella. Let's do some shoppin'. What d'ya say?"

The child held out his arms, and the sheriff picked him up and held him steady on his hip before retrieving his phone to call Kinsley. While taking care of children wasn't new to him, he had been in the service and was often away when Thomas was this age. Reinforcements would be necessary to complete this mission.

CHAPTER TWENTY-FIVE

Broken Promises

Gabby settled back in one of Kinsley's dining room chairs as she sipped her tea while listening to her best friend and Thomas banter back and forth about some issue with his school project. Her mind wandered to recent developments. Despite a promise to her dad, she and Dean had been lunching together nearly every day, with a few dinners thrown in. True to his word, he had been a gentleman, though, on many occasions, she'd secretly wished he would break that vow.

"Have you heard from Dusty?" Kinsley asked.

The question squelched what was quickly becoming a steamy daydream, and Gabby shifted in her chair to refocus. "No, but I didn't expect he would call. I've been avoiding our old haunts to give him some space. He'll come around. We both agreed it wasn't working."

Thomas turned toward Gabby and hooked an arm over the back of his chair. "Wait. I mighta missed something since the last time we talked. Dusty Reynolds officially broke it off with you?"

"It was mutual, but we did break up."

"Wow! How stupid is he? I have ten friends who'd chew their right arm off to be with you." He hesitated, and a sly grin played on his lips. "I'd throw my hat in the ring, too."

Gabby burst into laughter. "Thomas, you're too much."

"I'm serious. Let's go out."

"Oh my gosh, stop! You're a mess. I'm old enough to be your…" Gabby searched for an appropriate age comparison "…well, your older sister, for sure."

"What does that have to do with the price of tea? Dad is eight years older than Kins."

Kinsley gave a good-natured shrug when Gabby looked to her for help. "I'm going to take the coffee cake out of the oven while you two discuss dinner plans," she said as she got up and headed for the kitchen.

Gabby couldn't keep from smiling as she addressed Thomas. "I probably shouldn't start dating someone so soon after a breakup. I do appreciate the offer." He sat back and studied her, as she tried to let him down easily. "You're a handsome guy and any woman would be lucky."

"Oh, this isn't over. I'm pretty charmin'." Thomas winked.

"Don't I know it? I've heard every girl in town is a fan."

"What's with the big biker you've been hangin' with?" he asked.

The question knocked Gabby sideways. "Uh, Dean is a friend of my father's." She looked down at her shirt and brushed away imaginary crumbs. "When did you see him?"

"I saw the two of you in the park eatin' lunch a while back," Thomas replied.

"He's just a friend," Gabby reiterated, but his question made her wonder who else had seen them together.

"Who are you talking about?" Kinsley asked as she

returned and placed plates along with a warm breakfast cake on the table.

Thomas chuckled. "Some Harley rider who beat me to the punch with Gabby."

A frown creased Kinsley's brow. "What?"

Gabby scrambled to stop her worlds from colliding. "Dean McCormick. He's a friend of my father's—but nothing is going on with me and him."

"How do I not know about this?" Kinsley pinned Gabby with her look.

"I didn't think it was important. It's just a short visit and he'll be on his way."

Kinsley slowly took her seat. Gabby could almost see the wheels turning in her head, and she knew her friend wasn't one to let things go easily. If Lincoln found out, everything would come apart. A change of subject was in order. "Frank has had me at every opening in town lately, campaigning. He concocted some of them just to get me out there. I'm exhausted," she said.

Her clumsy effort to get their minds off Dean did not go unnoticed by Thomas, who stifled a laugh.

"The man is a miracle worker. I'm glad he's helping you and Lincoln. He comes up with ideas I never imagined," Kinsley replied as she cut the cake, plated the first piece, and slid it toward Thomas.

"How does your dad know a biker?" Thomas asked.

Gabby meticulously arranged her silverware on a napkin, so she didn't have to look at her friends while she told a half-truth. "Dad knew Dean years ago when he lived in California, long before he and Mom came to Harlow. Dean was on his way east and stopped over for a few days."

Thomas quickly swallowed the bite of cake he'd taken. "That guy is nowhere near Reverend Chambers' age."

Good God, Thomas, let it go, Gabby pleaded silently. She looked up and noted Kinsley's raised eyebrows, but it was too late to turn it around now. "Dad was friends with Dean's uncle. I swear it's nothing." She could almost smell the stink of desperation that outed her as a liar.

"Okay, Thomas, we've teased Gabby enough. If we don't let her have her secrets, she'll never come to see us again."

Thomas looked from his stepmother-to-be to the blonde. "Sorry, Gabs. I was only kiddin'." He mustered his best roguish smile. "But since you're just friends with that guy, you have no reason not to go out with me. What time am I pickin' you up on Saturday night?"

The women giggled.

Much to Gabby's relief, a call from Lincoln ended their confab abruptly. She needed to put out this fire before her and Dean's secret plan to help those inside the compound blew up.

***

Gabby paced the floor of her father's country home while waiting for Dean to either show up or respond to the urgent text she'd sent before leaving Kinsley's.

A rumble of bikes in the drive had her running to the front window. Dean dismounted and made short work of approaching the house. Gabby rounded a couch and met him as he swung the door wide. "Are you okay?" he asked as he looked her up and down.

"Yes, but you have to get things done and leave town," she stated anxiously. "The sheriff's fiancée is my best friend. They know you're here. I lied, but Lincoln will find out."

"Shit, Gabriella, you scared me with your text." He ran his fingers through his hair as he exhaled. "Sheriff James and I are acquainted."

Gabby felt like she'd been gut-punched. "How did that happen?"

"A club as big as ours couldn't stay hidden in a small town for long." Dean moved through the open living room/kitchen combination, took a cup from the drain board, and drew water from the tap. "Sheriffs James and White paid me a visit." He downed the liquid and placed his glass in the sink.

Gabby plopped down on the couch, leaned back, and closed her eyes. She should have known they would be found out.

"I can see what kind of person James is," said Dean as he crossed the living room to join her. "I understand why you don't want to involve him." He sat and laid his arm across the back of the divan, gently smoothing the hair at her temple with the backs of his fingers. "But you do know he is a trained law-enforcement officer with more than ten years of service, right? This is his job."

Gabby opened her eyes. "He's a really good man, Dean. And I know he's supposed to take care of the bad guys, but something about this mess makes me fear for his safety."

"But not for mine?" he teased.

Gabby sat up and folded one leg in as she turned to face him. "Of course, for yours too, but he has to play by the rules. You can do whatever you want."

"I can hardly do *whatever* I want, or we wouldn't be sitting on this couch right now." Dean winked. "I was giving you a hard time. Did you know that James was a Navy Seal?"

"I didn't. That's impressive. But how did you find out?"

He shrugged. "I like to know who I'm dealing with."

Gabby rushed headlong into a conversation she could put off no longer. "Where would we be?"

Dean let his eyes wander over her face. "What do you mean?"

"If you could do whatever you want. Where would we be?" A smokey smile touched his lips and she moved to straddle his lap. "Somewhere around here?"

"I'm not going to try to talk you out of this, if it's what you're hoping for," he warned.

"Good." Gabby watched him steadily.

Dean placed his hands on either side of her neck, and his thumbs hooked behind her jaw as he brought their mouths together. One mind-bending kiss later, he asked, "Are you sure?"

"I thought you weren't going to try to talk me out of this." Gabby rocked against his growing erection as she explored the tanned skin at the edge of his beard with her lips. Tugging the hem of his shirt free she slipped her hands underneath.

"I probably should," he groaned.

She sat up and let his shirt fall back into place. "I've never felt this...this whatever it is between us."

"Wait. You're not a virgin, are you?" Dean sat up straighter and slid her back so that she wasn't nestled against his crotch.

A slow smile tugged at the corner of her mouth. "Do virgins scare you, Mr. McCormick?"

"It's not on my list to be someone's first, but I'd be up to the task," Dean replied as an impish grin played across his lips.

"Well, I'm not one." She kissed him softly. "There's something different about you." Sitting up she stripped her shirt off and tossed it on the couch beside them.

"Christ, woman, look at you." He moved in to kiss her throat and placed her arms around his neck. "Hold on to me."

Gabby wrapped herself around him as he stood and strode through the house into the master bedroom. Dean kicked the door shut behind them and laid her on the duvet, then stepped back and unbuttoned his denim shirt as his eyes roamed over her half-naked body.

"I never thought you'd take your time," Gabby said as she reached behind her to unhook her bra.

He watched silently as she tossed the white lace and satin creation aside. When he didn't move, Gabby sat up and laid an arm across her chest. "If it's me. I mean—I—" She grabbed a quilt that lay at the end of the bed and pulled it over her. "I'm sorry. I'm sure you're used to much prettier girls."

Dean tugged the covering away and placed his hands on either side of her as he leaned in and kissed her tenderly. Gradually she relaxed back onto the feather mattress. "You are beyond gorgeous. I'm just not sure this is the best thing for you."

"I'll be sorry for the rest of my life if we don't do this." She wrapped her fingers in his hair and pulled his mouth closer.

Dean kissed Gabby with an urgency that made her moan. He wrapped one arm around her back, moving her farther onto the bed as he joined her. "Talk to me," he whispered.

Gabby blushed and shook her head.

Running his fingers over her shoulder, he laid a trail of kisses across her collarbones and down the center of her chest. The calloused skin of his palm against her stomach set Gabby on fire. He nipped the underside of her breast, and she arched closer to his mouth. "I like your rough hands," she breathed.

As he moved to her other breast, Dean explored her body before he let his hand wander down the outside of her jeans. Gabby parted her legs, and, at her silent invitation, he slid his palm up the inside of her thigh, stopping just below the apex as he kissed her neck.

"Ah!" Gabby exhaled as she opened her eyes. "You are such a tease."

"I am completely serious, *ma chérie*." He pulled the button on her jeans and eased the zipper down. "Tell me what you want," Dean murmured as he slipped his fingers inside her panties.

"I want you to get the hell off my daughter!" Harold Chambers boomed.

Gabby and Dean jumped and whipped their heads around. There in the doorway stood a furious Reverend Chambers.

"Daddy—" Gabby attempted to cover herself.

"No!" Harold turned his back but didn't leave. "Gabriella, put your clothes on!"

"This was my idea, not his," she protested as she

slid from the bed, grabbed her bra from the floor, and searched for her shirt—before suddenly remembering it was in the living room.

"That's what they all think. I won't have it, Gabriella. He is not for you!" Harold stepped through the doorway into the hall. "I want you out here in two minutes!"

"Rev—" Dean began.

"I will hear nothing from you, McCormick. Nothing! I warned you."

"Rev, listen," Dean said as he sat up on the edge of the bed.

"Get out here, Gabriella. Now!" Harold slammed the door, leaving them alone.

Gabby opened the closet and removed one of her mother's shirts from a hanger. "I'm sorry. I'll talk to him."

"There is no need to be sorry." Dean pulled her into his arms and slowly tasted her lips. "You'll see me tonight?"

"He's going to kill us."

"He won't," Dean assured her as he tucked a lock of hair behind her ear. "You're a twenty-eight-year-old woman, not his little girl. He just needs a moment to see that."

Gabby let her eyes wander over his face. "Okay. Park in the garage. I'll leave the door open."

The corner of his mouth turned up to release his sinful smile. "I'll be there around dark."

Gabby escaped to the master bath while Dean slipped quietly out of the house through the back door. She ran a brush through her tangled locks and noted the red splotches the biker's beard had left on her neck and cheeks. He was not what she'd imagined; she had thought sex with Dean would be animalistic, but he had been gentle. A flash of heat burned through her. She would have her night with him no matter what her father said.

Entering the main living space, Gabby expected the worst, but instead she found her father sitting at the kitchen island, his shoulders slumped, head bowed. "Daddy…" she began.

He turned and opened his arms. Gabby stepped in, and he gathered her close. "I'm sorry, sweetheart. I brought this element into our lives, and I shouldn't have."

"I'm okay. It really was my idea. Dean tried to stop me several times. Please don't be mad at him. I'm sorry I broke my promise to you."

Harold sat back. "My little girl is grown up. I shouldn't have asked you to promise such a silly thing. It's just that I've lived the life McCormick lives, and it's a hard one. I don't want that life for you. You deserve more."

Gabby listened quietly as he continued. "Dean is a good guy—a womanizer, but he has a heart of gold. If I thought he could be loyal to you, that he would leave behind the life and make a new start, I…" He let out a heavy sigh.

"I know, Daddy."

The reverend nodded in defeat. "I'm sorry I lost my temper."

"Thank you for being the best dad." Gabby hugged her father tightly. She knew everything he'd said was true, and this insane relationship with Dean should stop. But Gabby had always taken the safe path and made the appropriate choices. This time, she was going to do what she wanted.

CHAPTER TWENTY-SIX

From The Mouths Of Babes

Kinsley walked the breadth of the local general store looking down each aisle until she found Lincoln pushing a cart through the healthcare section with a package she had never expected to see. When she reached him, he gave her a swift kiss in greeting before she turned her attention to the third member of their group.

"Who's this little fella?" Kinsley smiled at the babbling toddler. When the child held his arms out, she lifted him from the buggy. "You don't have much of an outfit on, do you sweet boy?"

Lincoln smiled at them. "I was out conductin' interviews when this unexpected passenger cropped up. I have a social worker comin' to the office, but as you can see, he needs some essentials. I hoped you could help me."

Kinsley shot Lincoln a quizzical look. "That must have been some interview."

"It's a long story." Lincoln smiled at a worker arranging cans on a shelf nearby and lowered his voice. "We can discuss the particulars at home later."

Kinsley glanced at the store employee, who had been listening to their conversation, and gave the lady a friendly nod as they passed. The child put his head on her shoulder and began sucking his thumb. "What's this little one's name?"

"His name is Levi," Lincoln replied.

"Do you need somewhere to stay, Levi? I know just the place. My friend Frank will adore you." She kissed the child's forehead and pulled her phone from her back pocket. "He and Darren just finished their foster-parent classes. It's perfect timing." Kinsley put the phone to her ear and smiled at her fiancé as the child clung to her.

The sheriff shook his head in wonder. There wasn't anything Kinsley couldn't fix.

As she conveyed the information to Frank, a tremendous squeal came over the line. She ended the call and hugged the boy. "Frank is so excited."

"Yeah, everyone in the store heard," Lincoln teased.

He dutifully pushed their cart as Kinsley filled it with diapers, baby food, and other supplies. She asked the toddler what he liked to eat. Levi watched her with interest, though he had nothing to say.

"Hey, Gabby was at the house earlier and told me some friend of her dad's is in town. I guess he's a biker. She was reluctant to give me much info. Do you know what that's about?" Kinsley asked.

"I don't know exactly," Lincoln said. The fact that the woman who shared the minutiae of her life with Kinsley at every opportunity was now keeping her out of the loop only confirmed that something sinister was afoot with Chambers and McCormick. "But good luck to 'em hidin' whatever it is."

Kinsley stopped, put her arm around Lincoln's waist, and gave him a quick squeeze. "They don't stand a chance with you around."

She picked up a box of animal-shaped crackers and

struggled to open it with one hand while she held the child. Lincoln came to the rescue, and offered a cracker to Levi, which he wolfed down enthusiastically.

As Kinsley continued to shop and Lincoln followed, he realized how out of sync he felt with everything that was happening in Harlow. No matter how hard he chased, he just couldn't keep up. He took a deep, cleansing breath as they went around the end of an aisle—and nearly flattened Trenton Crawley.

"Imagine running into you shopping in the middle of the day, Linc," Trenton sneered. "Earning that county dime while spending time with your family?"

From the corner of his eye, Lincoln saw Kinsley move the child to her hip and step forward. "He's working, and I'm helping," she stated. "Likable people have helpers, though I'm sure it's nothing you've ever experienced." She sashayed past him and into the next aisle.

The sheriff couldn't contain his grin as he watched the color rise in Crawley's face before he cut a path around the speechless man. He caught up to Kinsley, put his arm around her shoulders, and kissed the crown of her head. "I wish I had your smooth way of puttin' people in their place. Thank you."

"You're welcome." She looked up at him, then peeked back to see if they were being followed before whispering, "That guy makes me so mad. I want to punch him into next week."

Lincoln chuckled. "Me too, darlin'. Me too."

CHAPTER TWENTY-SEVEN

Not So Silent Night

From his spot on their porch, Lincoln rocked slowly as he watched the traffic pass by on Main Street. Planters filled with red geraniums lined the edges of the veranda and their peppery scent clung to the still evening air.

Kinsley was out delivering a casserole she'd made for Frank and Darren, claiming her purpose was to relieve the stress of having a new toddler to care for, but Lincoln knew it was an excuse for her to play with Levi. Her reaction to the child had surprised him. There was a time when Lincoln had dreamed of having a large family, and, while the subject of Kinsley and him having children had never come up, his chance to be a father again was still possible.

Thomas came barreling out of the house, letting the screen door slam shut behind him. "See ya, Dad. I'm going out to Phil's place. I'll probably stay the night."

Lincoln watched the blur that was his son as he leaped from the porch deck to the sidewalk. "Be safe!" he called out.

"Always!" Thomas shouted back. He got in his well-used pickup and cranked the engine over. The whine that followed made Lincoln flinch. Kinsley was right. They needed to help his son get a new vehicle before the one he had left him stranded. Lincoln waved as Thomas drove away.

The unmistakable growl of a Harley sliced through the peaceful evening. As the motorcycle drew near, it wasn't difficult to identify McCormick as the rider.

Pushing out of his rocker, Lincoln hurried to his pickup and waited until Dean was a few blocks away before he pulled out of his driveway and followed. As soon as the biker took a left on Seventh Street, the sheriff had no doubt about Dean's destination.

Lincoln drove one block further, turned onto Eighth, then came up Adams Avenue and pulled in next to a curb half a block from Gabby Chambers' house. He killed the engine and watched as McCormick closed an attached garage door where he'd parked his bike.

The lights coming on inside outlined the occupants' progress through the dwelling. When the couple reached the living room, a set of sheer white curtains covering a picture window did little to hide their passionate embrace. Lincoln shook his head as he looked away. It was difficult to believe that Reverend Chambers would bless the union of his only daughter to a motorcycle club president.

He started his pickup and drove away, giving the couple their privacy. He hoped Gabby knew what she was getting herself into.

Lincoln prowled the nearly empty streets as a sinking sun left touches of gold along the edges of feathery clouds that floated aimlessly in a late-summer sky.

A baseball game was in progress, and Lincoln parked near the entrance of the gravel lot that surrounded Harlow's sports complex to watch. He breathed in the toasty smell of popcorn that filled the air as a sharp crack reverberated off surrounding buildings when the batter made a hit—the onlookers cheered. Scanning the grounds, the sheriff watched half a dozen kids sporting cherry-red smiles as they sat in the grass near a shaved-ice stand. He'd made his home in Harlow, and this was where he was going to stay.

Retrieving his phone, he scrolled through his contacts, and pressed the call button when he found the name he sought. Transferring to hands-free, he dropped his pickup into gear.

"To what do I owe a call from the best sheriff in seven counties?" Frank's teasing tone came through the pickup's speakers.

Lincoln chuckled. "I'm on board. Do whatever ya need to do to win this damned election."

"You won't be sorry," Frank enthused. "I'll make you even more famous than you are already!"

"I just want to be sheriff. You can keep the famous." Lincoln couldn't help but smile at his friend's excitement. "Thank ya, Frank."

The men said their goodbyes as the sheriff turned off the blacktop and took a dirt road deeper into his county. It was time to restore Harlow to its former glory, but to do that he would have to be its sheriff.

CHAPTER TWENTY-EIGHT

On The Block

Pulling off the two-lane road, Lincoln parked on a gravel shoulder and sipped his coffee as he watched a sky-blue Audi in his rear-view mirror. The car slowed, then stopped. Despite the sheriff's choice of some of the roughest back roads he could find, he could not shake the man while out in the county on his early morning rounds. It was time to see what Crawley wanted.

Lincoln exited his pickup and signaled for the driver to pull in behind him. Trenton parked and slithered out of his car.

"Just what is it you want?" Lincoln asked as he approached his stalker.

"I'm simply taking a drive in the county. Is that against the law?" Trenton returned with a challenging glint in his eye.

"Interferin' with police business is against the law. You, sir, are ridin' a thin line, and you're about outta road."

"Why, James, you look positively livid. Go ahead—hit me. An assault charge would look pretty on your record and set my win."

Lincoln studied his adversary as he considered how satisfying it would be to wipe the pie-eating grin off the man's face. Sadly, losing the election for one moment of satisfaction was not a smart trade off.

The sheriff's phone rang. He retrieved it from his shirt pocket, glancing at the caller ID before he took the call and headed back to his pickup, giving an open-handed wave to Jack Levine, who gawked at the two candidates as he drove past.

"Hey, Charlene. Great timin'," Lincoln said as he hopped into his vehicle and struggled to let go of his irritation.

"You sound stressed, Linc. What's going on?" she asked.

"That idiot Crawley is followin' me all over the county. I was real tempted to clean his clock just before ya called."

Charlene cackled. "While I would love that, your campaign may not survive another scandal. Have you seen the paper today?"

"Shit," Lincoln spat, and put his phone on hands-free as he took off. "No, I haven't."

"Crawley is calling for an investigation against you for sexual harassment."

Lincoln tried to process what he'd just heard. "Who's been sexually harassed?"

"Sheila Clark."

"I've never been alone with that woman for a minute! His bull won't get too far."

"No, it won't," Charlene concurred. "But that's not why I called. There is some kind of disturbance at the sale barn. Butch needs you."

"I'm five minutes out." Lincoln pressed on the accelerator leaving Trenton behind.

"Don't worry about Crawley. His chickens will come home to roost soon enough, Linc."

"I know you're right—" Lincoln's words trailed off as he pulled into the sale barn lot. There, amid the dust and trailers, were dozens of men in a full-on brawl. "Damn! Send Dixon to the sale barn. We're gonna need help." He disconnected the call and jumped from his vehicle to rush into the fray.

Lincoln eyed the restrained men who were sitting with their backs against Butch's SUV: a mixture of bikers and men from the settlement. "Am I glad to see you," his undersheriff wheezed. "I'm out of restraints."

A crowd had gathered around one large man. McCormick was knocking back all challengers like a god swatting away gnats. It was too bad he didn't put some of that power to good use; he'd make one hell of a deputy.

Lincoln approached the outer ring of onlookers and forced his way past. "McCormick!" he boomed, bringing everyone to a standstill. "Knock it off!" He caught a grin peeking at the corner of Dean's bloodied mouth. "I mean it! These folks aren't any match for ya." He pushed through to the center of the gathering and approached the bleeding biker.

"No, they certainly aren't," Dean replied, sizing up the men who were circling him. "I didn't start this, but I can't imagine you'll believe me."

"I don't play favorites." Lincoln waved for McCormick to follow. "Come on. We'll sort this out at the station."

Dean wrapped his hands around the edges of his leather vest and shook it, sending a cloud of dust into the air. "I came here to check out a genuine cattle auction with the Rev. Next thing I know, all hell broke loose."

Lincoln's eyes widened when Harold Chambers

stepped around the biker with a look that was more devilish than godly. At that moment, he realized that Reverend Harold Chambers was a stranger to him.

***

Gabby peeked around the end of a cattle trailer where she and Amos had been hiding while she pressed him for more information about the group that was staying at the settlement. "Shoot! The sheriff is here now. You have to go, and I need to make myself scarce. If Lincoln sees me, he'll be full of questions I don't want to answer."

"Give us a hug, Sis." Amos pulled her tightly to his chest.

"Promise me you'll be careful and keep your head down, Amos," his sister pleaded. "We're working on a way to get those guys out of there."

"Yah, I'll be gud." He grinned as he set her away from him.

"I love you." Gabby pressed her lips together to keep her emotions in check.

Amos brushed back a stray lock of her hair. "An' I you."

Gabby snuck to her car, which was parked behind the sale barn, and waited. Once she saw Lincoln leave, she drove back to her office thinking about the new information her brother had provided about the routine of the gang that lived inside the compound.

Amos had told her that a truck came in from Texas once a month but never on any set day or time. It was filled with people he assumed were fleeing Mexico, and boxes with unknown contents. He believed the settlement was being used as a distribution hub because, in the days following a shipment, the new arrivals and those boxes were taken away by friends of the gang.

Amos confirmed that a dozen of these 'friends' had taken up permanent residence after Jacob was murdered. The only activities the undesirables participated in regularly were trips to the bar in Harlow, harassing people at the settlement, and sleeping until noon. It wasn't a ton of information, but it was something.

Gabby smiled as she thought about the dust-up at the sale barn. It had been Dean's idea to create a distraction so that she could speak with Amos. It had worked well—almost too well.

Bypassing the main courthouse entrance, she slipped in a side door and went straight to her office wondering if she would get a call to bail her dad and Dean out of jail. Her mother would give them all a dressing down when she learned of their antics, of that Gabby was sure. If Dean and her father weren't incarcerated, dealing with a mad Marilyn Chambers might make them wish they were.

CHAPTER TWENTY-NINE

What Lies Beneath

Lincoln stepped through his front door and stopped in the foyer to listen as Kinsley explained a line of code to his son that sounded a lot like a foreign language. Thomas joined in, and they discussed a way to write the line that would apparently make the operation more efficient. How he had been so lucky to have these two people in his life Lincoln would never know, but he sure was glad.

"Honey, I'm home," he called out doing his best imitation of Ricky Ricardo—which was so awful it sent his family into fits of giggles. Kinsley stood to greet him, and Lincoln swept her into a dance around the table. Her wide smile said he was ridiculous, but she loved it.

"You two are too much. I'm gonna shower before dinner." Thomas shut his laptop and stuck it under his arm. "Back in a flash."

"Don't leave your wet towel on the floor, please," Kinsley called out as he left the room.

Lincoln nuzzled her neck as a torch song played softly through the speakers on her workstation and they swayed to the music.

"My, my, Sheriff. What did I do to deserve this?" she asked.

He raised his head and watched her for a minute. "Ya think I can win this sheriff's race?"

"I'm positive." Kinsley brushed the backs of her fingers over his jaw. "People here see right through Crawley." A grin lifted the corners of her mouth. "I might have let it slip to May Lester that he said her secret chicken casserole was dry but it's one of your favorite dishes."

Lincoln feigned shock. "Kinsley! I can't believe you'd spread gossip."

"It isn't gossip, it's the truth, and it's not something devastating. Well, at least not to you." Her slate-gray eyes twinkled. "Besides, Crawley said it in front of everyone at the bowling alley. Thankfully, he's never mastered the art of keeping his mouth shut."

"That'll put a dent in his popularity. May is on the board for the fair."

Kinsley gave an exaggerated wink. "Kiss me and go get ready. Frank and Darren will be here in an hour. We'll get this campaign wrapped up, then we can move on to getting married."

"Mmm, I can't wait." Lincoln bent and softly explored her lips. "You could shower with me."

"Now, Sheriff." Kinsley leaned back and gave him a playfully stern look. "You know I'd love nothing more, but dinner isn't going to cook itself." She slipped out of his embrace and swatted his butt with a backward swing of her arm as she headed for the kitchen.

"Hey!" Lincoln exclaimed. "I'm not your sex toy, Ma'am." Her laughter made him chuckle as he headed for their bedroom to gather his clothes.

Thomas exited their one shared bathroom, and steam

rolled into the hallway. "You better not have used all the hot water," Lincoln warned. Thomas snorted as he made a beeline for his room.

Lincoln's thoughts bounced between the race for sheriff, Miller's murder, and the band of bikers connected to Harold Chambers. Mentally turning each piece over in his mind as he stood in the shower, he looked at the individual parts from every angle as he tried to see how they all fit together.

Dean McCormick was well-spoken, which came as no surprise after Charlene had uncovered the man's Harvard education when she'd investigated his attorney status. When Lincoln and Butch had brought everyone into the station after the skirmish at the sale barn, McCormick had explained that two local men had taken offense to bikers attending an auction. When Reverend Chambers stepped in to calm the men down, it had only inflamed the situation.

In the sheriff's opinion, that seemed like a flimsy excuse to start a fight, but he had no proof it wasn't true because the men who had started it were from The Order and had refused to say anything.

Lincoln had charged them all with disorderly conduct and turned them loose; they'd pay a fine when they showed up for court, and he would have a list of names on file should anything happen in the future.

Then there was Jacob Miller, a man from a religious sect murdered in a scene staged to look like a gang-style hit. As their investigation continued, the number of people who had despised Miller for various reasons increased—if something evil or underhanded had been called for, it was a good bet that Jacob was the man on the job. But after extensive interviews and alibi checking, they had no one who could be held up as a solid suspect in Miller's murder. Most days Lincoln felt like they'd taken one step forward and ten steps back.

He finished his shower, dried off, dressed, and joined Kinsley in the kitchen. "What can I do?" he asked as he wrapped his arms around her and kissed her temple.

Kinsley relaxed back into his solid warmth. "That's a good start." She broke free and turned to face him. "Hey, Thomas filled me in on the guy Gabby's been seeing. She insisted this person was a friend of her father's, but he saw them making out in Gabby's car after they had lunch at Mario's."

Lincoln struggled to hide his surprise. "Interestin' that Thomas knows about Dean McCormick."

"You know, too?" Kinsley placed a fist against her hip. "How am I the only one who doesn't know my bestie has a new boyfriend?"

"If I were guessin', I'd say she didn't tell you so that ya wouldn't tell me."

"Why would this guy be a secret?" She moved to the island to arrange vegetables on a relish tray.

"I saw Harold, Gabby, and McCormick circling the settlement the other day. I have a feelin' him bein' here has somethin' to do with Jacob Miller's murder."

Kinsley stopped what she was doing and looked back at Lincoln. "You think Gabby's new boyfriend is the murderer?"

"It crossed my mind, but McCormick was in California at the time. He swears he never set foot in

Harlow or Stevens County until a couple of weeks ago, and I have no reason to doubt that."

"I don't get it. How *is* he connected, then?"

Lincoln shook his head. "I can't quite put my finger on the why of it. Gabby did say she was promised to Miller. Maybe he found her and was gonna force the issue. With him dead, problem solved."

"You can't think Gabby has anything to do with this murder!" Kinsley protested. "You didn't see how shocked she was that day in your office when she saw the sketch of Miller. There's no way she did anything to him."

"I know she's your best friend, but I can't dismiss the fact that she's connected to the deceased."

Kinsley sighed. "I understand her connection, but I'll never believe Gabby is a murderer." She moved around the kitchen while processing this new information. "You don't think she's in danger with this biker, do you?"

"No. Harold Chambers used to run with this club, and he knows McCormick. They've been staying out at his place in the country."

"What the…?" Kinsley turned to face him. "Reverend Chambers was a *biker?* And there's a club staying in his country house?"

"Yep." Lincoln grinned. "Chambers' history was news to me, too."

Waving for Lincoln to follow her to the dining room, Kinsley opened a drawer in the buffet and tossed a folded white tablecloth onto the table. Closing her laptops, she gathered her paraphernalia and stored it neatly inside a cupboard. "Help me, please?"

Lincoln grabbed a corner of the cloth and pulled it to

the other end of the table while Kinsley held her end in place. "I never would have imagined Harold and Marilyn were biker types," she said. "He's such a jolly guy, and Marilyn is a textbook preacher's wife."

"I don't know that Marilyn was part of it, but Harold fessed up. Said he and McCormick's uncle were tight back in the day."

"This town is chock full of secrets. What are you going to do about this club?" Kinsley retrieved a stack of plates, topped by silverware, from the sideboard and moved them to the table.

"Nothin', unless they do something illegal. They haven't broken any laws that I can prove."

"And you know for a fact Gabby is dating this Dean guy?"

Lincoln nodded as he gathered the silverware Kinsley had laid out and carefully arranged it next to the plates she was placing around the table. "I followed him to her house the night you went to Frank's to see Levi. He parked his bike in her garage and went in."

"Jeez, I don't have a clue what's going on around here."

"Gabby not tellin' ya points to their so-called innocent visit not bein' snow white."

"We should invite Gabby and her beau over for dinner," Kinsley suggested. "He might let his guard down in a relaxed setting, and you could get something out of him."

"Maybe you shoulda gone into police work instead of computer programmin'." Lincoln winked. "I would love it if you could get them here, but McCormick said he'd be leaving soon. Time may not be on our side."

Kinsley chewed her bottom lip thoughtfully. "I'll call Gabby and invite them for dinner tonight."

"You're somethin' else, Kinsley Rhodes." Lincoln took her hand and spun her around into his arms. "Thank you."

"Don't thank me yet. I'll get them here, but you'll have to use your mad detective skills after that."

***

It took every persuasive trick she had—and more than a bit of guilt—to talk Gabby into bringing her new pal to dinner. Her reluctance to introduce Dean to them had Kinsley constructing all manner of behind-the-scenes evil. She and Gabby talked about everything, so why not Dean McCormick? She was determined to find out the truth where her best friend was concerned, even if she had to forgo tact and ask outright.

Her ponderings were interrupted by the doorbell. Thomas went to let in their first guests as Kinsley finished filling an ice bucket. She hurried to the living room and placed the silver vessel on a bar next to crystal decanters filled with various types of alcohol before turning to greet their friends.

"Frank, Darren, welcome. How's Levi?" She smiled as the men approached and gave her a quick squeeze in turn.

"He's a joy," Darren replied.

"And he is wearing us out," Frank added as he wiped fake sweat from his brow, but his toothy smile told Kinsley all she needed to know.

"He's a doll. I'm glad he's with you. I hope you don't mind, but I've invited Gabby and her new boyfriend to join us."

Frank's eyebrows shot up. "Cinderella has been hiding a man from us?"

"Apparently."

Thomas joined in. "You guys wait until you get a load of this dude. He blocks out the sun."

Frank and Darren looked from Thomas to Kinsley with furrowed brows. She shrugged. "I haven't seen him, but reports are that he might be part titan."

Lincoln cruised into the room. "What can I get everyone to drink?"

"I'll have some of that Macallan scotch. Thanks, Linc. I hear we have a new kid in town, and he makes you look tiny," Frank teased.

"McCormick is a big ol' boy." Lincoln confirmed as everyone approached the drinks table.

Darren added his order for bourbon. "When did Gabby and Dusty break up?" he asked Kinsley.

"It had been coming for a while. They were better friends than lovers, and neither one is mad about the split. Still, I'm surprised she's taken up with a stranger so soon afterward. Gabby has always been very conservative when it comes to men."

"You'll get it when you see him," Thomas said.

The doorbell rang, and Kinsley experienced a tingle of anticipation as she went to answer it. Taking a deep breath, she dropped a smile in place and pushed open the screen door. "Come in, you two. Thanks for dropping your other plans to come hang out with us."

As they gathered in the foyer, Gabby's nervousness could have powered a moon rocket, but her calm and collected companion showed none of his cards.

Gabby spoke up. "Kins, this is Dean McCormick. He's a friend of my dad's."

"And yours, it seems," Kinsley teased. "Dean, good to meet you." She held out her hand in greeting.

"Miss Rhodes, a pleasure," Dean returned as he shook her hand.

"Please, call me Kinsley. Let's go on through. Everyone is anxious to meet you."

With a half-cocked smile, he replied, "I can only imagine."

As Kinsley led them into the living room, everyone turned and stared. Lincoln stepped up to break the ice, "Dean, what can I get ya to drink?"

"I'm not much of a drinker, but I'd take some iced tea if you have it, water if you don't."

"Be right back with your tea. I'll leave the introductions to you, Linc," Kinsley said as she headed for the kitchen.

"Damn! Up close, you really are king-sized," Thomas exclaimed. "Now I get why Gabby picked you instead of me." He laughed and held out his hand. "I'm Thomas James. Welcome to Harlow."

Dean looked briefly at Gabby before shaking Thomas's hand. "I wasn't aware Gabriella had other suitors."

Thomas winked at a deeply embarrassed Gabby. "Yeah, but it was just my dream and her nightmare." His comment brought about a flurry of chuckles from the other guests.

Kinsley returned and handed Dean his glass of tea, then moved to the far side of the room to join her fiancé near the bar. Lincoln was surreptitiously watching their newest guests field a plethora of questions. She said quietly, "The steaks are ready when you are. I suspect he won't be an easy nut to crack."

"You're right about that," he replied before slipping out through the kitchen to the backyard to put steaks on the grill.

Kinsley joined the group. Their interrogation tactics would have put the CIA to shame, but Dean was easily navigating the barrage of questions.

Frank looked around the room and asked, "Where is that man of yours, Kins?"

She gestured with her thumb toward the back of the house. "He's the grill master tonight."

"Oh gawd, I'd better help him. Our steaks were charcoal briquettes last time we left him on his own."

As Frank hurried away, Kinsley waded into the conversation. "So, Dean. President of a motorcycle club. What's that like?"

He took a sip of his tea then cleared his throat. "A bunch of boring guys and gals who love to ride."

"I doubt boring is a word ever used to describe you," Darren commented. "I'm interested in your lifestyle, if you'd be willing to share more about it."

Dean placed his glass on one of the coasters on the coffee table. "There are only a handful of old-timers left," he began. "The new club consists mostly of professional men and women who generously donate their time to keep it alive."

Darren nodded thoughtfully. "That isn't what I expected."

"I know what people think of us, and twenty years ago they wouldn't have been wrong. But times change.

Our organization has a diverse portfolio, thanks to a member who is an investment broker. We do quite a bit of charitable work in our community. When I became president, the club was already moving in a different direction. I simply made sure that continued."

"What about you? What do you do for outside income?" Kinsley asked.

"I manage the businesses the club owns. We have quite a few." He paused, met her gaze, and grinned. "All legitimate, I assure you."

"Gosh, you guys act like you've never met anyone before," Gabby protested. "Dean has a law degree from Harvard. That should satisfy your questions."

Thomas, who had been listening intently, spoke up. "Harvard? Wow! I'm never gonna win Gabby after that."

Dean laughed. "I doubt you have a shortage of ladies. You could leave me this one." He took Gabby's hand.

Kinsley could take the suspense no longer. She stood abruptly and announced. "Gabs, I need help in the kitchen. Can I get anyone anything?" They all assured her they were fine.

Once they were out of earshot in the kitchen, Gabby jumped right in. "I know what you're going to say, that I should be careful, and I don't know him. But Kins, he is…" she paused "…he is irresistible. I know it sounds ridiculous, but I had to have him. I'm well aware that it's going to hurt when he leaves, but I couldn't live the rest of my life with 'what if'."

The women locked eyes as she continued. "Can't you just be happy for me and let it be? He's not a bad guy, and he'll be gone soon."

"Okay." Kinsley retrieved an embossed metal serving tray and laid it on the counter. "So, what's that beast like in bed?"

Gabby fought it, but her grin flourished. "Not like I imagined, but mind-blowing."

Kinsley watched her friend's eyes shine knowing that when Dean left town, there would be a river of tears to dry. "I'm happy for you, Gabs."

"I'm so glad you know. I've hated keeping this a secret." Gabby grabbed her in a hug.

"So why did you?" Kinsley stepped back, donned oven mitts, and took foil-wrapped baked potatoes out of the oven. When no answer came, she looked over her shoulder and watched as Gabby chewed her bottom lip.

Kinsley turned to face her. "You know you can tell me anything."

"I knew you'd be worried about me, and I thought it would be over before you found out. You have a lot on your plate with the election, your job, your upcoming wedding..." Gabby suddenly took a keen interest in the no-wax flooring at her feet. "He's a temp. He'll be gone in a few days, and our lives will return to normal."

"Gabs, we both know you're not a temp type of girl. But I'm here for you, no matter what." Kinsley turned back to her task. Gabby was lying to her, and she had no intention of letting that stand; she was also concerned that Dean could be involved in nefarious activities that might put her friend in a precarious situation.

An email to her private investigator was in order. Gabby could try to hide the truth all she wanted, but Kinsley intended to find out what was what.

CHAPTER THIRTY

One Thing Leads To Another

Lincoln relaxed onto their soft mattress and pulled Kinsley close to his side, slipping his free hand under his head as he reflected on the conversations during dinner. Frank was confident they could win the sheriff's race by a landslide; Gabby was utterly in love with McCormick, and Kinsley was worried. The mystery of why the biker was in town had not been answered, and if anything, there were now even more questions.

"Tell me what you're thinking." Kinsley slowly traced an outline around the tail of the snake tattoo that decorated his stomach.

"'Bout a hundred things."

"Me too. Mr. McCormick was unexpected in every way. He's very intelligent."

"Yeah. He knows right where the line of the law lies, and, as far as I know, he's stayed on the legal side of it."

"Maybe he is just here visiting Reverend Chambers, like he said."

"I wish with everything in me that was the truth," Lincoln replied. "But I know in my gut it isn't."

Kinsley slid the sheet down as she raised up on her elbow and let her hand wander over the flat expanse of his lower abdomen. "Why don't we talk about something else?" She bit her bottom lip and watched his face as her hand explored.

"That's a conversation I'd love to have," Lincoln smiled and tugged at the hem of her nightgown. "Let's get rid of this and have an in-depth discussion."

"Sheriff, you have the best ideas." Kinsley grinned as she wiggled out of her gown and tossed it on the floor. "Let's see if I can make you forget your troubles for a while."

Lincoln rose over her and stroked her cheek with his thumb. "Darlin', you already have."

She slid her hand over his burgeoning need. "It seems like you have something you want to share with me."

Leaning in for a kiss, he whispered, "I confess. I do."

Kinsley let go a blissful sigh before their lips met, and she melted into his embrace.

***

Startled awake by the rumble of a semi-truck barreling down Main Street, Kinsley blinked a few times before focusing on the ceiling. As she listened to Lincoln's deep, even breathing, her thoughts turned to Gabby and Dean. Being around them was like watching her best friend step in front of an oncoming train and being powerless to save her. There was no doubt in Kinsley's mind that Gabby would be devastated when the biker left, but she would just have to be there to pick up the pieces when that day came.

Kinsley gave up on sleep, slipped out of bed, and put on her robe before heading to the kitchen. Retrieving a glass from the cabinet she grabbed a carton of orange juice from the fridge and poured herself a drink. Her initial idea of having Dean investigated returned: It would put her mind at ease to know more about the man who had turned her best friend's head.

She padded softly into the dining room and left her glass of orange juice on the table. The light from the kitchen was enough for her to retrieve her laptops from the cupboard and reassemble her workspace. Her screens flickered to life, pushing back the darkness with their soft blue glow. She typed an email to her attorney, Bill Schneider, asking that he tap their private investigator, Sean Young. Maybe finding out more about Dean McCormick could also benefit Lincoln.

Next on her list was Lincoln's campaign website. Frank had devised a genius idea of offering free rides to the polling stations on election day for those who couldn't drive themselves. Kinsley, Thomas, and several of Thomas's friends would arrange for pick up and drop off. She quickly added a page where people could enter their name, address, and choose from a list of pickup times.

After publishing the new site, she surfed the internet until she found Trenton Crawley's blog. The latest entry burned her to the ground. It was a picture of Lincoln in what looked like an altercation at the sale barn; the caption read: *Do you want a criminal for a sheriff?*

Kinsley scanned the photograph and picked out Dean and Gabby's father. The rest of the people were either members of the settlement or friends of McCormick. Trenton must have been stalking Lincoln's every move to get the shot.

She returned to her email, typed another missive

to her lawyer, then reread it before hitting send. It was past time for Crawley to get a taste of his own medicine. Lincoln deserved to be sheriff, and she would make sure that happened.

Smiling, Kinsley closed her laptops and went back to bed. As she cuddled in next to her fiancé, a feeling of confidence that the plans she'd put into motion would bear sweet fruit solidified—and the sooner that happened, the better.

CHAPTER THIRTY-ONE

Hidden In Plain Sight

With only the moon for company, Lincoln cruised Smuggler's Run, a name given to a stretch of lonesome blacktop that ran past Weatherby's land and continued into the Oklahoma panhandle. Henry used to tell stories about this infamous road and the part it had played when prohibition was in full swing. It had been a bootleggers' paradise; supposedly, the dastardly duo of Bonnie and Clyde had traveled this way and lived in Harlow for a time. Bonnie Parker was said to have operated a café, while Clyde Darrow worked for a local farmer. Whether or not the tales were true, the notorious name had stuck and, unfortunately, many unlawful activities with it.

Since the day they had discovered Jacob Miller's body, Lincoln had spent time parked somewhere along this road, but he had not seen a hint of criminal activity, with the exception of the Ray brothers hunting. And while Scott Weatherby had reported that all had been well of late, the atmosphere felt unstable.

When sunrise broke, Lincoln took Second Street toward town for a change of scenery instead of his usual highway route.

A beat-up blue, late-model Ford pickup parked alongside the road had him easing his vehicle onto the shoulder behind it. Lincoln radioed his position and a description of the pickup, including the fact that it wasn't tagged. Then he reached over to the backseat and retrieved his gun belt.

He left his truck cautiously and buckled his belt in place as he approached the Ford. Glancing into the pickup bed, he spotted a couple of crushed beer cans near the cab but nothing else. The back window was tinted nearly black, and his inability to see inside put Lincoln on edge.

He unsnapped the thumb break that secured his sidearm in its holster and approached the driver's door. Seeing no one inside, he tried the handle—only to find the door locked. It seemed out of sync that someone would secure this vehicle because the inside appeared as wrecked as the exterior. Even the radio had been removed from the dash, and wires were hanging limply through an empty hole. The silver-colored seat cover sported a multitude of dark stains that made the thought of sitting on it wholly undesirable.

Lincoln retrieved his phone, called dispatch, and asked them to send out a wrecker. As he continued around the front of the pickup, he laid his palm against the hood; surprisingly, it was warm.

An eerie feeling of being watched took hold as an ill-tempered wind tore across the prairie, stirring up a dust devil. The sheriff scanned the surrounding farmland. A person on foot would have nowhere to hide in the flat, treeless landscape, but there wasn't a soul about. "You're being paranoid," he admonished himself.

As Lincoln returned to his vehicle, he double-checked the surrounding area, unable to squash the feeling that he was being led down a rabbit hole at every turn. Seeing no one, he started his pickup and followed the two-lane blacktop into Harlow.

After a quick stop at the donut shop for pastries, he pulled into his spot at headquarters, slid the gearshift into park, and gazed at a sign affixed to a cinderblock wall in front of him.

Reserved Parking
Sheriff Lincoln James
Don't even think about parking here

It had been a gag gift from Charlene and Butch a few years back, and they had left it in place. Lincoln smiled as he retrieved the donut box from the passenger seat and headed inside. He greeted Charlene as he placed the pastries on her desk and opened the lid to make his selection.

"What are you so happy about this morning?" she asked.

Surprised by the question, Lincoln met her gaze. "Can't a guy be happy?"

Charlene chuckled as she leaned over and examined what was inside the box. "You haven't been that cheerful lately, Linc. Not that I don't understand why, but it's good to see your grin again. I've missed it."

His smile widened. "Can I get ya some coffee?"

"Holy crap! What's going on? Are you firing me or somethin'?" Charlene stared at him.

Lincoln laughed. "Can't I be nice without the world fallin' apart?"

"Sure, you can, but ease me into it, won't ya? It's too early for all this frivolity and niceness."

"I'll try to remember that." He crossed the open space to the kitchenette. "So, coffee, or no?"

"Yes, please," Charlene replied. "We have Ivan Parker coming in shortly for his interview. Do you need me to do anything?"

"Nope. I can't imagine it's gonna yield any information about Miller that we don't already know, but the manager at the hardware store told me Parker hired Jacob for odd jobs, so I thought I'd take a shot."

No sooner had Lincoln finished his sentence than the outside door opened, and Mr. Parker ambled in. He approached the bulletproof-glass divider and bent nearly in half to put his mouth to the speak-thru. "I'm h-here to see the s-sheriff."

Lincoln crossed to Charlene's desk and into the visitor's line of sight as he handed her a cup of coffee. The dispatcher released the lock on the secure door, and Lincoln pushed it open, waving Parker through. "Hey, Ivan," he said as he joined the new arrival. "Can I get ya some coffee or a donut?"

"N-no thanks," Ivan stuttered. "I d-didn't know Miller that well."

Lincoln smiled disarmingly. "Let's head back to my office and talk."

Wide-eyed, Ivan glanced from Lincoln to Charlene and bowed his head like a naughty schoolboy who'd been caught doing something wrong. Nevertheless, he tagged along behind the sheriff.

"Please, have a seat." Lincoln moved to the other side of his desk and settled in. "I'd like to know anything you can tell me about Jacob Miller. From what I've heard around town, ya hired him pretty regularly."

Ivan parked himself in a club chair facing Lincoln and gazed at the items on the desk. Lincoln sipped his coffee and waited patiently, but finally he had to ask, "What did ya hire Jacob to do?"

"N-nothing, really," Ivan said while avoiding eye contact.

Lincoln could see this was going to be a struggle. "Was he a good worker?"

"I d-didn't p-pay him for fa-farmwork." Ivan's focus dropped to his hands, which were clasped and resting in his lap.

"What did ya pay him for?"

The whisper-thin man slowly looked up. "I d-don't want t-ta be in t-trouble."

Lincoln's eyes narrowed. "Why would you be in trouble, Mr. Parker?"

A shiver rattled Ivan's frame. "I h-hired an associate of h-his."

"And what did this associate do?"

The man's shoulders slumped, and he shook his head. "I'm lonely. Jacob h-helped me from t-time to t-time."

"Helped ya how?" Lincoln watched Ivan closely. This was certainly not the conversation he had expected to have.

"A w-woman."

"I don't understand," The sheriff's brow furrowed as he tried to unravel what Ivan was trying to convey.

"H-he brought h-his friend Lily over s-sometimes."

"And what happened when he brought Lily over?"

"S-she cleaned and t-talked t-to me," Ivan confessed.

"And?" Lincoln prodded.

"S-she cooked me suh-supper and ate w-with me," Ivan replied.

Lincoln watched him fidget in his chair. "I don't understand why hirin' a house cleaner would get ya into trouble."

"I p-paid for h-her t-time. S-she s-stayed all evening."

It dawned on Lincoln what Ivan was trying to say. "Was Lily a prostitute?"

"I d-didn't touch h-her, I s-swear. We tah-talked is all. S-she was nice t-ta me."

"Ivan, do you expect me to believe you didn't know she was a prostitute, and all ya did was pay to talk to her?" Lincoln returned.

"I su-supected s-she was a p-prostitute." Parker met Lincoln's gaze. "But I d-didn't do n-nothing but s-spend time with h-her. S-since my w-wife died, I've been s-so lonesome."

Lincoln dropped his eyes and focused on the blotter on his desk as he considered the situation. "I understand, Ivan, but payin' to eat dinner with a woman—even if you don't do anything else—will get ya in hot water. I don't want that for you."

They looked at one another, and Ivan nodded.

"Why don't ya try the monthly dinner down at the Methodist church? It's a safer place to find a lady to chat with," Lincoln suggested.

"I'm n-not a Methodist." Ivan shrugged and focused on his slacks, brushing away imaginary lint.

"Aw, I bet they'll let you in. They gladly take all comers." Lincoln smiled as Ivan's head whipped up.

"Da-do you t-think it'd be okay?"

"I do. Now ya have to promise me you won't pay for company anymore, and we'll put this behind us."

"I p-promise, S-sheriff. I s-swear t-ta God I w-won't d-do it again." Ivan beamed.

Lincoln rounded his desk, and walked Parker to the front office. "Ya might want to keep that swearin' ta God to a minimum when you're at the church." He winked as he pushed the secure door open and held it.

Ivan grabbed Lincoln's free hand and shook it vigorously. "T-thank you, S-sheriff. T-thank you s-so much!"

"You're welcome, Mr. Parker. Thank you for comin' in."

Ivan scurried out the door and into the warm morning beyond.

"What did you do to get him so excited?" Charlene asked sarcastically as she shuffled paperwork.

Lincoln gazed out the front windows and watched a blackbird peck at the gravel lining the parking lot's edge. "I told him where to meet ladies who like to chat," he replied absently. His thoughts were consumed with the information Ivan Parker had shared.

The dispatcher stopped working and looked at her boss. "You did what?"

Lincoln rejoined Charlene at her desk. "Ivan's a good guy, just a little lonely. I told him to give the Methodist dinner a try. Those ladies will talk his leg off." He gave his confused employee a lopsided grin. "Let's get the paperwork together for a search warrant. It seems Jacob Miller might have been a pimp on top of everything else, and I finally have the probable cause I need to get into the settlement."

"What?" Charlene gasped. "There are prostitutes in the religious compound? That doesn't even make sense."

"It's a great place to hide 'em. Who's gonna look there?" Lincoln returned to his office satisfied that the long shot with Ivan Parker had paid off and given them their first big break in the case.

***

Gabby considered how her pale skin contrasted with Dean's deep tan as she lay with her head on his chest and fantasized about a life that would never be.

"That was an unusual dinner party," Dean remarked as he twisted a tendril of her hair around his finger.

"Uh-huh," she replied. Professional investigators would have been less thorough than her friends had been last night. "They care about me. Please don't think badly of them. They're really great people."

He squeezed her to his side. "I know they are. *I* wouldn't want someone as wonderful as you with someone like me."

Gabby moved her head and looked up at him. "You're a terrific guy."

"Rose-colored glasses, *ma chérie*. Rose-colored glasses..." His sly smile prompted her to slide up and kiss him.

"Harlow isn't such a bad place to live, you know." She propped herself up on her elbow and watched him.

"My life is in California. People depend on me." He hesitated while his eyes roamed over her face. "I'm not built for small-town Kansas life."

Gabby colored at his confession. "Oh, I didn't mean. I mean...I..."

"I know what you meant." He pushed her hair over her shoulder and his eyes followed his fingers as they stroked her skin. "You are a brilliant, beautiful woman, Gabriella."

Gabby laid down with her cheek to his chest so he couldn't see the truth in her eyes. "You're one of a kind, Dean McCormick."

"Of that, I am sure," he replied. "I should go. The town will be awake soon, and I'm not exactly inconspicuous."

Gabby sat up and watched as he slipped from her bed to dress. She grabbed a robe from a hook on the bathroom door and followed him to the front of the house. Dean turned, took her in his arms and rested his chin on top of her head for a moment as they soaked in the perfect silence. She turned her face up to kiss him before he left.

When the rumble of his motorcycle had faded, Gabby went to her spare bedroom, which she had converted into an office, and folded herself into her desk chair. As she waited for her laptop to come to life, she considered the twists of fate that had brought Dean McCormick into her life. Jacob Miller's death had felt a little like a macabre blessing when it had thrown them together, and now that there was an expiration date on her and Dean's relationship, Miller once again had her by the throat, but this time from the grave.

"Curse you, Jacob. Curse you and good riddance!" Gabby declared as she turned away from the gathering darkness and focused on her overflowing email inbox.

CHAPTER THIRTY-TWO

What Is Sown

There had been no word on the search warrant Lincoln had applied for based on the information provided by Ivan Parker that suggested Miller had been operating a prostitution ring from inside the compound, but Judge Goodale was on vacation. All the sheriff could do was wait with his fingers crossed and hope that the judge would grant his petition when he returned.

As he sat at the kitchen island, absently chewing a bite of toast, Lincoln wondered how much it would hurt him to go into this election with an unsolved murder on the books; by the way things were going, solving the case anytime soon would take a miracle.

A report on the abandoned pickup he'd found on Second Street had come back with a salvage title. The vehicle had previously belonged to a man who had passed away several years ago and had no connection to Jacob Miller, so that lead went nowhere. Lincoln could have sworn that pickup was somehow connected, and his gut instincts were usually spot on. He hoped he wasn't losing his touch.

They had found hairs that didn't match Miller's on his shirt, but no alarm bells rang when they were entered into the national DNA database. That meant whoever the hairs belonged to had never been jailed for a serious crime, since it was common practice to take DNA from anyone arrested for a felony.

There were also fibers from what looked to be a horse blanket on his clothing, but the type was so common that they were untraceable. The only thing they were certain of was that more than one perpetrator was involved because there was every indication that Miller's body had been carried into that house. The different-size footprints found at the scene suggested at least two people and, after closer inspection, they were leaning toward three. But for now, those responsible were in the wind.

"Something I can help with?" Kinsley reached out and stroked his shoulder.

Lincoln shook his head. "Nope."

"I know you're worried about the election, but don't be. People love you, and they won't let you down."

He smiled and rotated his barstool to face her. "It's just a job. If I lose it, there'll be another."

Kinsley slid off her stool and stepped between his legs. "You and I both know that isn't true. You love being sheriff, and Harlow is lucky to have you."

Lincoln brushed her lips with his. She was right, but he had to leave a way out mentally should the win go to Crawley. "I could be your coffee boy," he joked.

"Mmm." Kinsley waggled her eyebrows. "That would be some steaming hot coffee. I wouldn't get any work done." She picked up their breakfast plates and moved to the sink to clean up. "I can hardly believe the response we've received for the ride round-up. We want to make sure to get every voter to the polls. Primary elections tend to draw a lighter crowd."

When she looked back over her shoulder at Lincoln, her smile faded. "What's wrong?" Kinsley picked up a towel to dry her hands and hurried around the bar to him.

Lincoln cradled his head in his hands. "This town has had two murders in as many years. I struggled so long solvin' Henry's that you were nearly killed. Now there's this Miller mess. Maybe I'm not cut out to be sheriff." He raised his head and watched her closely. "Everything was great when there wasn't much goin' on, but what have I really done?"

"Nothing much went on because you were out there for years keeping the bad guys in line. You can't expect perfection. The world is changing, and there are a lot more baddies. Even so, Harlow is as nice a town as anyone could hope for, and that's down to you and your team." She smoothed her hand over his cheek. "You'll find out who killed Jacob Miller and stop them from doing anything else. You're the best sheriff. Don't you doubt it."

A tiny grin lifted the corner of his mouth. "You're one hell of a cheerleader."

Kinsley gave him a quick peck. "Now get your sexy butt in gear and let's get this day started."

A twinkle returned to his eyes. "Yes, Ma'am."

Lincoln watched her move around the kitchen cleaning counters. As she worked, he listened to her line out their upcoming activities, which included lunch with the Rotary Club a week from Thursday, and dinner with Thomas and his friends at Mario's on Friday. "I've invited the Lamar boys. They love pizza, and I know they'd like to see you." Kinsley looked up from scrubbing the kitchen sink. "What's that look for?"

His smile spread as he pushed back his chair and closed the space between them. "Thanks for bein' you, Kins."

She rolled her eyes and hugged him. "You need to save that charm for the rest of the world. You already have me."

"I hope they serve Mrs. Perry's roast beef at the Rotary lunch."

Kinsley burst into laughter. "You've just had breakfast. How can you think about food?"

"It's one of my special powers. I'll see ya later, gorgeous." As Lincoln turned to go, he called out, "Come on, Maizey girl." The pup scampered behind him, and they headed for the front door.

He crossed their adjoining lawns to his pickup, which was parked in his driveway, and breathed in the muted tones of a predawn town—until the rumble of a Harley in the distance cut through his peace like a razor blade. McCormick: Another mystery he had yet to solve.

Maizey whined at him.

"Can we catch ourselves a killer today, Maiz?" The pup danced around his legs until he opened the pickup door, and she loaded up. "Let's see what we can find in the country, girl. Seems like nothin' but trouble out there."

He slid into the driver's seat, patted the dog, and dropped his truck into gear. "You can help me sniff it out."

***

Kinsley finished cleaning the kitchen before going into the dining room to start her working day. When she opened her email, she was thrilled to see a response from Bill Schneider. There was no dirt on McCormick yet, but the email outlined a plethora of underhanded and downright criminal acts perpetrated by Mr. Crawley during his law-enforcement career in other counties. While he had been too slick to be convicted of doling out 'special favors', letting this information leak into Harlow's community would put a black mark on his campaign.

She knew all too well how Lincoln would feel about her being involved in releasing information about Crawley to the public, but then again, he had told Frank to do whatever he had to do to win. Her fingers hovered above the keyboard as she considered the consequences of her actions. If Lincoln never found out, there would be no problem. Trenton had been feeding falsehoods about Lincoln to the local news for quite some time and had put enough lousy karma out there that he deserved to reap what he had sown.

Kinsley started a reply to her lawyer, asking that he choose only those actions that had made it into newspapers at the time and find a way to leak those stories so that they could find new life in local publications.

CHAPTER THIRTY-THREE

Leader Of The Pack

It had been nearly a week since Kinsley's dinner party, the longest Gabby had gone without talking to her best friend since Kinsley had moved back to Harlow. Even so, avoidance was a better choice than continuing to lie and failing miserably. Maybe she should just tell the truth and let the chips fall where they may, as Dean had suggested more than once.

"You really need to quit being a wuss," Gabby grumbled aloud. She slammed a file drawer shut and traipsed through the records room into her adjoining workspace.

The warm, toasty smell of cinnamon and dough drifted into her office, waking her stomach, and she smiled when she heard Frank's boisterous good mornings echoing down the marble-lined corridor as he approached.

The person who entered the room with Frank was a bit of a shock. "Lincoln, I didn't know you'd be here." Gabby rounded her desk to greet the men as other courthouse employees, tempted by the promise of a treat, began to file in.

"Frank is like a pied piper with those homemade cinnamon rolls," Lincoln joked.

"I am irresistible!" Frank placed two large, tinfoil covered pans on a long table that sat against the far wall.

"My accoutrements if you please, Sheriff James."

Lincoln stepped forward and surrendered two tote bags, from which Frank produced plates, napkins, and plastic utensils.

Stepping out of the way of the growing crowd, the sheriff moved next to Gabby. "McCormick is quite a fella," he said.

Gabby shot him a sidelong glance. *Oh Lord, here it comes*, she thought. "Yeah, he is."

"You plannin' on seeing him as a permanent thing?"

Gabby shifted her weight uncomfortably. "Dean's leaving soon, and he lives twelve hundred miles away. I doubt we'll see each other again. Are you getting into the match-making game in case sheriffing doesn't work out?"

Lincoln chuckled as he studied her. "Naw. Just interested in what my friends are doin'."

Gabby was beginning to understand what an ant must feel like when caught under the burning ray of the sun through a magnifying glass. "My life is boring."

The sheriff tucked his thumbs in his front jeans pockets as his gaze wandered to the activity around Frank. "I doubt that. I could use your help again. Would you come over to headquarters after this is done, please? I promise not to keep ya too long."

"Sure," she replied, wishing she could think of a reason to say no.

"I appreciate it. We best step in here and shake some hands, or Frank will give us what for."

Gabby swallowed hard as she watched Lincoln join the gathering. With a practiced smile, she smoothed her hands over her blouse and stepped forward. Keeping the sheriff at bay would not be easy, but she would have to try for a while longer.

***

Lincoln hummed along with the tune on the radio as he drove out into the country thinking about the half-truths Gabby had shared with him after their campaign session with Frank.

When he'd revealed that she and her compadres had been spotted circling The Order's compound, the look on her face had been one of utter panic. Gabby had stuttered through some feeble excuse that Dean had wanted to see where she'd grown up.

It was time for Lincoln to accept that Gabby Chambers might be more involved with Jacob's death than he'd first imagined, and that he had ignored the signs because she was Kinsley's best friend.

When Gabby had initially divulged her connection to the deceased, she had said that she was with Dusty the night Miller was killed. Lincoln had taken it at face value, but now he had tasked Butch to dig into her alibi. He hoped that it checked out; he liked Gabby, and if she were involved it would devastate Kinsley.

The sight of Crawley and his sky-blue Audi in a standoff with Weatherby on his red roan mare snapped Lincoln back to the present. He parked in a shallow ditch, hopped out, and approached the scene with a determined stride.

Trenton Crawley was using an open car door as a shield, but his confidence grew when he saw Lincoln.

The sheriff looked up at Scott Weatherby, whose ears

were the color of a ripe Bing cherry. He was standing in his stirrups and holding the horse's reins tightly as the mare pawed at the ground. "Linc, you better get this pompous jackass off my land. He ain't welcome here," he growled. The muscles in Scott's jaw were working overtime as his glare centered on Crawley.

"As you can see, I am on the county access and not actually on Weatherby's land," Trenton shot back.

"Cuz I backed ya off my land. Marney left a gift fer ya there on yur hood."

Lincoln glanced toward the Audi and noted a hoof-size dent in the otherwise pristine metal. *Crawley must be one sandwich short of a picnic to rile up folks the way he's been doing these last few days*, he thought.

"Yes, and it's something you'll be paying for." Trenton turned to Lincoln. "I wish to file a formal complaint."

Lincoln's cheeks ached from holding in his pleasure at seeing Crawley put in his place. "Seems you were trespassin'."

"It's my word against his that I was on his land," Trenton spat.

Pulling his hat a little lower, Lincoln addressed the rancher. "Hey, Scott, do ya still have those trail cams pointed this way?"

Weatherby plucked his phone from his shirt pocket and swiped across the screen. "Sure do. I'll get that footage pulled up."

Lincoln watched as Trenton started to squirm. "Ah, yeah, okay. We can forget this happened. I won't press charges," Crawley sputtered.

Scott continued perusing his phone. "Ain't no reason

to leave this up in the air. Let's see what's what. Maybe it'll be *me* pressin' charges."

Lincoln waved to a passing local who had slowed to get a better look. "Crawley, I'd say you've pushed your luck about as far as ya should. Apologize to Mr. Weatherby and stay the hell off his land before you get somethin' worse than a hoof print in your hood."

Crawley mumbled under his breath.

"What's that? You'd like to check out the facilities at the jail?" Lincoln reached for his handcuffs. "Nothin' would please me more than to show ya our accommodations."

"No, no, that won't be necessary," Trenton replied. "I was just trying to help catch a murderer, but it looks like no one really cares about solving crimes here."

"That didn't sound like much of an apology." The sheriff pulled his cuffs and started around the car.

"All right. All right! I'm sorry! Dammit!" Crawley shouted, then mumbled something else.

"I didn't catch that." Lincoln raised an eyebrow but only received an evil look in response.

Crawley got in his car, slammed the door, and cranked the engine. He threw dirt as he reversed off the grassy verge onto the blacktop. Through the lowered window, he took a parting shot. "I said you're a bunch of redneck dickheads!" Then he nailed the gas before the sheriff had time to react.

Lincoln shook his head. "That man is a menace." The mare nuzzled his arm when he approached, and he rubbed her velvet nose. "Do ya wanna make a formal complaint?"

"Naw," Scott said. "Ya handled it right. We won't see

him out here again. He wouldna made it twenty feet in that frou-frou car he drives anyhow."

The men chuckled in unison. "Did Crawley say what he wanted?" Lincoln scratched the horse's neck to distract the animal from chewing on his shirt pocket.

"Said he was investigatin' the murder, but I knew that was bull. You'd never hire someone like that, so I backed him off my land." Scott patted his horse's shoulder lovingly. "Marney don't like him neither."

"Who does?" Lincoln smiled. "Anything else goin' on out here I can help with?"

Scott hesitated, which prompted Lincoln to look up. "What is it?"

Weatherby met his gaze for a moment before looking away. "Everything has been real quiet. A bit too quiet." He fiddled with his reins. "Thanks fer all you're doin'. I know you're out here every mornin'."

"Of course. I want your family to be safe," Lincoln returned.

Scott clicked his tongue and tugged on the reins to turn his horse toward home. "Win that election, or this whole place is goin' ta hell," he said before he urged Marney into a canter across an open field.

Lincoln surveyed Weatherby's vast expanse of land until mariachi music caught his ear. He turned his head to watch a Chevy Suburban approach, filled to the brim with young men. The driver took a long look at the sheriff as they passed.

An alarm began to beep, and Lincoln pulled his phone from his pocket. Lunch with the Rotary Club and the promise of a prime roast-beef dinner were next on his list.

He climbed into his vehicle and fell in behind the Chevy that had passed him. Out of curiosity he followed them into town and watched as the driver parked in front of Pete's Tavern, the only local bar. It wasn't out of the ordinary for people from neighboring towns to come into Harlow for a good time.

Lincoln pulled in at the curb in front of Pearl's a half a block away and counted eight men in total as they unloaded. He retrieved his phone from the console and made a call.

"Hey, Sheriff. How may I help you?" Dusty answered.

"Hey, Dusty. Who is available right now?" Lincoln studied the young men as they laughed and pushed one another around before disappearing into the pub.

"Ben, and he's sittin' right here."

"Great! Please tell him to meet me in front of the diner. He'll be tied up for a while."

"Will do."

Lincoln ended the call and texted Kinsley to let her know he would be late for lunch. These fellows were probably up to nothing more than some daytime drinking, but with all he had going on in his county it was better to be safe than sorry.

CHAPTER THIRTY-FOUR

A Fox In The Hen House

Kinsley placed a call, put it on speaker, and continued to work on a line of code she'd been struggling with for a while.

"Good morning, m'lady. How are things in Hooterville?" Bill Schneider answered with his usual flair.

"Chaos reigns supreme, as always. How are you?"

"Busy as a nine-tailed cat in a room full of rockers."

Kinsley hooted with laughter. "You've been hanging around me too long. You've picked up my grandpa's sayings."

"It fits," Bill replied.

"It does. Hey, I sent you the purchase contract for the old department store building with the changes I'd like you to review," Kinsley said. "We can't keep meeting in the church basement. Dr. Towner needs space to set up shop, and though that place is in dire need of new plumbing and a facelift, it's big enough to split and put in a small free clinic. I'm not crazy about becoming a landlord, but the town could use it."

Bill let out a deep sigh. "The rent is too low, but I know I'm fighting a losing battle to try and talk you into raising it."

"You sound tired, Bill." Kinsley stopped typing, picked up her phone, and took the call off speaker. "Is everything okay?"

"You're busy down there in Nowheresville. Are you ever going to slow down?"

She cradled the phone against her shoulder and smiled as she raised her arms and stretched out her back. "Not likely. Hire someone—or two someones. You know who we can trust." Her attorney didn't respond. "Bill, what's going on?"

"Your company is growing at an astronomical rate. On top of that, your interests are all over the place." He paused. "I'm treading water just on the farming jargon. It would be best to have a team specializing in these different areas. I'm a general practitioner, and you need brain surgeons."

"I know I've put a lot on you. Pull together a proposal and let's talk about getting what you need to keep everything rolling."

"I feel like I'm letting you down," he admitted.

"Are you serious? You've done more than anyone else could or would have done for me. I don't want to lose you, Bill. We've been together since the beginning, and we still have a long way to go. Send me your recommendations and let's do it."

Kinsley listened as he tapped his pen steadily in the background, holding her breath for what might come next.

"Miss Rhodes, did I ever tell you how glad I am that you stumbled into my grubby little office?"

Kinsley relaxed as she heard the smile in his voice. "Literally stumbled." She laughed. "That freak downpour was the best rain I've ever been caught in."

He hummed in agreement. "I'll get something together. Thank you, Kinsley."

"I look forward to it. And you're welcome. We're a team. Talk soon." She disconnected the call.

Frankly, she was surprised it had taken him this long to bring up the need for help. The programming part of her company alone was a huge undertaking; add to that the large chunk of the county she'd purchased over the past year, the computer student internship with the college that would begin in the spring, and becoming a business landlord with the building she'd just purchased to start a partnership with Dr. Townsend. It was no wonder that Bill was overwhelmed.

The doorbell broke into her contemplation and sent her scurrying toward the front of the house. Kinsley raised to her toes and looked through the peephole. The woman on the other side looked vaguely familiar. Sensing no real threat, she opened the interior door but kept the screen locked between them.

Maizey growled and Kinsley reached down and scratched the tense pup as she addressed the woman. "Hi, can I help you?"

The stylish blonde looked down her nose at Kinsley. Her short locks were expertly shaped in a style that said 'day-at-the-beach', and a row of perfect white teeth peeked out from behind her glossy rose lips. "I'm Jeannie."

The blood drained from Kinsley's face. This was Lincoln's ex-wife—and she was a knockout.

She had forgotten that Jeannie was in town to spend the day with Thomas; even so, she never imagined the ex-Mrs. Lincoln would darken her door after the horrible things she'd said and done when Kinsley and Lincoln's engagement was announced.

Convention dictated that Kinsley invite her in, but as she stood face-to-face with the woman who had caused Lincoln and Thomas so much pain, she struggled with propriety. "Thomas should be out any minute," Kinsley said as she decided to leave the fight for another day and opened the screen door.

"How cozy," Jeannie snarked as she prowled into the space like a big cat.

"We like it." Kinsley reached down to pet the still-growling dog that was sticking to her like glue.

They stood in uncomfortable silence as Lincoln's ex-wife inspected her perfectly manicured nails, and Kinsley wished Thomas would hurry the hell up.

"Lincoln told me you've set the wedding date." Jeannie's eyes narrowed as she scanned Kinsley from her bare feet to her ponytail. "I'm sure he tells you we talk quite often."

Squaring her shoulders, Kinsley met the challenge. "You have a son together, so I'm hardly surprised you'd have things to discuss," Maizey emitted a guttural groan and she knelt to calm her. "Maiz is usually very friendly. I don't know why she's acting like this."

Jeannie wrinkled her nose and scowled at the animal.

"Hey, Mom," Thomas said as he hurried into the room. His eyes darted between his mother and Kinsley. "I told you I'd meet you at Mario's."

Jeannie's top lip curled back on one side in a smile that looked more fiendish than friendly. "It was time I met the new woman."

"Her name is Kinsley," Thomas corrected.

"Yes, I know." Jeannie turned and strutted toward the door.

When Thomas looked to her for guidance, Kinsley rose from her kneeling position and rubbed his upper arm. "Go and have a good time."

"Thanks, Kins." He mouthed the words 'I'm sorry.'

Kinsley smiled and winked as she patted him lovingly.

Closing the door behind them, she placed her forehead against the solid surface. Maizey squeezed between her legs and the door, sat on her feet, and looked up.

Lincoln had shared how his ex-wife had a fondness for game playing, and she had a distinct feeling that if Thomas hadn't come out when he did, the game would have been afoot. Logically, Kinsley knew there was nothing to worry about, but trust was still tricky for her to master, especially when the ex-wife raised red flags in her face. *How well do I really know Lincoln?* she wondered.

Scratching Maizey behind the ear, Kinsley pushed back against her demons. "Come on, girl, let's get some lunch."

CHAPTER THIRTY-FIVE

Behind The Mirror

Lincoln pored over the dozens of interview statements his undersheriff and deputies had collected from the inquiry into Jacob Miller's death. Finding nothing new to pursue, he closed the folder and laid it on his desk.

Like an F5 tornado, Miller had torn a path of destruction through Stevens County, leaving behind at least half a dozen illegitimate children, most of whom were now being raised by their grandparents. Lincoln always did his best to see the good in people, but he had yet to discover even a spark of humanity in this man.

Butch had followed up on the tire tracks from the crime scene and concluded that they were common to nearly every all-terrain vehicle. Despite having a long list of ATV owners around Weatherby's farm, Lincoln tasked Deputy Adams to begin questioning the titleholders. The likelihood of striking gold was slim, but they could leave no stone unturned.

They still didn't know why Weatherby's abandoned house had been used as a dumping location for the body. After an exhaustive search, they had found no connection between Scott Weatherby and Jacob Miller. Weatherby was a congenial fellow whom people genuinely liked; for someone to try to set him up as a suspect in a murder case was mystifying.

Lincoln scrutinized the investigation board. Most of the people he'd questioned were involved with Miller for work or were the parents of a young woman who had been romantically connected to him. Everything they had pointed to a lot of people hating the guy, and hate was a powerful emotion. Any one of them could have killed Jacob, but there was no solid evidence to implicate anyone.

The sheriff stacked the files he'd been working on and set them aside before heading to the front office. Charlene was on a call, so he stepped into the kitchenette, took a glass from a cabinet, and got a drink of water while eavesdropping.

"I can tell you where you went wrong," Charlene said. "You have to sauté the onions in bacon grease before you mix them into the pork 'n' beans." A satisfied smile blossomed as she listened to the person on the other end. "Yep, makes all the difference. You're welcome. Enjoy those baked beans, Elma, and tell Destry hey."

Lincoln placed his glass in the sink and approached her desk. "That sounded like important police business," he teased.

"A bad batch of beans could cause murderous feelings," she returned without missing a beat. "What's up, Linc?"

"Apparently not a thing. I'm goin' to the barber shop if ya need me."

"Good idea. You're starting to look like a hippie."

He chuckled as he snagged his Stetson from the rack by the door on the way out.

***

Less than two minutes later, Lincoln pulled up in front of the only barber shop in town and killed the engine. Rolling down his window to get a better look through the shop's double-plate glass windows, he saw several men waiting their turn. Among them was Jack Levine. Lincoln grinned as he wondered what interesting things Levine would have to say; the man was never without a story to tell.

When Lincoln pushed open the door, he set off a tinkling of bells that caused a flurry of heads to turn. A warm, musky scent of shaving cream spiked with antiseptic wafted around him as he strode across the black-and-white checkered linoleum floor to a line of chairs set back against an achromatic wall.

"Sher'f," Floyd Grimes, the local barber, greeted him as he brushed hair from a cape draped around his current client. "Looks like you're overdue."

"That's a fact," Lincoln returned. He took the only empty seat in the thick of the other customers. "What's the latest, fellas?"

"A murder and a primary election runoff. Harlow hasn't been this excitin' since I don't remember when." Jack Levine closed the latest edition of the local newspaper and folded it up. "How goes it, Linc?"

"Never a dull moment."

"My ol' lady said she heard one a' them there satanic cults murdered that Miller kid." Jack gave Lincoln a wry smile. "That right? We got some a' them runnin' around town?"

"Naw, it wasn't a group like that," Lincoln replied.

The man who had just exited the barber's chair piped up, "What about them bikers?"

"Afraid not. They're as clean as a whistle. Nothin' to worry about," Lincoln confirmed.

The men said their goodbyes to the client who was leaving, and Floyd beckoned the next in line as he threw in his two cents. "If you ask me, he got what was comin'."

"Really? Did ya know Miller?" Lincoln asked.

"Not personally, but a lady I see—"

"Aw, Floyd, we all know you and Alma are doin' the horizontal shuffle," Jack teased.

The barber flushed red. "Alma would have yer hide for speakin' 'bout her that way."

"Shit. Me an' her dated in high school." Jack elbowed Lincoln and winked. "I mighta kissed her once or twice."

Floyd shook his head as a grin played along his lips. "You'd be a lucky man if ya had. Anyway, back to what I was sayin'. Alma's granddaughter messed around with that Miller boy for a while. He broke her heart."

"Yeah, he's got a reputation for doin' that," Lincoln returned. "What's her granddaughter's name?"

"Sara Peterson, but she won't be much help. She left town a while back."

"I do recall that." Lincoln nodded thoughtfully. "Her parents came in to see if we could help track her down. Since she was of age, and there was no evidence of foul play, there wasn't much we could do. They admitted she'd left of her own accord."

Lincoln remembered speaking at length with the girl's parents. They thought Sara had probably gone to Colorado to stay with relatives, but he had never found a shred of evidence to support that; the girl had just packed a bag and disappeared. He distinctly remembered asking if she'd had a boyfriend, but her parents had said no. It was interesting that they'd left that crucial piece of information out of their report.

"Did she ever contact her family?" the sheriff asked.

"Nope." Floyd urged the client in his chair to look down so that he could shave his neck.

"I'm sorry ta hear that." Lincoln made a mental note to check in with the Petersons. If Jacob were the reason their daughter had left town, he'd like to know why they hadn't said as much.

"Sara was a beautiful girl. The world was her oyster, but once Miller showed up, she changed," Floyd added.

"Changed? In what way?" Lincoln sat forward.

The barber reached for a can of baby powder, applied a liberal sprinkling to his customer's neck, whisked off the excess with a brush, then patted the client's shoulder to indicate he was through. The man stood up, dug a few wrinkled bills from his front jeans' pocket, and handed them over.

"Thank ya, Joe. See ya in a couple of weeks," Floyd said as the man left. "Jack, you're up."

Jack placed his liver-spotted hands on the chair's chrome armrests. With an oomph, he pushed himself upright before shuffling across the space to the barber's chair. With the graceful movements of a matador, Floyd unfurled a clean cape and draped it around him. "Let's see. Where were we?" he frowned.

"Sara changed," Lincoln prompted.

"Right. She was a ray a sunshine, but after datin' Miller, she became sullen. Them last months before she left were dark times." Floyd started cutting Jack's remaining fringe of hair. "Her parents were worried, but there was nuttin' they could do. A shame, really."

Jack spoke up. "That Miller was a pest. I ran him and his crew off my land a few months back. Worthless bunch. Always drinkin' and carousin'."

"They were trespassin'?" Lincoln asked.

"Yep. Fishin' in my pond—and they had a couple of them ladies o' the night with 'em."

Floyd was visibly shocked. "They brought prostitutes fishin'?"

"Sure 'nuff. I got an eyeful before runnin' 'em off," Jack confirmed.

Lincoln saw an opening to find out more about Jacob's side business. "Where do ya think they came across prostitutes?"

"They're around." Jack sported a mischievous grin. "There's nothin' wrong with a little fun."

Lincoln stifled a laugh as he shook his head. "It isn't legal. At least not here."

"I remember the days when my daddy ran a moonshine still, and us boys bootlegged his licker all over this part of the country. Us Levines are nothin' but outlaws." The old man cackled as Floyd dusted him off.

Jack stood, produced a bifold wallet from his hip pocket and extracted several bills. "Thanks for the cut, Floyd." As he moved toward the door, he thumbed over his shoulder toward Lincoln. "Make him presentable, if ya can."

"I'm not a miracle worker, Levine," the barber joked as Jack shuffled out the door.

Lincoln stood, placed his hat on the seat he'd just vacated and moved to the barber's chair. He got comfortable as Floyd put a fresh cape around him. "Where do ya think Sara went?" he asked.

"Can't say," Floyd replied. "Miller ruined her. She loved the boy, though I never could see the why of it."

"How did her father feel about their relationship?"

"He threatened to take a gun full of salt to the kid's backside more'n once," Floyd revealed. Lincoln met the barber's gaze in the mirror. "I—I'm not sayin' he'd really do it. But from what Alma said, he didn't like Sara bein' with the guy."

Floyd chattered on about local gossip as he finished Lincoln's haircut, but as the sheriff left the shop his thoughts were on the fathers in town who might have liked to fill Jacob Miller full of more than salt. It was possible one of them had finally snapped.

CHAPTER THIRTY-SIX

Time In A Bottle

Gabby lined up her peas around the edge of her plate with a fork as she listened to Dean. He was giving her father a rundown of what the club had found when he and some of his men had sneaked into the settlement in the early morning hours on a scouting mission.

"Amos was right—it doesn't look like there are that many armed men out there. The people are easy to control. We located the houses where the undesirables are staying, thanks to the directions your brother shared," he said. "I must hand it to them—they've found a good place to hide while they sell their drugs, and traffic people into the States. I'm still of the opinion that we should tell Sheriff James what's going on."

Harold looked down at the table. "As you said, we're interfering in police business. Unless we want to go to jail, we'll have to keep Lincoln out of it. Do you have a final plan yet?"

Dean watched Gabby's activity for a moment before turning back to Harold. "Will those people at the settlement participate in the upcoming election?"

"Some of them, but the town is puttin' on a big do downtown that includes a farmers' market. They'll come in for that." Harold smiled as he caught on to Dean's idea.

The biker nodded. "The fewer innocents inside when we go in, the better. Most of the armed men are young, and you never know what a kid will do when the heat is on. Gabby, what do you think?"

She stopped playing with her food and focused on Dean. "What?"

"Will most of the people from the settlement come into Harlow on election day?" he asked.

"I can get a note to my brother asking him to urge people to attend the election day events."

Dean squeezed Gabby's hand under the table. "It's settled. Marilyn, can you put up with me for a while longer?"

"You could stay here permanently, and I'd be just fine with that."

Dean winked at her, and Marilyn melted into giggles. "Mr. McCormick, you are too much," she said as she recovered her composure. "We should celebrate with peach cobbler and some vanilla ice cream." She rose and started to gather plates. "Anyone interested?"

Dean stood up to help, but Gabby put her hand on his shoulder and urged him back into his chair. "Stay here and entertain my father or he'll get into trouble."

Harold chuckled as his daughter and wife took the dishes to the kitchen. "How's things at the farm?"

"Peaceful," Dean replied. "I don't know why you don't move out there. At night, I swear I can see every star in the universe. How did you end up with that property?"

"Alvin Gunderson owned it. He was a bachelor. Marilyn took him under her wing, and he became a part of our family over the years. When the cancer got him,

Marilyn practically lived there while she nursed the poor fella. We had to bring him to town to live with us at the end." Harold pulled a thread at the edge of his cloth napkin. "We had no idea he'd left us his place. Alvin was a good man."

Dean nodded as Harold continued. "I thought Gabby could have it when she gets married. She loves it out there. I'm more of a city dweller."

The women returned with their dessert, and Harold eyed the fruit-filled confection as he patted his stomach. "You've outdone yourself, babe. This looks delicious."

Gabby's head was filled with too many thoughts as she returned to her place at the table, but one stood out above the rest. Eventually, Dean would pull out of her driveway and never return. What they'd shared had blown a big hole in the center of a life that, until now, had been satisfying. His stories of the places he'd traveled and adventures he'd experienced had put a sharp point on the fact that she'd been sitting still in Harlow for far too long. It was time to get out before it was too late.

CHAPTER THIRTY-SEVEN

Turning Over Rocks

Rain beat a trance-inducing rhythm on the roof of Lincoln's vehicle as he sat parked along a lonely dirt road near the settlement. In the murky pre-dawn, even a pinprick of light would have been easily detectable had there been any. The empty landscape left him with little to do but stare into the darkness and ruminate on their unsolved case.

They had unearthed quite a lot of information about The Order since Jacob's death. The founding members previously belonged to a group of Amish in Pennsylvania until a disagreement over their belief system had caused several members to split. The Order had been established in Stevens County in the late 1980s, when an inheritance of a section of land had given the fledgling congregation a perfect place to begin.

The settlement had started with a few houses and a community barn, but over the years it had grown to fill half a section, all fenced in like a modern-day fortress. Working as farmhands and handymen, the males did most of the money earning, while the women took care of their family and home-schooled their children. They even had a midwife and a birthing center on the property.

Abraham Miller had been one of the founding members and remained the head minister. It was usually a pretty good bet that if you followed a corrupt kid home, you found corruption somewhere in their upbringing; however, Jacob had been raised by a super-religious father with a core belief of 'love thy neighbor,' so Miller's reported actions seemed out of step with Lincoln's usual philosophy.

Gabby had mentioned that Jacob had a dark side; perhaps he was a sociopath. He had many of the markers: a Jekyll and Hyde personality, no sense of right or wrong, and a lack of remorse or empathy. Many of the women interviewed had described him as handsome and charismatic, but the same had been said about every deadly cult leader on record.

Lincoln wrapped his arms around the steering wheel and stretched; he wished they could solve this case sooner rather than later because these stakeouts were killing his back. He tried to find a comfortable position as he settled into his seat, unscrewed the top of his coffee thermos, and continued his deliberations.

The perplexing side investigation by Harold Chambers and Dean McCormick continued to stump him. Even with Kinsley's help, Gabby had been unwilling to divulge information. But then again, what harm could they really do?

Lincoln knew that Dean was not the murderer because he'd been in California when Miller was killed. Dusty had provided Gabby with an alibi that had checked out, and there was no way the Reverend had done the deed: He'd been in Dallas at a church conference the week Jacob died. What they were up to remained a mystery, but they were doing something sneaky no doubt.

Answers about what exactly was going on behind the chain-link fencing that surrounded the compound, and whether it had led to Jacob Miller's death, were still just out of reach. Judge Goodale was stalling on the warrant, which made Lincoln wonder if the judge was in someone's pocket.

A sudden shrill ring startled him. He retrieved his phone from a cupholder in the console, checked the caller ID, and glanced at the time before answering. "You're up early."

Thomas chuckled. "Surprised?"

"Absolutely floored. What's up, kiddo?"

"Can you come get me, Dad, please? My pickup won't start. I'm at Phil's."

Lincoln started his vehicle. "That's the Faulkner kid, right?"

"Uh-huh," Thomas confirmed. "I stayed out here last night. I need to get goin' or I'm gonna miss my first class."

"I'm only a few miles away. Be there shortly." Lincoln ended the call, turned his pickup around, and made tracks toward Faulkner's farm. Whatever he was looking for wasn't going to show up here—at least not today.

The rain picked up as Lincoln neared his turn, and he slowed to a crawl, straining to see the entrance through the deluge. He took a right, then navigated the long drive that led to Faulkner's house. He barely had time to unlock the passenger door before his son came bounding down the driveway. "You're full of energy this mornin'," Lincoln teased.

"I was ready to get out of there. I shoulda come home last night, but it was really late so I stayed. Phil's parents are different."

Lincoln turned down the radio, made a three-point turn, and started toward town. "Different, how?"

"I dunno. Like everything is sinful." Thomas shrugged. "Speakin' of sin, have you read the latest edition of the paper?"

"Nope. I haven't had time."

"Well, you should. Mrs. Faulkner was reading it to us last night after dinner. There is an article about Crawley sayin' he got caught doin' some mayor's wife while he was supposed to be investigating her husband for a string of robberies. It says he was suspected of being in on the heists, but they couldn't prove it. Then Crawley left town."

Lincoln looked at his son then back at the road. "Are you serious?"

"Yep. It's all there in the paper. You should check it out. That's great news, isn't it?"

"It's somethin'. I wonder where they got the information. You know, it might not be accurate."

"I bet it is. That guy is a creep!"

Lincoln grunted in agreement as he pulled into Kinsley's driveway. "Thanks for tellin' me. That won't do him any favors at the polls if it's true."

Thomas grinned. "He never had a chance. Thanks for the ride, Dad. Hey—"

"Yes, I'll have your pickup towed into Junior's garage," Lincoln replied before Thomas could ask.

"You're the best! Catch ya later." Thomas opened the passenger door.

"Tell Kins I'll stop by for lunch, please."

"Will do!" Thomas replied as he slammed the door

shut and sprinted through the rain toward the house.

The sheriff backed out onto the street with a whole new outlook. If Crawley really were corrupt, the proof coming out now would surely put a win in Lincoln's column. On the downside, he could imagine the rumor mill in Harlow churning out the gossip that the leaked information had come from him. He didn't relish the idea of people thinking he would resort to damaging someone's reputation just to win an election.

CHAPTER THIRTY-EIGHT

Fits Just Right

"Your dad said you could use his pickup for the voter round-up tomorrow since your truck is still in the shop." Kinsley said and pursed her lips. "Junior sure takes his sweet time about fixing anything. He's had it for—what? A week?"

"He does, but I can't say I hate driving your Range Rover." Thomas gave her a toothy grin as he grabbed his can of pop and took a swig. "Speaking of the election, every buddy of mine is lined up to roust folks and get them to the polls."

"That's great news."

Kinsley added a few finishing touches to the updates on Lincoln's website and sat back to inspect her work. He had agreed to let her showcase his charitable acts, but with one caveat: The news had to have appeared in a local paper. The sheriff had thought he was being clever with this proviso since the editor of Harlow's newspaper wasn't a fan of Lincoln after he'd arrested her boyfriend for cattle rustling. However, once Kinsley expanded her search to surrounding towns, Lincoln was surprised by how many times his good deeds had been reported.

She smiled with satisfaction and moved on to check the ride-request database. Finding a few new names, she added them to her spreadsheet and published the changes.

"This election came up way too quickly. I can hardly believe how time flies," she said.

"That's what all old people say," Thomas teased pulling a chuckle from Kinsley.

He sat back, and two little lines formed between his brows. "Dad loves his job. What'll happen if he loses?"

"We have to keep the faith that won't happen. I can't see Trenton Crawley beating Lincoln. He's a worm and your dad is—"

"Oh jeez, don't get all mushy about Dad!" Thomas interrupted, making them both laugh. "You're right, I shouldn't worry."

Kinsley changed the subject. "How is your project going?"

"Great! I'm almost finished. It's really gonna be a winner."

Relief washed through her at the news. She had been concerned that his proposal might be a bit ambitious for a novice to take on. "You'll finish junior college soon. Have you considered going to a four-year school? I can make some calls. I know a few people at Carnegie Mellon."

Thomas squinted at her, downed the remainder of his pop, and set the empty can aside. "CMU? Really? You think I have any chance of getting in there?"

"Your flawless grade-point average will speak for itself, but you'd better not wait to apply if you want to go in that direction. Are you interested?"

The boy looked at his computer screen. "I'd hate to leave you and Dad, but that school has an impressive program."

"It would be a great opportunity," Kinsley agreed. "We should talk to your dad first."

Thomas sat back and chewed his bottom lip before he spoke. "I was planning on taking a break from school. I'm ready to get on with livin'."

"Since you started Juco in the fall semester, you'll have a six-month break after graduation," Kinsley threw in. "I thought as your graduation present it might be nice for you to take a trip abroad, see a different part of the world. I understand wanting to get on with living, but there'll be plenty of time to do that when you've finished school."

Thomas's eyes sparkled. "Gawd, I'd love to travel! England, maybe?"

"Sure, England is great. You could spend a little time in France, too. Maybe Italy."

"Damn. I never thought I'd see any of that. Yeah, I'd love to go. Thanks, Kins."

She smiled. "You're welcome. We've had a heck of a year. We all need to unwind."

"And it ain't over yet," Thomas added.

Kinsley contemplated the next day's election, and their wedding planned for a few weeks afterward. If Lincoln lost his bid for sheriff, it would turn their world upside down. Staying in Harlow might not be best for any of them. *Getting married right now might not be the right thing either*, she lamented.

"Hey, Kins, did you hear what I just said?"

She looked up from her computer. "Sorry, I was lost in thought."

"I'm gonna marry Gabby," Thomas repeated matter-of-factly.

Kinsley closed her laptop and frowned. "You've asked Gabby to marry you and she's said yes?"

"Well, no, not yet. But I *am* going to marry her."

"Are ya now?" Kinsley relaxed as she realized this was just his crush running away with him. "I believe a woman has to agree before a marriage can take place."

"She will. You just wait."

Kinsley gave a non-committal shrug. "Knowing what you want is half the battle. I wish you Godspeed, young Skywalker."

Thomas laughed. "You're such a nerd, Kins. Right now I don't have a chance in hell, but once I'm out of school and working full-time, she'll change her mind about me."

"What if she marries someone else before then?"

"She won't. She keeps datin' non-committers."

Kinsley cocked an eyebrow. "Ya think?"

"It's true!"

Kinsley struggled not to laugh; her stepson was a corker. "I admire your confidence."

Thomas went on, "Gabs took my breath away the first time I saw her. She's the one."

"Hey, you'll get no argument from me—Gabby is great. I just don't want you to be disappointed. She's pretty hung up on Dean."

"Not a problem. She'll get that bad-boy phase out of her system." Thomas gave her a thousand-watt smile as he pushed back his chair. "Don't you dare tell her my plan."

Kinsley smirked as she pressed her thumb and index finger together and dragged them across her lips.

Thomas chuckled and bent to pet Maizey, who was waiting patiently at his feet. He closed his laptop and placed it in his bag. "I have to go to school."

She slid her key across the table. "Take care of my car, and fill it up before you bring it back, please."

He hauled his backpack over his shoulder and winked. "You know I won't."

Kinsley shook her head. Maizey crawled under the table, and she rubbed the pup with her feet while she contemplated a relationship between Gabby and her stepson. Thomas had less than a snowball's chance, but it would be interesting to watch. He was a handsome young man with excellent prospects; stranger things had happened.

***

Lincoln placed his elbows on his desk, bent his head forward, and ran his fingertips over his scalp. Too many things were bearing down, and even with a full staff there wasn't enough of him to go around. He needed a vacation. Once he cleared his list, he and Kinsley were going to rent a cabin somewhere quiet where they could sleep in, fish, and do a whole lot of nothing.

The intercom buzzed, interrupting his daydream. "Linc, you have people here to see you," Charlene relayed. "It's Abraham and Rachel Miller."

"I'll be right there." He hurried out to greet Jacob's parents, the two people he never thought he'd have an opportunity to speak with.

Lincoln pushed past the secure door and greeted them warmly. "Mr. and Mrs. Miller, please allow me to say how sorry I am for your loss. Thank you for comin' in." He held out his hand to shake. Mr. Miller ignored it, his stony look unchanged.

The sheriff overlooked the slight and swept his arm toward the security door. "We can speak privately if you'd like to come to my office."

"Nah," Miller responded quickly. "Sheriff James, we're comin' ta claim da body of our son."

"We have an investigation into his death. I could really use your help," Lincoln said, treading carefully into the conversation. The couple looked on stoically, never quite meeting his gaze. He tried again. "May I ask why it's taken ya so long to come see me?"

"We 'oped dis business would pass, and we could claim 'im without da police. But da coroner said we 'ave ta talk ta ya," Mr. Miller stated.

"I see. If we could please sit down for a few minutes, your insight could be invaluable."

"We 'ave na answers. Our son was 'is own man, and we can't tell ya who da murderer is," Abraham said curtly.

"I understand you're upset, Mr. Miller, but I would like to get justice for Jacob."

Mrs. Miller murmured under her breath as she stared at her shoes.

"I'm sorry. I missed that," Lincoln said as he leaned closer.

The woman stiffened her spine and raised her head, looking past the sheriff at some spot on the wall behind him as she spoke. "I said Jacob was not a gud man, Sheriff James. 'E did bad, and da Lord punished 'im. It was God who did da killin'."

Lincoln studied the Millers, who were showing zero emotion over the loss of their only child. *Perhaps Jacob didn't fall far from the tree after all*, he thought. "I respect your beliefs, but God didn't do this. I need to find out who did."

Miller put his hand on his wife's shoulder. "When we can 'ave 'is body, send word. We can't talk ta ya." He and his wife turned to go.

"Please, wait. If your son had enemies, knowing who they were will help us find his killer."

"Gud day," the man said. He motioned to his wife, and she hurried out of the building ahead of him.

Lincoln watched them load up in an old black sedan and drive away. "That was a disaster," he grumbled as he passed through the secured door and stopped at Charlene's desk.

"It sure was," she said. "What was that God business about? A call came in, so I couldn't listen to what they were sayin'."

"They said God killed Jacob."

"God?"

"Yep." Lincoln ran his knuckles along his jaw. "Those people were more than standoffish. I'd say they were scared." He strode to the kitchenette to get some water. After taking a long drink, he set the empty glass in the sink, and turned to his colleague. "What's that missin' piece, Charlene?"

"You'll find whatever it is, Linc," she reassured him. "Or it will find you."

He was beginning to have his doubts that they would ever discover Jacob Miller's killer; having a ton of suspects was almost worse than having none.

CHAPTER THIRTY-NINE

Fish In A Barrel

The normally peaceful country setting of her father's second home felt oddly unsettling. Gabby bounced her legs nervously as she sat on the edge of a rocking chair waiting for Dean and his crew to return. They had taken an early morning excursion to the settlement with a plan to rid The Order of its criminal element.

A heavy morning dew sparkled on the grass as her worrisome thoughts flitted between the election and what might be going on within the compound at that very moment. Whatever was happening was taking much longer than she'd imagined, and some truly horrific scenarios were beginning to form. If Dean or any of his men were killed or hurt, how would she live with herself?

Gabby stood up, then paced from one end of the porch to the other until she caught sight of a swirling dust cloud in the distance. As a line of cars drew near, she recognized her parents' van in the lead and rushed out to meet them in the driveway.

Dean parked his borrowed vehicle and exited just in time to catch Gabby as she jumped into his arms and hugged him tightly. "I've never been so scared," Gabby whispered against his cheek. She let go, slid to the ground, and stepped back to give him a once-over. "You're not hurt, are you?"

His barely visible crow's feet deepened as he tucked her hair behind one ear. "I'm fine."

Gabby urged him toward the porch. "Sit here and tell me everything that happened. Don't leave out anything."

With a twinkle in his eye, Dean got comfortable and began. "We took a quiet approach and used the element of surprise as a weapon..."

"You're going to drag this out, aren't you?"

"Patience is a virtue, my dear."

Gabby snickered. "I'm neither patient nor virtuous. Out with it!"

Dean took her hand between his as he granted her request. "We approached from the rear of the property and dropped off a few of my men. They headed for the hole in the fence you'd mentioned while the rest of my crew continued to the entrance. I expected resistance from the guard, but no one was posted, so we rolled back the gate and drove right in."

"Easy-peasy!"

"Yes—but I became concerned that everyone had gone into Harlow. And then I heard it." He stopped as if reflecting on the scene.

Gabby's eyes widened as she held her breath. Dean hesitated so long that she cried in exasperation, "Oh, my God! Tell me what!"

His rich laughter vibrated through her. "Music."

"Music?"

"That wild, energetic, mariachi-type music. I had a feeling that the people behind it were the ones we were looking for. We parked and walked toward the center of the settlement. There, spread out on tables, were bottles of tequila and an abundance of tarts."

Gabby frowned. "By tarts, I assume you mean women and not dessert."

Dean sprouted a devilish grin. "No, I mean dessert. There wasn't a soul in sight. Someone had left the music playing, a feast had been abandoned, and the compound was empty."

Gabby chuckled at his play on words before she stood up, leaned against the handrail, and began to wring her hands. "What are we going to do now?"

He looked out across the land. "I assume they're in town. We'll have to meet them there or wait for another day."

"You can't wait. Kinsley and Lincoln won't leave me alone about why you are here, and I'm about to break. I'm not good at this espionage crap."

"Are you anxious to get rid of me?" Dean teased.

Gabby looked down at her shoes. "You know I'm not. If I could find a reason to keep you here, I would." The color rose in her cheeks. "And I probably should have kept that last bit of information to myself."

He opened his arms, urging her onto his lap. Gabby settled in and put her head on his shoulder as they tranquilly rocked.

"You have an election to attend, and it looks like the boys and I are going to a celebration in Harlow after all." Dean leaned Gabby back and gave her a sigh-inducing kiss before helping her up and running his hand over her rear. "Get your gorgeous derrière into town before you're late for work."

As she hurried to her car, she watched Dean mingling

with his men. Gabby blinked several times to clear the mist that was forming in her eyes as she slid into the driver's seat. Catching her reflection in the rearview mirror, she said, "Buckle up, buttercup. You knew what this was when you started it."

***

Lincoln pulled Henry's old pickup into a parking space next to the sheriff's office and shut off the engine. He got out, rested his hip against the bed of the vehicle, and watched the crowd that had gathered at the courthouse waiting to cast their ballots. Excited chatter filled the air; there was even a hotdog vendor who had set up shop on a corner of the courthouse lot to tempt voters with his savory fare.

He felt a mixture of discomfort and a thrill of the unknown. It was odd to entertain the idea that very soon he might not be Sheriff Lincoln James. The title didn't define him, but it did fit him like a pair of well-worn gloves.

Lincoln pushed himself upright and sauntered toward his destiny. It was time to cast his vote and let The Fates sort out the rest. He'd never been inflexible when it came to life's twists, and he wasn't going to start now.

He swiped his keycard at a side door and slipped inside, intending to vote then make himself scarce. He wouldn't have Crawley and his cronies accusing him of electioneering.

"Linc!" Dusty fumbled to retrieve a ballot paper and pen and hand them to the sheriff. Lincoln offered his driver's license as proof of identity, and Dusty scanned it into the machine on the table.

"Lotsa folks are here already, I see." The sheriff nodded toward the voters as they milled around chatting.

"Yep. No one wants to leave this one up to chance. After those news articles, Crawley has lost his support." Dusty beamed at his boss. "You can use that station right over there." He indicated a voting cubicle against a far wall.

"Thanks." Lincoln waved to several citizens who were trying to get his attention as he made his way to the podium-height stand. Pulling the red, white, and blue privacy curtain around him, he smoothed the ballot paper against the wooden top. As he read the document, his eyes rested momentarily on his name printed above Trenton Crawley's, then he made his selections, left the voting booth, and fed his completed ballot into the collection box.

Escaping the hubbub, Lincoln walked several blocks toward a cordoned-off portion of Main Street. Vendors and food trucks lined two blocks of downtown, and a mini car show had been pulled together to round out the festivities.

As the twangy sound of a local singer covering an old country tune drifted among the tents, Danny Singleton, the town's most senior police officer, spotted Lincoln and rushed up to greet him. "Howdy, Sheriff," he said, hooking his thumbs behind his wide gun belt.

"Hey, Danny," Lincoln returned.

"We got things under control here. No trouble," said Danny as he sniffed confidently.

"Looks like it. How've ya been? I haven't seen ya around."

"Oh, ya know. I'm livin' the life. Things have been pretty busy for the past year."

Lincoln nodded. "How's everythin' goin' with the new police chief?"

"Good, good. Chief Bretz is a ringtail twister, but I like workin' for her."

Lincoln chuckled, knowing Danny was right on track with his description of Yolanda Bretz, who was one of his own former Navy pals. He couldn't have been more delighted when she had accepted the position of police chief in Harlow and moved her family to town. "Yolanda is a good egg. I'm glad things are workin' out. Have ya seen Butch?" he asked.

"He was down by Pearl's not that long ago."

"Thanks, Danny. I better let you get on. Take care now."

"Sure 'nuff. See ya, Sheriff."

Lincoln skirted the crowd and continued to the next block, where he found his undersheriff shooting the bull with two men in the parking lot of Pearl's diner. "Hey, fellas," he said as he joined the group.

"Word is you got this election in the bag, Sheriff," one of the men said.

"I hope what you're hearing is right." Lincoln shook hands with each of the men.

The locals wrapped up their conversation and wandered off in search of food, leaving Butch and Lincoln to watch the crowd. "I'm surprised Crawley ain't struttin' around here," Lincoln observed.

Butch nodded. "That is a surprise. Come to think of it, I haven't seen hide nor hair of him today. That's outta character."

"Sure is. Mind if I borrow your unit? Thomas has my pickup, and I need to take a spin around the county to clear my head."

Butch fished around in his front jeans' pocket and produced a key. "I'm helping the city with crowd control here, so I ain't goin' nowhere."

"Thanks." Lincoln held out the key to Henry's pickup and told Butch where it was parked. "It'll get ya where you're goin', but I wouldn't take it too far outta town."

"Roger that." The undersheriff playfully saluted his boss as they parted ways.

Lincoln cut down an alley to where Butch had parked, unlocked the SUV, and hopped in. Exhaling as he pulled out of the lot and took City Limits Road out of town, he tossed his hat onto the passenger seat, then rolled the windows down and let the warm wind blow away his cares.

As he turned onto the dirt road that led to Henry's farm, memories flooded in of the first time he'd taken this route with Kinsley the previous year. She was a bobcat back then, and while she had mellowed a degree or two, he could never see her being docile. He admired her independent streak; he had no use for a shrinking violet.

Pulling into Henry's property, Lincoln parked beside a tailwater pit and got out. He, Kinsley, and Thomas had planted a row of evergreens along the south end of the manmade pond. In a few years, those tiny trees would make a perfect shelter belt against the stiff south winds that often ripped ferociously across this open land.

Kinsley had talked him into helping her erect a shade structure, and they'd finished it off with a concrete-topped picnic table and benches. On many occasions they had gone there to watch the sun go down while they fished. Kinsley had expressed a desire to build a house out here; although Lincoln had never lived in the country, it was an appealing notion.

He sat on the tabletop, faced the pond, and rested his forearms on his thighs as he considered what tomorrow might bring. No matter how hard he tried, he couldn't reconcile himself to conceding his job to Crawley; it would be hard enough to give it up to a good guy, but Trenton would be nothing but a glory-grabbing sham of a sheriff.

Lincoln watched the sun sparkle off tiny ripples on the surface of the pond. "Henry, my friend, I wish you were here to give me some good advice." A fish leapt out of the water and then disappeared under the surface. "We sure do miss you."

His phone vibrated against his chest, and he retrieved it from his shirt pocket. "Hey, darlin', I was just thinkin' about you."

"Oh, were ya now?" Kinsley replied with a smile in her voice.

"Always. What's up?"

"I had a call that Thomas hadn't picked up the remaining people on his list. Last I heard, he was going to get his pal Phillip Faulkner, but now he's not answering his phone. They're probably horsing around outside. Would you please go out there and see if you can find him for me?"

"Sure can. I'm a few miles away, but I'll head over."

"You're the best! Love you."

"Ditto," Lincoln returned. He ended the call and got into Butch's unit. Today promised to be the longest day of his life.

CHAPTER FORTY

This Too Shall Pass

With the noise from a crowd of voters who had all but taken over the courthouse, and the early-morning failed eviction operation by Dean and his pals, Gabby's nerves were fraying. She got up from her desk and looked out of the windows that lined one wall of her office. From her second-story perch, she people-watched while reflecting on her current circumstances.

Dean had tried again to persuade her to tell Lincoln what she knew, but Gabby, like her father, feared they had already gone too far. She had been horribly dishonest with her best friend and their relationship was strained; another serious blow could kill it. Her recent choices could indeed lead her straight to the devil by the time this drama ended.

"Hey, Miss Commissioner, I've cast my vote. What say I take you to lunch?" Kinsley said as she breezed into the room.

While her friend's visit was unexpected, it was a welcome surprise. Gabby forced a smile before she turned to straighten her desk. "At least I know I have one vote for sure. Where are we going?"

"I thought we'd try Pearl's. Since the change in wait staff, we're less likely to get our food with a side of spit." Kinsley winked, which made Gabby giggle. "I'm in the mood for a big ol' cheeseburger and fries."

Gabby placed her hands over her belly. "I don't know that I could eat a thing. My stomach is full of butterflies."

"I get that. I have two of you to worry about." Kinsley jerked her head toward the door. "Let's forget for a while."

The ladies wove through the crowd and cut across the courthouse lawn to a sidewalk that took them away from the election crush. "So, how's everything going?" Kinsley asked.

"Okay, I guess. Work is slow," Gabby replied.

"Are you seriously going to talk to me about work when you have that hunk of a motorcycle rider taking up space in your bed every night?" Kinsley teased. "Is he staying?"

As they rounded the red-brick building that housed Pearl's, Gabby assured her that Dean would be leaving town very soon. A note on the diner's door stated it was closed for the day.

"Well, that was a bust. I guess we could get something to eat at one of the food vendors," Kinsley said as she turned to check out a mass of people milling around on the next block, and a smile began to blossom. "I spy with my little eye something that starts with D."

Gabby scanned the crowd as the object of her affection spotted her simultaneously. He waved for them to join him. Kinsley linked Gabby's arm and urged her forward. "Come on, lover girl. Your man is waiting. Maybe we can talk him into buying us lunch."

***

As they lunched with Dean and his crew, which included Kenny Cooper and his new puppy Cash, Kinsley traveled every conversational avenue in an attempt to draw McCormick into divulging even the smallest tidbit of information, but the man was as sharp as they came. He wouldn't be tricked into revealing anything he wasn't of a mind to share.

Kinsley accepted her free lunch with a side of defeat and accompanied Gabby back to work, where she left her friend to her tasks.

The crowd at the courthouse had thinned. She scanned the area in search of Thomas before calling his phone again to no avail. It wasn't like him to shirk his duties; he'd never been out of contact for so long.

Kinsley got in her car and called Lincoln, only to reach his voicemail. Her stomach churned as his name faded from her phone screen. Scrolling through her contacts, she found just the man who could help. She pressed the call button and prayed Butch would answer.

CHAPTER FORTY-ONE

Trial By Fire

As Lincoln approached his turnoff, he waved to a female in an oncoming car and admired the antique Cadillac she was driving. Its black, mirror finish reflected the barbed wire-laced land that surrounded it. Stopping on the road, he took a second look in his rearview. A person didn't see a 1958 Caddy in pristine condition every day. Then he remembered that this wasn't every day; there was a car show in town.

The sheriff returned to the business of finding his wayward son. The long, dirt driveway that led toward Faulkner's homestead was riddled with potholes, and he maneuvered around as many of them as he could, while tapping his fingers to Patsy Cline's silky voice coming from his vehicle's speakers. He rounded a bend lined by monstrous red oak trees and caught sight of his pickup, flanked by a sky-blue Audi, both parked in front of Faulkner's house. Lincoln eased his vehicle to a stop and hopped out.

A stiff wind was whistling down a corridor between a windbreak of evergreen trees and Faulkner's brick ranch-style home, stirring up a pile of dead leaves that had taken shelter under an Adirondack chair at the end of the porch. Adjusting his gun belt to a more comfortable position, Lincoln approached the front door and knocked. As he looked around for any signs of life, a hoot owl called out solemnly from a hidden perch.

He walked the length of the dwelling, peeking in windows to see if anyone was home. Seeing no activity inside, he stepped to the end of the veranda and looked down a dirt path that led to several outbuildings. Exiting the shelter of the porch, Lincoln rested his hands on his hips as he scanned Faulkner's land for a clue to where everyone had gone.

A sudden burst of shouting came from inside the barn, and Thomas's voice in the ruckus had Lincoln sprinting across the dirt lot. As he stepped through an open door into the building, the mossy scent of fresh hay did little to cushion the shock of seeing Crawley sprawled on the ground and Thomas kneeling in front of a pacing Phillip Faulkner, who was holding a rifle.

Lincoln's senses sharpened, and he pulled his sidearm from its holster. "Put the gun down, Phillip."

"Dad!" Thomas scrambled to his feet.

Startled, Phillip whipped around and fired. The bullet whizzed past Lincoln's head and sent chunks of wood into the air as it hit the wall behind him. The sheriff winced as the dry shards of shrapnel tore through his shirt and peppered his side and back.

"Thomas, get down!" he barked before addressing Faulkner. "I don't want to shoot ya, Phillip, but I will. Lay your weapon on the ground."

"I cain't," Phillip responded.

While Lincoln held Faulkner in his gun sight, he heard Butch calling from outside. Cold gripped his soul as Phillip's aim swung wildly toward Thomas, and then centered on the open barn door.

With his back to the wall, Lincoln skirted the edge of the open space, "Talk to me, Phillip." Faulkner shook his head slightly as his rifle veered toward the sheriff. "You let my son and Crawley go, and we can discuss what's goin' on."

Phillip's eyes flicked toward his hostages before returning to his most significant threat.

When Lincoln reached the rear of the barn the boy was forced to turn his back on his captives to keep the gun trained on him. "I'm a bigger prize than either of them. You've got my attention." He jerked his head toward the door. "Go on, Thomas. Take Crawley with ya."

Phillip whipped his gun toward the fleeing pair.

"Talk to me, Phillip," Lincoln said, pulling the shooter's attention back to him. "What is it ya want?"

A tear squeezed out the inner corner of Phillip's eye and ran down his nose. He dashed it away with the back of his hand. "Ya cain't help me. It's gone too far."

"Nothin' is as bad as all this," Lincoln assured him. Over the boy's shoulder, he could see Butch framed in the doorway with his sidearm drawn. He exchanged a quick look with his undersheriff.

"I don't want to shoot ya, and I don't think you want to kill me, Phil," the sheriff went on. "You're Thomas's friend and mine. We can work out whatever is botherin' ya." As he spoke, he felt blood trickling down his side and back.

Faulkner stared down the barrel of his rifle. Lincoln caught the flicker of a final decision being made in the young man's eyes an instant before he heard the shot.

CHAPTER FORTY-TWO

Don't Mess With The Bull

With the multitude of voters coming to and going from the courthouse, Gabby was unable to concentrate. Add to that a note Amos had passed to her by way of the lumber-yard owner while she and Kinsley were lunching, which gave the location of the people they sought, and her focus was shot. She'd sent Dean a text, and his reply let her know that their plan to rid the settlement of its unwanted guests was back on.

Gabby watched from her office until Kinsley had driven away before she begged off work for the rest of the day and left to meet Dean and his crew.

Classic rock and cigarette smoke boiled out onto Main Street when Dean opened the door to Pete's Tavern. His men and Gabby stepped inside. As her eyes adjusted to the neon-lit interior, she scanned the stools at the bar filled with familiar faces. Most of the action was happening at the back of the establishment, where a group of young Mexican males were shouting boisterously to one another across pool tables while others dirty-danced with scantily clad women.

A member of the rowdy group downed his beer and spiked his glass mug, smashing it on the establishment's concrete flooring, which drew hoots of laughter from the other members of their crowd.

Dean ushered Gabby to a single empty stool at the end of the bar. "Stay here. If everything goes sideways, run." She nodded as a lump in her throat threatened to choke her.

Acknowledging the bartender with a nod, Dean stepped into the fold of his men, and they advanced toward the back of the bar. "Who's in charge here?" he asked loudly.

In response, a string of Spanish expletives was thrown his way, but he would not be dismissed that easily. "We've heard you're leaving town today. We're here to show you the way."

"We ain't leavin', *pendejo*!" One of the men, soaked in the ignorance of youth, cut away from the collective and swaggered up to the bikers.

Dean stood his ground. "You're mistaken. You *are* leaving, and you won't be coming back."

"Who's gonna make us?" the man hissed as his friends gathered behind him.

"I hoped you'd see the light and leave with your teeth intact, but we're happy to help you make the right decision." Dean's lips peeled back into a sinister smile. The motorcycle club members fanned out on both sides of him.

McCormick watched calmly as the young man facing him slid his hand around his waist to his back. "Don't pull that gun. You won't win this fight. The people at the settlement want you out, and I am here to ensure that happens. You are leaving Harlow. How much blood you lose on the way is up to you. Make the smart choice."

The young man assessed the bikers who had unholstered their weapons and were holding them low.

"*Cabrón!*" he shouted. He put his hands out to his sides to show that he was not holding a weapon.

"Call me what you like. It's time to go," Dean returned.

"Ya heard the man. We've had enough of y'all's shit!" A new voice entered the conversation, and all heads turned to see who it was. The bartender, whom Dean had acknowledged when they'd entered the bar, was holding a shotgun loosely in one hand. "You've been comin' in here an' bustin' up my place fer long enough."

Faced with an overwhelming show of force, the leader bowed his head. "We'll get our stuff an' leave tomorrow."

"José! Shoot him!" came a shout from someone within the group, followed by a chorus of approving grunts from his *amigos*.

"José," Dean said coolly, "your friend is stupid, and he will get you killed. You'll leave today."

"We have to get our stuff," José whined.

"You'll buy new stuff. Are you going to take the hard road?" Dean stepped closer so that the boy had to crane his neck to see his face.

José took a giant step back and everyone behind him did the same.

"Give me your guns," Dean demanded.

"*Pinche cabrón!*"

"Indeed. Hand them over, and let's get you back on the road to wherever you came from."

***

Gabby ran to her front door when she heard the rumble of Dean's motorcycle. As he pulled into her drive, she stepped out and waited for him on the stoop. "That took longer than I thought it would," she said as they entered her house together.

"We had to gather the rest of their crew from the party on Main Street before we could send them on their way. It took us a while to find them all. We followed them until they left Oklahoma and headed south into Texas." Dean tossed his bag on her couch and pulled Gabby into his arms. "Shower with me before this bash?"

She grinned. "Aren't you even the least bit upset by what happened in the bar?"

"It went much better than I'd imagined. The bartender—correction, owner—joining in was a perk. He said he would call in the incident once we were gone and turn the weapons we collected over to the police. He agreed to leave our club out of his story. The generous tip I left might have helped." Dean winked.

"Everyone in the bar was so shocked that no one moved an inch," Gabby observed.

Releasing her, Dean retrieved his bag. "They were punk kids, not much of a gang. Don't get me wrong, I'm relieved they gave up so easily."

"You're just a big bad biker," Gabby purred as she smoothed her hands over his leather clad chest.

He grinned and took her hand to lead her to the bathroom. "Come on, gorgeous. I have something big to show you."

Gabby followed him down the hall. For the first time since the day she'd seen the sketch of Jacob Miller, she felt the tension drain away. Now that the problem at the settlement was resolved, she would never have to tell Kinsley anything, and Lincoln would quit asking questions. The uneventful day-to-day of living could return.

CHAPTER FORTY-THREE

A Price To Pay

Kinsley cursed under her breath when the doorbell rang and sent the tinkling sounds of 'Für Elise' echoing down the hall to the bathroom where she was hurrying to get ready. Her afternoon had been an endless stream of visitors dropping off celebratory food offerings for Lincoln because, so far, the election was tipping toward an overwhelming victory in his favor.

She quickly finished her final application of mascara and jammed the wand back into the container before tossing it into her makeup bag. "Good Lord," she grumbled as she rushed through the house to answer the door.

Her phone rang as she reached for the knob. Fumbling it from her back pocket, she pulled open the door. The call number set an uneasy tone as her eyes met those of the last person she expected to see: Casey No-Last-Name was standing on the other side of the screen door.

Kinsley smiled as she pushed open the barrier and both women looked at the phone in Kinsley's hand as it rang for a second time. "I'm sorry. Just one second. Hi, Butch. Did you find them?" As she listened, her smile faded. "I'll be right there."

Panicked, she reached out and squeezed the hand of her unexpected visitor. "Lincoln and my son are at the hospital. I have to go!"

"Oh, God, no!" Casey uttered.

Kinsley ran into the house, grabbed her purse and keys from the dining-room table, and sprinted for the door. "I don't know what's happened. Do you want to come?"

"No, no," Casey responded hurriedly as she backed toward the porch steps.

"I'm so sorry, Casey. Please come by again!" Kinsley shouted over her shoulder as she reached her SUV.

Kinsley hopped in and peeled out of the drive. Looking in her rearview mirror, she saw Casey still watching from where she'd stopped on the sidewalk. She could guess how much courage it had taken her new friend to reach out, only to be turned away so abruptly, and that knowledge caused a hefty dose of guilt. Surely, the woman would understand and try again.

***

Lincoln squeezed one eye shut as another stitch went in. "Damn, Doc. Dig in there, why don't ya?"

"If you'd let me give you a shot, this wouldn't hurt," Dr. LaRay chided.

Thomas was watching the operation intently. "That old barn got ya good."

"Coulda been worse. At least Faulkner was such a bad shot he missed me both times." Lincoln looked down at his side. "It screwed up that tattoo over my ribs. Kins won't be happy. She loves that snake."

"You two are so weird," Thomas snickered.

His father winked, then winced as the doctor continued to close his wound. "Any news on the Faulkner boy, Doc?"

"Quit breathing so deeply. I'm trying not to mess up your snake so your sweet lady will keep bringing me apple pies," LaRay replied. "I heard Faulkner was released into Butch's custody. You barely scratched the outside of his shoulder. He has fewer stitches than you."

"That's good news." Lincoln relaxed on the hospital table with his hand behind his head and began fitting together the pieces of what had happened in Faulkner's barn.

Phillip Faulkner had undoubtedly gone off the rails today, but his confession that he had murdered Jacob Miller had topped it all—and stunk of lies. The kid had to be protecting the real killer, but the question was why. Who could be important enough for Phillip to go down for murder?

Kinsley blew into the room, worry etched on her face. She grabbed Thomas and hugged him. He returned her embrace. "We're okay, Kins."

"Thank heavens." She let him go and cast her eye over him. "You're not hurt?"

"Nah. Phil kept apologizing to me. I can't imagine what got into him. He told Dad he killed that Miller guy, but there is no way."

Kinsley took his hand and they stepped to his father's bedside. When Lincoln winced as another stitch went in, she did, too. "What happened here?"

Dr. LaRay smiled at her briefly. "He's fine. I had to dig out some old barnwood, and we'll need to watch for infection, but he'll recover."

"You took five years off my life today. No more of this, Lincoln James."

He laughed lightly. "I'd be okay if this never happened again."

"Your mom and dad called as I was pulling up. They're in town for the post-election party. I sent them to your house. Maybe we should cancel."

"Doc said all is well. Right, Doc?"

"You still have an election to win. You can't die on us now," Dr. LaRay returned.

Lincoln closed his eyes and exhaled. With everything that had happened, he'd forgotten about the election. *If I lose to Crawley, that would be the crap cherry to top off this shit day*, he thought.

CHAPTER FORTY-FOUR

The Hero Rides Away

Lincoln climbed painfully out of his pickup and approached headquarters. As he stepped inside, the look of horror on Charlene's face gave him back his grin.

"Oh my God, Lincoln!" she exclaimed as she rushed through the secure door and held it open, extending a hand to help him. "What in the world are you doin' here? It's only been a few hours. You should be at home."

To avoid what felt like shards of glass ripping through his side and back where the doctor had stitched him together, Lincoln kept his laughter light. "Aw, it ain't as bad as all that." He squeezed her fingers as he passed, then placed his hand on a wall to take a breather.

Charlene put a fist to her hip. "Does Kinsley know you're here?"

With a jerk of his head, he indicated his entourage who were approaching the building. Charlene abandoned her boss and rushed to greet Lincoln's parents. "Connie and Dale, I'm so happy to see you." She ushered them into the front office.

Dale James balanced several pizza boxes on the palm of one hand while he pulled the peppery redhead in for a hug with the other arm. "We came up for the election party and found our son shot, but he just had to get back to work. You know how he is."

Charlene glanced at her boss, and he grinned sheepishly. "Y'all set up at that table in the kitchenette, and I'll help this nut back to his office," she ordered.

Lincoln made it to his office and exhaled heavily as he relaxed in his chair. Charlene was close behind him. "Now you stay put. Tell me if you need anything, and I'll get it for you. I'll call Doc LaRay to see if there are any prescriptions or special instructions. If there are, I'll send Dixon to get them."

Lincoln gave an impish smile as Charlene fussed over him. "I like this treatment."

"Don't get used to it," she grumbled, moving around the office to retrieve scattered files and bring them to him. "Here is everything Butch has gathered so far, Phillip Faulkner's confession and interview notes. What else do you need?"

"This is a good start." He flipped open the top folder and skimmed Faulkner's signed confession to the murder of Jacob Miller. "Thank you, Charlene."

She busied herself stacking some random papers. "Just so ya know, if you go and get yourself shot again, I'm quitting. You scared the bejesus out of me."

When Lincoln looked up, unshed tears were shining brightly in her eyes. She blinked rapidly to keep them in check. "Technically, I wasn't shot," he said, doing his best to lighten her mood. "The barn got me pretty good, though."

"Just don't do anything that'll kill you," she huffed. "I'll tell Butch you're here."

Lincoln picked up the first file Charlene had gathered and quickly read the interview notes with Faulkner and

Crawley. Then he closed his eyes and laid his head back against the headrest.

According to Phillip, he had murdered Jacob because of some unresolved feud from years ago. What the fight was about wasn't clear; Lincoln suspected that was because Faulkner was making up the story on the fly, and he wasn't very good at it.

Phillip claimed that he'd caught Crawley poking around their barn. When Crawley started questioning him about the proximity of their farm to the murder scene, Phillip thought the man had some authority and was there to arrest him, and things got out of hand. Thomas was just in the wrong place at the wrong time.

Crawley's statement outlined where his mistakes had played into the events of the day. Needing tools to fix a faucet at his residence, Trenton had helped himself to Faulkner's setup in the barn, and Phillip had discovered him raiding their tools. When Crawley had asked questions about Jacob Miller's murder that were none of his business to be asking, Phillip had started a fight that escalated into Trenton pulling a pistol. In return, the boy threw a punch that landed, and retrieved a rifle to defend himself. Crawley had walked away with a broken nose—but it could have been much worse.

Lincoln opened his eyes when he heard Charlene's soft footsteps approaching. She deposited a fresh mug of coffee on his desk. "What's your take on this confession?" he queried.

She shrugged. "I'm no detective."

"You're one of the best detectives I know," Lincoln returned. "Your gut feeling."

"It seems like a load of bull," she stated. "The way Phillip talked about Miller—at least, what I heard when he was talkin' to Butch—it was like he had never actually met the man."

Lincoln soaked up Charlene's take on the situation as she continued. "But why would he confess to a murder he didn't do? He's not a stupid boy." She shook her head. "I heard Butch tell Phillip not to sign that paper, that he would go to prison if he did. But he seemed determined to throw his life away."

"Love, loathin', or loot. We'll know the answer if we can determine which one it is." Lincoln grunted as he sat forward to pick up his coffee cup.

"That's a pretty short list. Why just those?" Charlene asked.

"Generally speakin' the motive for murder is usually on that list. In this particular case, I'd say the reason for Phil's false confession fits in there somewhere." Lincoln raised his mug toward her. "Thanks for the coffee."

"Knowing what I know about Miller, I'll bet it's loathing. Everyone I've talked to thought he was a jerk." The phone rang, cutting their conversation short. "Oops! Gotta go." Charlene hurried out to the front office.

The sheriff returned to the paperwork. Phillip would certainly be locked up for what he'd done, but if they found that the boy had actually murdered Jacob Miller, Lincoln would eat his hat.

"How are you doing?" Kinsley asked as she came into his office and stopped beside him.

Lincoln addressed the worry she couldn't hide. "I can't just sit around doin' nothin' when we're so close to solvin' this murder."

Kinsley shook her head, and a smile peeked at the corner of her lips. "I know. I assume Phillip has given reasons for this insanity?"

Lincoln shifted in his chair and bit back a groan. "His confession says he did it because he hated Miller, but somethin' doesn't sit right. He doesn't give any valid reason for hating the man."

Kinsley chewed her bottom lip. "What's on your mind?" Lincoln asked.

"I'm trying to remember anything Thomas or Phillip said when I was around." She frowned. "Other than the remark about strangers being on their land since the murder, Phillip wasn't much of a talker. I didn't get any weird vibe that he might be dangerous, and my bad-guy detector is pretty good."

Lincoln tapped the file that held Phillips' confession with his index finger. "The kid volunteered the whole story to me while we were at the farm and again when Butch interviewed him here. We thought he might be loopy after I shot him, even though it was only a scratch, but the doctor assured us that neither the shock of being shot nor local anesthesia would make someone delusional enough to make up a story about committin' murder. All I'm saying is that the statement wasn't coerced in any way. If anything, he's been given every chance to back out. He has to be protectin' someone—but who?"

"Maybe you should talk to Thomas. He might know who is important to Phillip. They're pretty close." Kinsley placed her hands on the arms of his chair, and leaned in. "Good job not killing the kid."

He cupped her jaw and pulled her in for a kiss.

"Oh—uh—uh, sorry." Butch stammered as he stopped in the doorway.

Kinsley laughed and turned her head toward him. "Hi, Butch." She stood up and laid a hand on Lincoln's shoulder. "I was just leaving, but this guy is on restriction. No going out on investigations. I don't want him talking you into anything that will get you in hot water with me."

"Yes, Ma'am." Butch grinned.

Kinsley gazed down at Lincoln and rolled her eyes when she saw his rascally smile. "You be good. I'll take your family home and get them settled, and we'll see you in a few hours, if not sooner. Don't forget the party at Darren and Frank's tonight."

"I'll be home soon. Promise," Lincoln replied.

Kinsley patted his arm before she headed for the door. "You're a complete mess, Sheriff James."

Butch pulled out a chair at the small round table near Lincoln's desk and took up residence. "Damn, am I ever glad you're okay. You sure were cool while Phillip had you in his sights. I was more than a little nervous."

"Thanks for backin' me up. I've been in similar fixes before. And no matter how it looked, I didn't welcome the idea of gettin' shot."

They fell into quiet contemplation for a moment before Lincoln said, "Where are we on this confession?"

"We're nowhere." Butch bent forward and rested his forearms on his thighs. "You don't have to tell me Phillip is lyin' to us. I tried more than once to talk him out of signing that paper. His parents sent a lawyer in, and he tried to tell Phillip, too. But the kid just won't listen, and I can't figure out who could be worth life in the penitentiary."

"His brother?"

"Nope. I thought that, too, but his parents told me Phillip's brother was in Manhattan when Miller was killed. He's at K-State taking summer classes—gonna be a veterinarian. I called up there and got his class schedule for the time frame. I'll follow up, but I have no reason to doubt it'll clear him. From what I understand, he's been gone a few years and doesn't come back to Harlow except for holidays. He and Phillip aren't close."

Butch cleared his throat. "Mr. and Mrs. Faulkner have alibis that I'm certain will check out. They were on a cruise ship headed to Jamaica for their wedding anniversary. They were beyond shocked by what was happening with their son."

Lincoln shrugged. "Maybe he did it, and we're lookin' a gift horse in the mouth."

"That would tie up nice and pretty. But when does that ever happen?" Butch groused.

Lincoln rocked back in his chair and studied the whiteboard. "Lotsa folks had every reason to want Miller dead."

Butch's gaze followed his boss's. "And the man we have locked up in back seems to be the only one who had no reason at all."

"Does Phillip have a girlfriend?"

Butch shook his head. "I asked. He said he doesn't."

"Let's take a ride out that way," Lincoln suggested.

"Kinsley said no investigation," the undersheriff warned.

Lincoln grinned. "We aren't investigatin'. We're just lookin'. If we keep it quiet, there won't be any trouble." The painful process of standing scuttled his amusement.

Butch grimaced. "I'm not sure this is such a great idea, Linc. I can go look at whatever you want me to."

"Once I'm up, I'm good," Lincoln wheezed. "What we need to solve this case is out there, I'm sure of it. And I don't want to sit around thinkin' about the election results."

"Oh, you don't have anything to worry about there. I didn't talk to a single person today who voted for Crawley. That no-good so-and-so is on his way out."

"He didn't seem too keen on stayin' around after he got his block knocked off by Faulkner." Lincoln chuckled, then flinched and placed a hand on his injured side. "A stiff wind could blow that kid over. Crawley needs to toughen up."

"As long as he does his toughening up somewhere other than Harlow, I couldn't care less what that snake does," Butch added.

"I second that."

As they left the station and got into Butch's vehicle, Lincoln pondered the possibility of Crawley staying in Harlow if he lost his bid to become sheriff. The man had been nothing but trouble looking for a place to land; add a dash of pissed-off, and that was a pot full of mayhem they didn't need in town.

CHAPTER FORTY-FIVE

Game, Set, Match

Frank shushed those gathered for Lincoln and Gabby's election party as an announcement came over the radio. Ninety percent of the vote had been counted, and Lincoln had secured his position as the primary winner for sheriff of Stevens County.

Lincoln relaxed in his seat and placed his forearms on the picnic table. Bowing his head, he listened to the buzz of the crowd who had chosen him to move forward. He would run without opposition in the general election in November. Suddenly the shadow cast by this race for sheriff retreated.

Kinsley slipped her hand into his. "Congratulations, Sheriff James."

He looked up and smiled at her. "Thank ya. I couldna done it without you."

She perched on the picnic bench beside him. "Are you feeling okay? We can go home. Everyone will understand after the day you've had."

"Gabby's race is close. Shouldn't we stay and support her?" Lincoln asked.

Kinsley searched the gathering until she saw her friend cuddled into the crook of Dean's arm, chatting with a few co-workers. "She'll understand."

People converged on Lincoln to congratulate him,

and he winked at Kinsley before he stood and greeted his supporters.

"Make way, make way!" Frank shouted above the commotion.

As the sea of well-wishers parted, he and Darren presented a large sheet cake with *Congratulations, Sheriff James* written in cursive. Sparklers had been strategically placed to surround an expertly piped gold sheriff's badge that stood out against a field of white frosting.

"You couldn't lose with me behind you, so I ordered the cake early." Frank elbowed the sheriff teasingly as he placed the dessert on the table.

"That's a fact." Lincoln's smile widened. "Thanks for all ya did for me."

Darren pulled out the sparklers, cut the cake, and handed out pieces as Lincoln looked on with a light heart. The people of Harlow still believed in him, and he didn't intend to let them down.

CHAPTER FORTY-SIX

A Bird In The Hand

Gabby stared blankly out the kitchen window of her father's country house as she filled the coffee decanter with water and thought about how quickly life could change. Two weeks ago, she had been in a new relationship and on the political trail; now she was alone and had lost the race to be commissioner by a hair. Unfortunately, close only counted in horseshoes and hand grenades.

Cold water splashed from the overly full carafe onto her hand, bringing her musings to an end. She sat the pot in the sink, dried her hand, and returned to filling her coffee maker. Pressing the power button, Gabby moved around the granite-topped island and stopped at her open laptop. Scanning her updated résumé, she spotted a couple of errors and quickly corrected them.

Her phone began to buzz against the counter. With a smile, Gabby took the call. "Don't you ever sleep?"

Dean's velvety laugh came over the line. "I'd sleep better if you were here wearing me out."

Gabby crossed to the coffee maker and poured the small amount that had already brewed into a mug. "You've only been gone a week. You can't possibly miss me already."

"If I admit to missing you, it will ruin my horrible reputation."

"No one will hear it from me." She quipped. "To what do I owe the pleasure of this early morning call?"

"I emailed you a plane ticket. Come to Cali for a visit. We can go to the beach. You said you've never seen the ocean."

She took a sip of her coffee and gazed out the front window. A deer cautiously entered the yard and stopped to graze on the cultivated grass. "I'd love to see you. You know I would. It's the goodbye that kills me."

"It doesn't have to be goodbye. It could be, 'See you later'," Dean offered.

"A great argument, Mr. McCormick." Gabby had run through many scenarios that involved her visiting California, but each one ended with her in tears on a plane home. "I would if I could." She left it at that before too much was said.

Dean moved the conversation forward. "How is everyone?"

"Mom, Dad, and Kinsley are good. Lincoln is recovering. And Thomas is up to his usual antics."

"Still trying to get you to go out with him?"

"Of course." She smiled, thinking about Thomas and his plot to make her his. "I've been staying at my folk's house in the country. The weirdness at work after I lost the race is beginning to fade." Gabby's mind wandered to her CV. She still had no solid plans, but she was sure that a new life was out there somewhere waiting for her.

"Sounds like everything is settling down. Have you heard from your brother?"

"I got a note a few days ago. All is well. He told me to say hello. You made quite an impression."

Dean laughed. "I tend to leave a mark."

"That you do."

The line went quiet for longer than was comfortable. "I'd better get with it," Gabby said. "I have a list of good-daughter tasks. The church craft bazaar and Kinsley's wedding are coming up soon."

"Uh-huh," Dean rejoined. "If you change your mind about that visit, you'll let me know?"

"I won't change my mind." Gabby didn't want to leave him with any question about her intentions. "I'd never want to leave, and then what would you do?" she joked. Dean's uncomfortable silence had her rushing to fill the void. "It was nice to hear from you," she added.

"Take care of yourself, Gabriella. It was wonderful to hear your voice." Dean's tenderness spanned the distance between them and made her heart squeeze painfully.

"Thanks for calling. Bye, Dean." Gabby ended the call. As she blinked back tears, she focused on the deer that had moved closer to the house. Her father's minivan rolled up and sent the animal bounding away.

"Gabs!" Harold hollered as he came into the living room.

She covered her true feelings with a smile. "Can I get you some coffee?"

Her father moved into the open kitchen and placed a pan on the counter. "Thanks, but I hafta get back. Your mom sent me out with some cinnamon rolls."

"Tell her thanks, and thanks for checking on me." Gabby came around the bar and hugged him.

He held her tightly for a moment before he set her away. "Are you not with Dean because you think it will make me happy?"

She busied herself with straightening up the napkins in a holder on the island. "No. Why?"

"Look, I might have been wrong about him," Harold admitted.

Gabby pivoted to face him. "Where is this coming from?"

He brushed back her hair. "You're so sad since he left. If Dean is the one, be with him, sweetheart. All I want is for you to be happy."

"Oh, Dad," she whispered and stepped into his embrace. "I'm not with Dean because that is how it should be. It's not your fault."

"Good." Harold kissed the top of her head before he released her. "I need to meet some people at the church, so I better skedaddle."

Gabby walked him to the door and waved as he left. She took a deep breath and tried not to think about that plane ticket in her email. There was no future for her and Dean, and dwelling on it wouldn't change a thing.

With a quick text to Kinsley to remind her of their brunch plans, Gabby traipsed through the house toward the shower. It was time to get on with living and leave her dreams of Dean McCormick behind.

CHAPTER FORTY-SEVEN

The Scales Of Justice

Kinsley replied to Gabby's text and got back to work. With the primary election in the bag, and Crawley off to parts unknown, life had returned to its average level of insanity.

She emailed Bill about candidates for his team. Once they'd settled on who to hire, a trip to Kansas City to meet everyone and sign paperwork would be necessary. She looked forward to seeing the expanded office space he'd rented. But until Miller's murder case was officially closed, Kinsley planned to stay put in Harlow.

Phillip had remained true to his original confession. Lincoln, certain the kid was lying, had stalled the trial arraignment as much as possible whilst he and his team kicked over every rock in search of Miller's real killer.

Kinsley opened an email from private investigator Sean Young and read through his findings. It seemed that Dean McCormick was not only well-educated, but he was also well-off financially. His parents had been real-estate developers in California, and Dean had inherited their empire when they had perished in a car accident. He was a baller in biker's clothing; Gabby had landed herself quite a catch.

Footsteps on the porch drew her attention. She looked up to see who it was, but the filmy curtains didn't allow for a clear view. Gabby was the only person on her list today, and it was much too early to be her.

Kinsley locked her computer and ran for the front of the house before whoever it was woke Thomas by ringing the bell. Whipping open the door, she was so stunned by her visitor that it took her a moment to recover. "Casey. What a surprise."

The girl glanced back over her shoulder. "Are ya here alone?"

Kinsley let the door partially close as a streak of fear prickled over her skin at the unusual question. "No," she said as she scanned her unexpected guest for signs of a threat. Kinsley felt guilty for being suspicious, but she'd ignored her gut instinct before and paid a hefty price.

Casey shifted uncomfortably. "I mean, is the sheriff here? I want ta talk ta ya without him."

Kinsley wasn't convinced that was the reason. "Thomas is home. Why don't we sit on the porch, and I'll get us something to drink."

Casey nodded as she looked at the porch swing and rockers. "I didn't mean ta scare ya."

"It's okay. I'm easily spooked." Kinsley took a deep breath and smiled reassuringly as she let it out. "What would you like to drink?"

"Nothin'. I don't have too long," Casey said as she started toward the seating area at the other end of the veranda.

Kinsley stepped out and let the door shut behind her; she feared the girl would disappear for good if she did not engage her this time. As they sat side by side, Casey gripped the arms of her chair and slowly rocked while they watched children playing in the churchyard on the other side of Main Street.

A shiny antique Cadillac was parked in front of the house. "Is that your car?" Kinsley asked.

Casey studied the vehicle. "It belonged to a happy girl I used ta know, but she's gone now."

Kinsley puzzled over the curious answer for a moment. "What can I do for you?"

"Have ya seen Phil? Is he doin' okay?"

"I haven't seen him, but I hear his shoulder is healing well," Kinsley replied.

"Good." Casey closed her eyes as she continued to rock.

Kinsley watched as a tear squeezed from between the girl's lashes and streaked down her cheek. "You can tell me anything. Let it go, and we'll deal with whatever it is."

Casey pressed her lips into a thin line and forced back a sob.

"Do you know something about Phillip and the murder?"

The girl nodded.

Kinsley took her hand and held it while she waited for more information. When it didn't come, she fed the fire. "My friend Gabby was promised to Jacob Miller before she left the settlement years ago." Casey's eyes went wide. "She told us how cruel he could be. I wouldn't be surprised if he did something awful to Phillip."

Casey looked down at her lap. "Phil and I had a thang for a long while when we were in high school. He still loves me."

Unsure what to say, Kinsley rubbed the girl's arm.

"He was good ta me." Casey dashed away another tear with her free hand.

"Is Phillip the father of your baby?"

Her hand fell to her slightly protruding belly. "Naw. He woulda been a good 'un."

"I'll do all I can to help. Please tell me what you need." Kinsley wondered what this testimonial about the man who'd shot at Lincoln had to do with Casey, and she searched the girl's face for a clue.

Casey squeezed Kinsley's hand and let go. Her voice was nearly a whisper. "My name ain't Casey, it's Sara Peterson. Phil's protectin' me."

"Protecting you from who?"

The girl straightened in her chair and met Kinsley's questioning gaze. Her mouth opened and then slammed shut.

"Casey—I mean Sara—Lincoln will keep you safe. I promise. Who is Phillip protecting you from?"

Something sorrowful passed over Sara's face as she swallowed hard and said, "Ya need ta take me ta the cops. I killed Jacob Miller."

CHAPTER FORTY-EIGHT

Ties That Bind

Kinsley texted Gabby and begged for a rain check, promising she would explain later. Picking up a magazine from a tile-topped end table beside her, she barely noticed the outdated cover. A year ago, she'd sat in this same waiting room while Lincoln gallivanted all over town; here she was, waiting for him again, but under very different circumstances.

Kinsley looked at the woman sitting to her left. "Would you like something to drink?"

Sara shook her head. She had gone silent after her confession. When they'd arrived at the sheriff's office, she'd put her head against the cinderblock wall behind her and closed her eyes.

"Do you want me to contact your parents?" Kinsley asked.

Again, Sara rolled her head back and forth against the wall. "I ain't talked to them in quite a while."

"They must be worried about you."

"They don't care."

"I don't mean to be harsh, but you must consider your child. Someone will need to care for you and your baby. Your mom and dad would surely want to be there for their grandchild, right?" Kinsley was doing her best to impress on Sara the severity of her circumstances.

Sara merely opened her eyes and focused on the stained ceiling tiles above her as she laid her hands on her belly.

Kinsley couldn't let the girl go down without a fight. "You shouldn't say anything without an attorney. I can call one for you."

"They got free ones, right?" Sara asked.

"Lawyers?"

Sara sat forward and nodded.

"If you can't afford an attorney, one will be assigned," Kinsley confirmed.

"I got no money. But I did what I did, so I don't see why I need one."

Kinsley took a deep breath. "Did you kill Jacob by accident?"

Sara studied her fingers that were laced together on her lap. "I left town a while back, but I ran outta money and had ta come home. I couldn't go ta my parents, and Phil was always there for me, but he didn't want me talkin' ta Jacob. Said Miller was no good. I begged him ta help me get Jacob alone so I could tell him about the baby."

Kinsley glanced toward Charlene, who had positioned herself directly behind the speaker hole in the bulletproof glass and was hanging on the girl's every word. "Sara, please let me call an attorney for you. I'm not the person who can help with this."

"I trust ya," Sara replied.

"I appreciate your trust in me, but confessing to murder will put you in prison. You understand that, right?"

"It's done. I cain't take it back." Sara's chest hitched.

Kinsley could see the burden she had carried and cautioned her again, but the advice went unheeded as Sara continued.

"Phil called Jacob and told him he'd won a church raffle. Said he'd meet up ta deliver the prize, but I went instead, and I told him 'bout bein' pregnant." Her chin trembled. "He—" she took a shaky breath "—h-he said I was disgustin', and he punched me in the stomach more'n once." Sara exhaled heavily. "Jacob said a whole lotta things he shouldna said ta the mother of his baby."

Kinsley retrieved a package of tissues from her purse and held it out. "I'm so sorry."

The forlorn girl removed a tissue and dabbed at her wet cheeks. "I thought he loved me."

Kinsley nodded. "Of course, you did. Anyone would."

"When he was laughin' at me as I was layin' there on the ground, I guess I snapped. His pickup was runnin', and I got up and—" she paused as a haunted look crept into her eyes. "I got in his pickup and ran into him with it. It weren't no accident, I wanted him ta hurt like I hurt. But I didn't mean ta kill 'im. He fell and hit a rock—" Sara's head drooped, and she covered her face with her hands as her shoulders shook with the depth of her sorrow.

Kinsley comforted her as best she could. She had lived with an inordinate amount of rage and hurt for a long time, and she understood how it could push a person to the very edge of sanity. Until she had been attacked the previous year, Kinsley couldn't have imagined taking a life, but shooting her attacker had affected her profoundly. No one really knew what they would do until they were chest-deep in a horrible situation, and it was not her place to judge Sara's actions.

The outside door opened, and Lincoln strode in with Butch on his heels. Sara's head whipped up, she took Kinsley's hand and held on.

"You need an attorney to represent you," Kinsley advised again. "Please don't say anything until you have one."

Sara's eyes flicked between her and Lincoln. "I'm scared."

"I know, and I'm sorry for that." Kinsley squeezed her hand tightly before she let her go with the officers.

***

Sara slipped into a chair in an interrogation room and bowed her head while the sheriff and Butch readied their recording equipment. Butch pressed a record button on a remote for the video camera and went to check that it was working.

Lincoln sat opposite the girl and watched her. His heart went out, but he had to do his job. "Sara, can I have someone call your parents? I know they'd want to see ya."

She shook her head.

Butch came back in and gave a thumbs up to indicate the equipment was rolling.

"I'm going to read you your Miranda rights before we start." Lincoln recited the lines as he'd done more times than he could remember, knowing that this particular instance would stick in his memory. "Do you understand everything I've said?" Sara nodded without looking up. "I'm sorry, but ya have to answer yes or no for the record."

"Yes. I understand," she sniffed.

"Do you want an attorney?" Lincoln asked.

Sara raised her head and looked first at Butch, who was standing near the door, and then at Lincoln. "What good would it do?"

"They can help ya. You need a defense."

"I did it. That's all there is to it."

Lincoln pulled a pen from his shirt pocket and slid a legal pad front and center. He took down highlights as Sara told them every gory detail of the beatings and sex orgies that Jacob Miller had subjected her to before she'd run away. Her story ended with the night of his murder on a deserted country road near Weatherby's farm.

"Nobody helped me. I killed him myself." Sara searched the sheriff's face. "Ya can let Phil go now, right?"

"How did you get him in that house by yourself?"

She broke eye contact, looked down at her hands and began picking at her nails.

"Where is the gun you used to shoot him?" Lincoln asked.

Sara raised her head and frowned. "I told ya I ran over him. I didn't shoot him."

"Someone shot him and did a whole lot of other things to him." Lincoln pushed a photo of Miller's deceased body across the table. "If it wasn't you, who was it?"

The girl broke down and laid her head on the back of her hands while she sobbed. Lincoln placed his clean white handkerchief on the table at her elbow, then turned to Butch. "Have one of the guys bring her somethin' to eat, please. She needs a break." He turned back and watched her for a moment. "Sara, we'll find out who helped ya. Not tellin' me is only delayin' the inevitable."

She shook her head and clammed up; even dinner didn't loosen her tongue. Lincoln was left with no choice but to end their interview and process her for lockup.

***

Butch met Lincoln in his office after they had settled Sara Peterson in a cell. "Holy shit, that Miller was some piece of work, wasn't he?" He took a seat next to Lincoln at the small conference table.

"You said it," Lincoln returned as he read through his notes. "He destroyed a lot of lives directly and indirectly—Phillip's, Sara's, and countless others." He handed over the paperwork.

The undersheriff whistled low as he read through Lincoln's notes. "I can't believe she hit him with his own pickup."

"Yeah, his tirade and beatin' were more than she could take, but that is quite somethin'. I've been mighty mad, but to run someone down is a whole other level of anger. I feel for the poor girl."

Lincoln ran his hand over his face. "Sara's missin' person's case is still open. I know she doesn't want her parents informed, but they'll find out one way or another. They're good people. I'd best go see 'em. It would be better coming from me than to read it in the newspaper."

"I'll go visit with the Faulkners," Butch offered. "It would be nearly impossible for Sara to have been stayin' in their mother-in-law's house without them knowin'."

"I doubt they'll admit to it, even if they saw her," Lincoln countered. "But it never hurts to poke around.

While you're at it, stop by Weatherby's place and question their son, Greg."

"What am I asking him?" Butch's eyebrows raised a notch.

"A while back I was out there lookin' around the crime scene to make sure we didn't miss anything. I saw who I now know was Sara walkin' through Weatherby's cornfield. When I asked Greg about havin' a sister, he acted odd and took off. I'm sure he knew Sara was stayin' at the Faulkners'. What else he knows I can't say, but let's find out."

Butch shook his head. "There are so many movin' parts to this one, Linc. How deep does it go?"

"Deep. Someone helped Sara stage that body, and she's never gonna tell us who. Faulkner was involved, but I know there is more. We'll have to dig up the evidence ourselves."

Lincoln wondered what Thomas knew. His son had spent quite a bit of time at the Faulkners' lately. "We'd better make a list of Phillip's friends and bring 'em in. Put Thomas on there. I don't believe he was involved, but he could have helpful information."

"Will do." Butch flipped to a clean sheet and began to write as Lincoln rattled off every friend of his son's he could remember.

The sheriff rubbed his eyes as he listened to the radio from the dispatcher's desk and the rhythmic scratching of Butch's pen against the paper. They had a way to go until this case was wrapped up.

"Ya know, we still have that biker rally goin' on," Butch added.

"Nope, we don't. The bikers left."

Butch stopped writing and looked up. "They just up and left? Nothing else happened?"

Lincoln nodded. "Not as far as any of us can tell. Most of them headed out after the election. McCormick and Gabby shacked up for a week at the farm before he went on his way."

"Hum," Butch replied. "Odd, ain't it? That they would just leave like that?"

"Not a day went by that one of us wasn't watchin' the settlement or Chambers' place," Lincoln pointed out. "It was about as borin' as watchin' paint dry. They never did anything we could catch 'em at."

"Maybe they were just here for a visit, like they said."

"Wouldn't that be somethin'?" A crooked grin bloomed across the sheriff's lips.

"It would." Butch snorted. "Sara said she hit Jacob with his pickup. Do we know where to start lookin' for it?"

"I'm pretty sure it's sittin' in the city impound lot."

"How do you know that?"

Lincoln inhaled deeply through his nose, then let the breath out as he thought about that pickup. "Because I had it towed there when I found it abandoned on the side of the road a while back. The title came back salvaged, but I'd be willin' ta bet it's his. We'll need to call in a forensics team to go over it with a fine-toothed comb. It's pretty beat up from one end to the other."

Butch nodded while making a note.

"I'll stop by city hall tomorrow, and the chief can let me in the lot." Lincoln rose slowly. "It's about quittin' time. I'm gonna catch Gabby at the courthouse before she gets too far. Maybe she'll tell me what Dean and his crew were really doin' here—but I'm not gonna hold my breath that will happen."

***

Lincoln's trip to the courthouse was a bust: Gabby had called in sick. Since word traveled faster than a wildfire in dry brush, heading out to the Petersons' farm to speak with them about Sara could not wait.

CHAPTER FORTY-NINE

The Messenger

A silvery-green backdrop of cottonwood trees showcased Peterson's pristine farmstead. Lincoln rolled to a stop at the top of their circle drive and shut off his pickup. As he looked out across the property, a collie rounded one corner of their house and raised an alert.

He got out and stooped to pet the pup before he navigated three steps to a concrete porch deck and knocked loudly on the front door. A steady thump of a hammer hitting wood drew his attention; when no one answered his summons, he went to investigate.

The source of the noise was coming from horse stables several hundred feet from the house. He trekked across the hard-packed earth and approached a set of open doors. Hunter Peterson was inside working on a stall. When he saw Lincoln, the rancher put down his tools and crossed the space to greet him. "Sheriff James, it's been forever since we've seen ya."

"It has, it has." Lincoln looked around the swanky stable while enjoying the butterscotch scent of fresh-cut yellow pine. "This is quite a place ya got here. Your horses are livin' the high life."

Peterson chuckled. "That they do. What can I do for ya, Sheriff?"

"Is your wife around? I'd like to talk to you both, if I

may." Lincoln tiptoed around the subject of his visit.

"Penny is up at the house." Peterson brushed wood shavings from his jeans. "Let's head up there and see if she has somethin' for us to drink."

Lincoln followed his lead as he thought about the best way to convey the information that he had to share with them.

They entered through a back door and stopped in the mud room. Hunter notched his heel in a boot jack, pulled off one and then the other boot, and set them neatly on a waterproof rug. "Sorry to insist, but my wife will lose her mind if we track through her house," he said, glancing down at Lincoln's feet.

"I get it. Kinsley's the same." Lincoln removed his boots and left them behind as they moved through a laundry room into a kitchen/dining-room combination.

"Penny, where are ya?" Hunter called. "The sheriff is here."

From somewhere beyond the kitchen, a boisterous rendition of a country tune about friends and low places was being sung off-key. "Shit, she's cleanin' the bathroom with her earbuds in. I'll go get her. Please, have a seat at the table." Hunter rushed down the hall and out of sight.

Lincoln wandered over to an antique sideboard at the other end of the room and looked at the pictures on display. The Peterson family smiled at him as they swam and opened presents, happy moments from a life they might never know again.

The couple came back into the room with Penny in the lead. "Sheriff James, I'm sorry I'm such a mess." She ran her fingers nervously through her shoulder-length auburn locks.

"Not to worry." Lincoln shook her outstretched hand.

"Can I get you some iced tea?" she asked.

"I'd love some. Thanks."

"Ya don't get out this way much," Hunter said. The question behind his statement was clear.

"You folks are pretty quiet." Lincoln placed his forearms on the table and studied the wood grain top. "I'm sorry to say today isn't a social visit."

Penny placed a tray of ice-filled glasses on the table and poured tea from a pitcher before sinking wordlessly into a chair. Her intense blue gaze made Lincoln squirm.

"It's about Sara," he began.

"You found her?" Penny breathed. She grasped the sheriff's forearm and squeezed. "Please, tell me she's alive."

"She's alive. No worries about that, Ma'am." Lincoln patted her hand. "But I do have some bad news."

Hunter put an arm around his wife's shoulders. "She's alive, that's the most important thing. Where is she? Can we see her?"

Lincoln's mouth had suddenly gone dry. He lifted his glass and took a large gulp before returning it to the table.

"Does she not want to see us?" Penny despaired.

"Mr. and Mrs. Peterson, Sara showed up at the station and confessed to killin' Jacob Miller." Lincoln spelled it out as quickly as he could. "She's in our jail, and you're welcome to come see her. She needs you both."

"What's gonna happen to her?" Hunter asked.

Lincoln studied their family pictures for a moment. "She refused counsel despite our advice. She's confessed, and more 'n' likely she'll be sentenced without a trial." He met their haunted stares and saw the weight of what he was saying sink in. "There's no easy way to say this. She's pregnant."

Penny let out a sob and turned into her husband's arms. Hunter squeezed his wife to him and kissed her head. "We knew she was pregnant when she left. It's Miller's, and we fought with her about him and the baby. We need to see our little girl, no matter what has happened."

Lincoln nodded and started to get up. Penny stretched out her hand to stop him. "Can we save her? Keep her from going to prison?"

"Sara needs an attorney." He squeezed Penny's hand before placing it on the table. "Please come to the station when you're ready." Hunter followed him to the back door and waited while he pulled on his boots. "I'm real sorry I had to tell ya this, Mr. Peterson."

"We appreciate you comin' out to tell us in person, Sheriff James. I know ya didn't hafta do that. We'll come into town shortly."

As he made his way to his pickup, Lincoln cursed life for being so damned hard on good people.

CHAPTER FIFTY

The Other Shoe

A vibrant sunrise washed everything in a tangerine hue as Lincoln pulled his pickup in next to the chain-link fence that surrounded the city impound lot at the edge of town. As far as he could see, the corn fields had traded their emerald leaves for the golden husks of maturity. Harvest crews would be pulling into town in the coming months, and the county fair was just around the corner.

A white police cruiser with a light bar affixed to the top came to a smooth stop at the closed gate. Police Chief Yolanda Bretz climbed out and adjusted her heavy leather gun belt on her slim hips as Lincoln approached. "Damn right, you brought me some breakfast after making me get out so early." She grinned as she accepted a to-go coffee cup topped by a donut.

Lincoln smiled. "You'd never do me another favor if I came empty-handed. How's things goin'?"

"Good, real good. I like it here. I wasn't sure I would when you called and said there was an opening, but dammit, you were right. Diego and the girls love Harlow, too." Yolanda took a monster-size bite of the donut.

"Always nice when the family is happy with a move. When I heard you were getting out of the Navy business, I thought it might be a good fit."

Yolanda swallowed before answering. "Missed me, did ya?" she teased.

Lincoln chuckled. "Ya know that's right. There isn't anyone around here who can outshoot me at the gun range."

"And drink you under the table. Let's not forget that, James," she joked, before shoving the remainder of the donut into her mouth.

"I had a hangover for days after that goin'-away party ya threw for me. I wish I could forget it."

Yolanda cackled as she fished a ring of keys from her front pocket. "Lightweight," she accused, and unlocked the gate. "What are we lookin' for?"

"A seventies' Ford pickup. Faded-out blue and beat ta hell. I had it towed in a while back."

"Yeah, I remember. Something off about it?" Yolanda asked. When Lincoln nodded, she led the way toward the back of the lot. "Hey, speakin' of bein' off, two days ago Pete Blanchette brought in a pillowcase filled with guns."

"Pete from the bar?" Lincoln asked.

"One and the same. Said he ran off a Mexican gang and they surrendered their weapons before he kicked 'em out."

Lincoln stopped short. "'Scared-of-his-own-shadow Pete ran off a Mexican gang?"

Yolanda glanced over her shoulder and saw that she'd left Lincoln behind. She waited as he shook his head and caught up with her. "That's what he said, and he stuck to his story. I didn't buy it either."

"Tell me more." Lincoln was anxious to hear where this tale would lead.

"The gang was frequently in his bar. He said it'd been goin' on for months. They were troublemakers, and he'd had enough."

"When did he take their guns and throw them out?" Lincoln asked.

"The day of the elections."

"Interestin'..." The sheriff scratched his chin then started to chuckle. "He brought a *pillowcase* filled with guns into the police station?"

"Yep. Said he couldn't find anything else to put them in. Some mighty nice pieces in there. And wouldn't ya know it, all the serial numbers are filed off." She gave a conspiratorial wink as they stopped in front of the vehicle they were seeking. "Here we are."

Lincoln had little doubt that this was the pickup that Sara had used to run down Jacob. The homemade diamond-plate push bar welded to the front bumper and the broken grill looked like a match to the marks found on Jacob Miller's body.

"This sure is a popular vehicle," Yolanda observed.

"Whaddya mean?"

"A guy came in askin' about it not too long ago." She tapped her chin thoughtfully. "The officer told me his name. Starts with a P maybe..."

Lincoln walked slowly around the pickup. "I've called in a forensics team to pull prints and evidence. I'm certain this pickup was used in our murder. Please make sure nothing happens to it."

"Jeb Paulson!" Yolanda suddenly shouted, then changed gears upon hearing what Lincoln had said. "Holy shit! Is Paulson the killer? He told my guy that he saw the truck in the lot and wondered if it would come up at auction. I'll station someone out here until you tell me it's all clear."

"Paulson isn't the murderer," Lincoln assured her. "But that is great information." His detective senses tingled. "Bretz, you and I need to talk more often. If ya need one of my guys to help cover the lot, please let me know."

As they strolled back to the entrance, Lincoln thought about the weapons that Pete had dropped off, and the bar owner's name was added to the list of people to question. "I'd like to take a look at those guns Pete turned in," he said.

"Sure," Yolanda replied. "Could one of them be the murder weapon?"

"The victim didn't die of a gunshot, but a gun was used. I'm tryin' to cover all the angles."

Lincoln suddenly remembered the SUV full of young men he'd followed to town not long ago. They had looked more like a group of pals out for a good time than the type of hardened gang members he'd encountered in the past. "Have you ever seen a Mexican gang around here?"

"I haven't, but let me ask my team. Someone might have." Yolanda pulled a pad and pen from her shirt pocket and scribbled down some notes. "We did see those bikers, but they were uncharacteristically mellow. Nothing to report there."

"McCormick and his crew weren't around when Jacob Miller was murdered."

"Damn, but you got a plateful, James."

"That I do. Thank ya for the help. Let me know if I can return the favor."

"Oh, you know I will." Yolanda shot him a toothy grin.

Lincoln loaded up and headed out with what he suspected was the last piece of their puzzle. He called Butch and asked that he meet him at Jeb Paulson's farmstead.

***

Twenty minutes later, the sheriff pulled into Paulson's driveway and watched as the tattered curtains that covered a dirty window swung back into place. Butch parked along the road, hopped out, and approached as Lincoln exited his vehicle. "What's up, Linc?"

"According to Chief Bretz, Paulson has been sneakin' around askin' about the pickup I had towed in."

"The one you think is Miller's?"

"Yep. There's a very good chance we've found our last member of the murder crew. Let's see what he has to say. They know we're here, so look sharp. We don't need another shootin'."

A diesel engine roared to life somewhere beyond the house. Lincoln and Butch ran the length of the building as Paulson came barreling out of his barn on a small tractor and headed across a field.

"We got ourselves a runner!" Lincoln shouted, as he and Butch turned and ran back toward their vehicles. "Let's get him!"

The sheriff tore across a freshly plowed field until he caught up and was keeping pace with Paulson, who had pushed his tractor to its top speed. Pulling ahead, Lincoln turned toward him forcing the farmer to make a choice: hit the sheriff's vehicle, or crash into a thicket growing near the edge of the field. Thankfully, Jeb chose the bushes.

Butch brought his SUV to a rocking halt behind the disabled farm equipment, effectively blocking him in.

The farmer leapt from the tractor and ran. Jumping out of his pickup, Lincoln made quick work of stopping him. "I didn't do nuttin'! I didn't!" Jeb shouted as he wriggled against the sheriff's hold.

"If that were true, ya wouldn't be runnin'," Lincoln puffed.

He and Butch secured Paulson in the back of the undersheriff's SUV. Lincoln stepped back and grimaced as he held his side.

"Ya all right, boss?" Butch asked.

"Them damn stitches." He straightened and took a deep breath. "For a little guy, Jeb sure can run. I'll meet ya back at the office, and we'll see what he has to say."

Butch saluted and crawled into his unit as Lincoln headed for his pickup. If his instincts were right, they would wrap up Miller's case by the end of the day.

CHAPTER FIFTY-ONE

Mercy

In the weeks since Phillip's confession on election day, the mystery surrounding the death of Jacob Miller had been uncovered piece by piece until they finally had the whole picture. Lincoln had released Jacob's body to his family and was relieved to be clearing up the case files that had dominated his office for far too long.

He reached into a box of new tabbed file folders Charlene had left on his desk and plucked one out. He laid it on the blotter in front of him and labeled it Paulson, Jeb. Picking up Jeb's signed confession, he read through it for the last time.

Thirty minutes into his interrogation, Jeb had broken and filled in what they had been missing. He had corroborated Sara's story that she had met with Jacob and subsequently killed him. In a panic, she'd run to Phillip, who had turned to Paulson to help dispose of the evidence of her crime.

With a family tie to Phillip as his cousin, and no love lost for Jacob Miller, Jeb had come up with a plan for staging the body in a gangland-style killing, complete with a torture element that he hoped would throw suspicion on the gang he knew was running things at the settlement. The shot to Miller's forehead, done with Paulson's own gun, was meant to cover a head wound inflicted when the victim had fallen and hit a rock. But it hadn't quite done the job.

The postmortem beating that the coroner had mentioned had come from an unstable Sara, who had flown into a rage as the men were loading Miller into his vehicle to move him. She'd picked up a shovel Jeb had brought along and whaled on Miller's corpse as if she wanted to extract revenge for what he'd put her through.

They had used Weatherby's abandoned property simply because it was adjacent to the murder location. In their haste to clean up what had happened, the secluded property had seemed like an excellent place to set their scene. According to Jeb, the choice had nothing to do with Scott or his family. The full palm print the officers pulled from a wall inside the house belonged to Paulson.

The all-terrain vehicle tracks Lincoln had followed into the brush were made by Phillip's four-wheeler. On the night of the murder, he'd gathered rope and a few essentials from his parents' barn and brought them back using an overgrown path through the field of sweet briar that connected the two farms.

If they had buried Jacob's body somewhere in the miles of sandy ground scattered with yucca plants that surrounded the dirt road where Sara had killed him, there was a good chance they might have gotten away with murder. It was unlikely that the residents at the settlement would have reported Miller's absence, and the inhospitable earth was unsuitable for growing crops. Jacob Miller would have simply disappeared. Thankfully, criminals weren't generally known for their intellect.

When Butch had questioned Greg Weatherby, he had

admitted that he knew Sara was staying with the Faulkner clan. He had kept her presence secret because she'd asked him to, but he knew nothing about what she'd done to Miller.

Thomas said he had met Sara just once when he was visiting with Phillip. Him being new to town, Thomas had no reason to suspect she was anyone other than who Phillip had said: a distant cousin. Kinsley had no idea the woman was lying about her identity because she had never met her before.

Sara Peterson's parents had eventually convinced their daughter to accept legal counsel, and her attorney was going for voluntary manslaughter, claiming the murder was a crime of passion. Sara could serve as little as two-and-a-half years if her defense team were successful. Her child was due in a few months, and her parents planned to take care of the baby until their daughter was released from prison.

While Lincoln agreed that the girl should pay for taking a life, his heart ached for her parents and the child who would be born into such difficulty.

He picked up a baggie that held the raffle stub he had pulled from Miller's shirt pocket on the day of discovery; it had been a very unlucky ticket for Jacob Miller. Lincoln dropped it into a bank box on his desk and closed the murder file. What a convoluted mess this case had turned out to be.

Butch strolled in and settled into a chair in front of Lincoln's desk. "It was mighty nice of you to testify in favor of the Faulkner boy. His parents would like to thank you in person."

Lincoln sighed. "Prison is still prison. Phillip isn't a bad kid, he just got caught up in an awful situation and made some incredibly stupid decisions. He apologized to me time and time again. I feel for him."

"He woulda got a dozen more years if you hadn't spoken up," Butch said. Then he huffed, "Just take the compliment, will ya?"

"Fine," the sheriff chuckled. "Hey, Jeb mentioned criminal activity out at the settlement. Do we know anything about that?"

"Not a peep from those folks out there. I swung by with the warrant you got and looked around, but there was nothing out of the ordinary. Just a bunch of folks livin' a simple life." Butch shrugged. "But Pete Blanchette may know something about it."

Lincoln sat forward. "Oh, yeah? What makes ya think that?"

"The other night in the bar, Pete let it slip to Dixon that the guys he ran off lived at the settlement. He also shut down one of his regulars when the man started talking about the day that gang left town, and how a huge biker had taken care of things."

"Now ain't that somethin'?" Lincoln smirked. "I knew McCormick was here for a reason."

"What can we do about it? It's hearsay."

"There's not a damn thing we can do unless something solid comes up. As far as we know, the bikers kicked 'em out of a bar without anyone getting hurt. There's nothin' illegal about that. Unlawful bouncin' isn't a thing."

Butch chuckled.

"It looks like Dean might have taken care of a problem

we didn't even know we had. I hope it doesn't creep back in. Let's keep a closer eye on things out that way, at least for a while." Lincoln realized that Gabby had been a little slicker than he'd given her credit for. "Anything on the schedule I need to know about?" he continued.

Butch pulled a notepad out of his shirt pocket and flipped it open. "Mrs. Paulson is signing away her rights to Levi. With Jeb going to prison, she has no income and no way to care for herself, much less a kid—not that she has any desire to. You need to give your statement to the judge on Friday."

Lincoln considered how Levi had flourished in Frank and Darren's loving home, and he hoped their plans to adopt the boy formally would come to fruition.

Butch adjusted his ball cap a little lower over his eyes as he fought back a grin. "Hum. Seems we have that thing on Saturday out by the cottonwood tree at Henry's farm."

A big smile lit Lincoln's face. "Yeah, *that* thing. I better not forget."

Butch laughed. "Kinsley'll have your hide if you don't show up to get married."

"I wouldn't miss it for the world. That reminds me, I need to go downtown and pick up my new suit jacket."

"The party after is gonna be quite a do. It's cool that Leon Boss is coming," the undersheriff added.

"He's givin' away the bride, but it was nice of him to offer to play at our reception. I hear the whole town is gonna turn up." Lincoln tapped the bank box on his desk. "I'm glad we solved this—it's a weight off. Thanks for all ya did, Butch."

The undersheriff gave a half-cocked grin. "You were a

man on a mission. I'm glad to back ya up, though."

They went through to the outer office and found Dusty at the helm. "Where'd Charlene go?" Lincoln asked.

"Her, Kins, and Gabby went to Liberal to have a girl's day out before you lock your fiancée down," Dusty relayed.

"There ain't a man in the world who could lock that woman down," Lincoln replied. "I'm headed out to do somethin', even if it's wrong. Call if ya need me."

CHAPTER FIFTY-TWO

Asking For A Friend

As she drove, Kinsley listened to her friends share the latest gossip about newly elected commissioner Josh Layton's sex scandal that had broken just days after his win against Gabby. Apparently, Mr. Layton had a habit of paying for a unique set of preferences when it came to closed-door activities. His dominatrix had spelled out everything in lurid detail to an undercover reporter.

What comes around goes around. One less evil bastard fighting for the crown, Kinsley thought.

Charlene turned sideways in the passenger seat and addressed Gabby, sitting in the back. "Does that mean you'll be appointed commissioner now, Gabs?"

"I assume a new election will have to be held, but I can't see myself running again," Gabby replied.

"You only lost by twenty votes. You'd win if you ran again," Kinsley protested.

The blonde stared out the window at the passing land. "I don't want to be stuck in Harlow forever."

"Ooh! Does this have anything to do with that handsome biker?" Charlene tittered.

"Not in the way you think. He and I—" Gabby paused. "—he and I have gone our separate ways. But being with him made me realize I've spent years waiting for my life to start when I had the power to do whatever I wanted all along."

Charlene raised an eyebrow. "Wow! He musta been somethin'."

"He was," Gabby said softly.

Kinsley looked in the rearview mirror at her friend in the backseat. Gabby had lost that spark of life that had always lit her up from the inside.

They pulled into Liberal, and Kinsley lined out the day ahead. "Okay, ladies, I have a list of last-minute wedding items. When we're done, I've managed to get us a table for lunch at that underground restaurant we've been wanting to try, so no sneaking into The Mercantile and stuffing ourselves with their delicious homemade confections."

Charlene giggled. "You'll have to drag me past that place. Their chocolate turtles are to die for."

"They are delish," Kinsley replied as she navigated the shopping mall's parking lot and found an open space. Her phone dinged; she retrieved it from her purse and responded to a text. "Let's get this party started."

They approached the mall like women on a mission but were soon distracted by a shoe store and then a dress boutique. When they came out of the second store laden with packages, Gabby grinned. "It is amazing how a new pair of shoes can adjust a bad attitude."

"You got that right!" Charlene nodded. "We needed some retail therapy."

Kinsley's phone trilled again. She pulled it from her back pocket and sent another text. "Shoot! It's getting late and we haven't even started on my list." She carefully tore it into three parts. "Divide and conquer. I'll meet you two back at the fountain in center court when we have what we need." Her phone sounded again.

"Dang, girl, you are popular," Gabby teased.

"I have lots of balls in the air," Kinsley replied. "Here we go!"

After Gabby took off like a shot in the direction of a craft store in another wing of the mall, Kinsley grabbed Charlene's arm to hold her back. The redhead threw her a questioning look. "I called Dean a few days ago," Kinsley confessed.

A mischievous smile crept across Charlene's ruby-red lips. "And?"

"He had sent Gabby a plane ticket to come see him, and he was going to ask her to stay in California, but I guess she turned down his offer to fly out. He mistakenly took it as an indication that she wasn't interested—but you and I both know she's been roaming around like a droopy dog since he left."

"Oh God! This is so exciting." Charlene clapped her hands.

"I told him the truth about how she feels." Kinsley smiled sheepishly. "I know it's a bit of a betrayal, but he needed to know, and she was never going to tell him. That's who I've been texting with."

"You're killin' me, Kins. Hurry up and tell me what's happened."

"Ladies." A raspy baritone washed through Kinsley like summer sunshine. They both turned and looked up at a grinning Dean McCormick.

"And he's flown in to surprise her," Kinsley finished.

"Yeah, that'd be hard to miss," Charlene replied sarcastically.

Kinsley crossed her fingers that her idea to straighten out her friend's love life wouldn't go horribly wrong.

CHAPTER FIFTY-THREE

The Last Supper

The sun gave its final hurrah as Kinsley pulled into a parking space at the Glockenspiel restaurant in Guymon, where their wedding rehearsal dinner was being held. She took a deep breath and killed the engine.

"Are you okay, Kins?" Gabby reached across the console and took her hand. "You look beautiful."

"Yeah, I'm good. And thanks. The weight of everything that has gone on lately—and now getting married—is finally hitting me. Marriage is a serious undertaking." She looked through the plate-glass window at her friends and family gathered inside.

"You still want to get married, right?"

"Did I tell you Lincoln's ex-wife came to the house and went on about how close they still are?" Kinsley turned to face Gabby. "You don't think I have to worry about that, do you?"

"Are you serious? No! Lincoln loves you. And you and I both know how he feels about the ex-witch."

"She is a knockout. I'm talking model pretty." Kinsley bowed her head.

"You're gorgeous, too. Besides, we know Jeannie's soul is black as tar. Are you looking for a way out?"

Kinsley gazed again at the people inside the restaurant,

then focused on Lincoln. "No. I love him. I'm just having some last-minute jitters."

"I'm sure that's normal. Is there anything I can do to help?"

Kinsley smiled and pulled Gabby in for a hug. "I'm lucky you're my friend."

"I'm lucky you're my friend, too. Thank you for calling Dean." Gabby squeezed Kinsley tightly.

"I'm so glad you weren't angry. I couldn't stand to see you sad for another day."

"I could never be mad at you. I wouldn't have had the courage to tell him myself. He's asked me to come to California to stay."

"Wow!" Kinsley replied. "I'm so happy for you. But I'll miss you."

Gabby squeezed her hand. "You'll just have to come out for a visit."

"Deal! Lincoln's brother, Grant, lives out there. I'd like to meet him, and I know Lincoln hasn't seen him in years." Kinsley opened her car door. "Let's do this."

***

Lincoln couldn't hide his smile as he looked around the table at the gathering. He was about to embark on a whole new adventure, and he couldn't be more pleased.

"Right, Dad?" Thomas asked.

"What's that? I'm sorry I missed what you said."

"I was tellin' Grandpa that those news reports about Crawley couldn't have come out at a better time. Now you have no competition."

"It was fortunate timin'," Lincoln replied. "I wonder

what possessed our paper to go diggin'. I thought the editor was backin' Trenton."

"With the internet, those articles could be easily found—everything printed in our paper had been in another paper before. Someone probably tipped them off," Gabby offered.

Lincoln's eyes slid to Kinsley, who was busy entertaining his mother. "I guess that's probably it."

Dale put an arm around Thomas. "No matter how it happened, it was fortunate. Not only for you but for the county. That guy was a crook."

"I'm gonna pay the bill for this feast," Lincoln said. He bent and whispered to his fiancée, "Kins, please come with me."

Kinsley looked at him and frowned. "Okay—"

He held out his hand and then led her through the crowded restaurant and out the entrance doors, where they had more privacy. "Did you or someone you know leak those stories about Crawley to the paper?"

She let her eyes roam over his face but didn't answer. "Because ya didn't believe I could beat him on my own merit?"

"I did believe you could win," Kinsley said. "But the town needed to know what he really was, and he was making up things about you. It pissed me off. Everything the paper printed about Crawley was true. I did it to help you, Lincoln."

"Ya had to know I wouldn't approve."

She looked out across the parking lot. "I just wanted to help you."

Lincoln smiled and shook his head. "Woman, I love

you madly, but you exasperate me."

Kinsley nailed him with her slate-gray stare. "Well, you know what? Your dangerous job and your model ex-wife exasperate me, too! I didn't do anything wrong, and I shouldn't be in trouble for trying to help you live the life you want. F-For helping you get the job you deserve. And certainly not the night before we are supposed to get married."

"What happened with my ex-wife?" Her angry outburst had blindsided Lincoln.

"As if you don't know since you two are so *close*," she spat.

Kinsley whipped around and headed back inside, stopping in the restroom to calm herself before rejoining their party. That disagreement was not the confidence builder she needed to convince her that getting married was the right move for them.

CHAPTER FIFTY-FOUR

Done And Dusted

Kinsley lay awake watching the moonlight surge and retreat across her bedroom ceiling as the south wind blew in through the open window and gently moved the curtains. She hadn't slept well.

Her fears about Jeannie and Lincoln were ridiculous. She'd known it even as the words flew out of her mouth, and she had told him as much before they'd left the restaurant.

Lincoln had insisted on riding with her after dinner and had sent Gabby with his parents. On the thirty-minute trip home, he had tried to settle everything, but his assurances had done little to alleviate Kinsley's fears that they might be making a colossal mistake by getting married.

As they'd pulled into her drive, she'd told him they were fine. Lincoln, at Kinsley's insistence, had reluctantly joined his parents and Thomas at his own house because of the silly superstition about not seeing the bride before the wedding. The last thing they needed was bad luck.

What surprised her most was that Lincoln had underestimated her so badly. Surely, he knew that she would never stand by and watch when someone she loved needed help? But he had carefully pointed out that she could alleviate problems by sharing her helpful deeds instead of letting him find out by some other means. Kinsley had to admit he was right, and that her way of helping might need some tweaking.

She swung her legs out of bed. Maizey rose from her place on the floor and padded over to her. "What am I gonna do, sweet girl?" Kinsley said softly to the dog and received an enthusiastic tail thump in response. "Yes, you're right. I should quit sabotaging my own happiness. How did you get so smart?" The pup nuzzled her hand.

After quietly letting the dog outside, Kinsley snuck into the bathroom so she wouldn't wake Leon, who was asleep in her spare room. She showered, dressed in jeans and a flannel shirt, grabbed her keys, and let Maizey back in to watch over the house and their sleeping guest. The farm was the best place for quiet contemplation, and she had until eleven to make up her mind about tying herself to Lincoln for life.

The predawn air blowing in through the vehicle's open windows had the crisp nip of autumn. Once the sun was up, the first glimpse that fall was on its way would be replaced with another scorching late-summer day.

Kinsley parked next to the tailwater pit and shut off the engine. While it was true that she had come a long way from the shut-down woman she had been a year ago, there were still broken parts of her that would likely never heal. It seemed unfair to expect Lincoln to navigate her scars for the rest of his life.

As the sun peeked over the horizon, Kinsley got out of her car and went to sit on the picnic bench. "Grandpa," she said aloud, "I'm supposed to get married today, and I might have hardheaded my way into believing it's a bad idea. I wish you were here to tell me what to do."

***

Lincoln walked into his kitchen and watched his mom scurrying about making breakfast. "Good mornin'," he greeted her. "Anythin' I can do?"

Connie smiled and pointed to a stool. "You can have a seat and relax."

"Where's Dad?"

"Oh, he's taken to sleeping in since retirement. You'd think he was royalty the way he lazes around," his mother joked.

"I am a prince, and you know it," Dale said as he entered the kitchen and pulled up a stool next to Lincoln. "Are you ready to take the leap again, son?"

"To be honest, I'm 'bout as nervous as I've ever been," Lincoln confessed.

Connie stopped in her tracks. "Do you not want to marry Kinsley?" she asked.

"More than ever. But I've been down this road before, and I don't know what I'd do if we don't make it."

Dale put his hand on Lincoln's back. "Kinsley is nothin' like Jeannie, but if you're havin' doubts, now is the time to get out."

Thomas strolled in. "Dad, if you don't marry Kinsley, you are the biggest fool in the world. She's amazing, and she loves you like nobody's business."

Lincoln pulled his son in for a side hug.

"I saw Kinsley leave about thirty minutes ago. She sure is an early bird," Connie remarked.

"Yeah, she runs early in the mornin'," Lincoln replied.

"No, she was dressed, and she left in her car."

"Shit!" Lincoln spat. He pushed off his barstool and snagged his keys from the island. Stunned by the sudden change in his demeanor, everyone stared.

Thomas broke the silence. "What's happened?"

"We had a misunderstandin' last night. I obviously didn't fix it, but I'm gonna. She's not gettin' away from me that easy."

Lincoln jogged across their adjoining yards and up onto Kinsley's porch. He was about to grab the door handle when a voice came from the direction of the rockers. "She ain't here," Leon drawled.

Lincoln turned and rested his hands on his hips. "Do ya know where she is?"

"If I were guessin', I'd say she's at the farm talking to Henry." Leon drank from a mug he was holding. "What goes on between the two of you isn't my business, other than I love and care about her, but being married to Kinsley isn't going to be easy. She's had a hard road, and her stubborn streak is a mile wide."

"I ain't lookin' for easy." A sparkle sequined Lincoln's eyes. He opened the screen door, whistled, and Maizey barreled out to greet him. "Come on, Maizey girl. Let's go get Kinsley." As he moved off the porch, he glanced back at Leon, who was grinning from ear to ear.

Leon rocked back and winked. "Yeah, you got this. I'll see ya at eleven."

CHAPTER FIFTY-FIVE

Every Good Thing

Lincoln pulled Henry's '69 Chevy pickup into an empty spot next to the VFW hall, killed the engine, shut off the lights, and reached across the bench seat to take his wife's hand. The couple peered into the hall through a set of open double doors.

From what little Kinsley could see, the venue was packed. White twinkling lights, gauzy tulle, and hay bales were giving their small-town wedding reception a touch of country class. "It looks like Frank has done it again. He's getting quite a reputation for party planning," she observed.

"Harlow is lucky he and Darren moved to town." Lincoln gently squeezed her hand. "Are ya ready for this?"

Kinsley smiled. "Our wedding came off nicely, didn't it?"

"It couldn't have been more perfect. You look like a dream. I nearly couldn't say my vows for starin' at ya. I'm glad ya decided to see things my way."

"Thank you. You're mighty handsome yourself, and you presented a compelling argument first thing this morning, Sheriff. Bringing our dog with you was a brilliant idea." Kinsley chuckled. "You've signed up for a lifetime with a slightly off-kilter woman who thinks you're about the best thing since sliced bread."

"I'm a lucky man." Lincoln tugged her hand, urging her across the seat toward him, and snuggled her up to his side. They waved to Dean and Gabby as the couple entered the building. "How's that goin'?"

"Who knows how it will shake out, but she's going to California for an extended visit."

"Dusty doin' okay?" Lincoln asked.

"Surprisingly well. He and Gabby had been friends for far too long. The reality of being together wasn't as sweet as the fantasy."

Lincoln opened his door and helped Kinsley out. They clasped hands again before they entered the hall. The music immediately tapered off. "Everyone, Mr. and Mrs. Lincoln James!" Leon announced.

The newlyweds made the rounds to thank people for coming. Once the hubbub of their arrival had died down, the band struck up a slow waltz, and Lincoln convinced Kinsley to join him on the dance floor. "What's on your mind, Mrs. James?" he asked as they moved slowly to the music.

Kinsley looked up at him and the twinkling lights reflected in her eyes. "I was thinking about how irritating you were when we first met."

"Whoa, buyer's remorse so soon?" he teased.

"I wouldn't have had it any other way," Kinsley said as a lopsided grin emerged.

Leon's band put on a stellar show, but after a flurry of two-steps and one Cotton-Eyed Joe line dance, they needed a break.

Kinsley stood aside as their large round table filled. Darren and Frank, with little Levi perched between them, reminded her that not everything Jacob Miller had left behind was evil. That boy was the light of her friends' lives.

Leon, Bill, and Butch were sitting with their heads together in what looked like a Masters of the Universe-style plot. Charlene gave Dean a friendly punch in the arm as he and Gabby laughed at something funny she had said.

On the opposite side of the table, Lincoln had his arm cocked over the back of his chair and was entertaining Thomas and his parents, while Maizey sat at his knee, patiently waiting for someone to drop a morsel of food.

Her focus was drawn to the last empty chair at their table, and she was suddenly overwhelmed with memories of the one person who would have completed their group. Grandpa would have loved to see her get married, but if there was any justice in the universe, he was watching from the great beyond.

"Sweetheart," Lincoln called to her, "why are you standin' there all alone? Come sit with us." He patted the seat next to him.

Kinsley smiled as she realized the vacant chair was hers. Despite Grandpa's absence, her circle was complete.

There is always another story waiting to be told.

ACKNOWLEDGMENTS

As I conclude this second book in the Rhodes series, I am filled with a sense of joy and gratitude. The unexpected return to Harlow, Kansas was made possible by you, dear reader. Your fondness for the town and its inhabitants, and your encouragement to write a follow-up inspired me. Revisiting Lincoln, Kinsley, and their crew was a delight. Thank you for sending me back. I hope the return journey was as enjoyable for you as it was for me.

My books would not be fit for public consumption without the fabulous folks behind the scenes who help me sand and polish the final drafts.

My soul sister Jill Corley, who stepped in again to read the first draft; your insightful feedback and unwavering support were invaluable. Myrna Christensen, my dear friend, bless your proofreading eagle eye and willingness to read for me. Mindy Reed hopped on board with her excellent developmental editing skills. And last, but by no means least, Karen Holmes, an editor of unequaled talent and a grand human being; you chipped away until the final draft sparkled. A simple thank you will never be enough for what each of you have done.

To Catherine, Charlotte, and the terrific team at 2QT Publishing, my gratitude to you for bringing all the individual pieces together to make my dream of publishing a reality again. I am fortunate to have found you!

I would be remiss if I didn't acknowledge the multitude of marvelous friends, acquaintances, coworkers, and book lovers who played a crucial role in spreading the word about 'Broken Rhodes' with their reviews and mentions on social media. The past two years have been a whirlwind, and the overwhelming support I have received has been truly humbling. Thank you all for giving my book wings.

If you've enjoyed 'Bullets in the Briar', it would be tremendously helpful if you would be so kind as to leave a star rating and a few words of review on Amazon or Goodreads to help other readers find the book.

Thank you for taking the return trip to Harlow with me. Perhaps we'll meet there again!

All the best,
Kimber

ABOUT THE AUTHOR

Kimber Silver was born and raised in Kansas and spent most of her childhood at her grandparents' farm. However, her love of travel has taken her on many adventures and broadened her horizons. Kimber lives with her husband and two rescue dogs in central Kansas.

www.kimbersilver.com

X: @kimber_silver21

Goodreads: Kimber Silver

Instagram: @Kimber_Silver

Facebook: AuthorKimberSilver

www.ingramcontent.com/pod-product-compliance
Lightning Source LLC
LaVergne TN
LVHW091712070526
838199LV00050B/2369